Won't Stop

Won't Stop

Clifford "Spud" Johnson

www.urbanbooks.net

Urban Books, LLC
300 Farmingdale Road, NY-Route 109
Farmingdale, NY 11735

ISBN 13: 978-1-62286-665-6
ISBN 10: 1-62286-665-7

First Trade Paperback Printing June 2018
Printed in the United States of America

10 9 8 7 6 5 4 3 2 1

Distributed by Kensington Publishing Corp.
Submit orders to:
Customer Service
400 Hahn Road
Westminster, MD 21157-4627
Phone: 1-800-733-3000
Fax: 1-800-659-2436

This book is dedicated to my aunt Linda Powell
for always believing in me even when I
didn't believe in myself.

Love is extremely painful.

—Hot Shot

Prologue

The first African American director of the FBI, Denver J. Johnson, was in his late fifties and had a solid reputation as a scrupulous and honest administrator. All he wanted in life was to do some good. Good for all Americans, but more so for African Americans in the urban communities across the U.S. That was the main reason he devised Operation Cleanup, a special assignment that was designed to rid the bad guys in urban communities by giving them a heavy dose of aggression. He felt the best way to deal with those types of men and women was to put in a deep cover operative who could deal with them on the level they were accustomed to. He sat back in his chair and smiled after reading the file that was e-mailed to him from JT. So far, so good. Special Agent Jason Gaines, also known as Hot Shot, had successfully completed his first mission in Dallas, Texas, and was now ready to proceed further with his next mission. Nodding his head in thought, the director of the FBI felt like a proud father. His idea and plans had finally started to pan out, and he felt good—real good. He had been somewhat hesitant of using Hot Shot with all of the emotional baggage he was carrying with the loss of his entire family. Something that tragic could cause a sane man to lose his mind quickly. He was glad he listened to JT because Hot Shot was the perfect man for Operation Cleanup, and the proof was staring at him right on the file he read. The man was good—extremely. It was time for the next mission and the director felt confident that Hot Shot would again produce positive, if not stellar, results in the state of Oklahoma. He smiled and thought, *Look out, bad guys in Oklahoma City; here comes Hot Shot.*

Hot Shot was standing in front of the mirror in his bedroom trying to calm himself down. He couldn't believe that Nola still refused to talk to him. He was losing his mind because never would he have thought she would just up and leave him for good. It had been over five months since she returned to Dallas to be with her brother, twin sister, and two cousins who were awaiting their court dates so they could surrender and start serving their time for the crimes they plead guilty to. Lola had to serve three years and some change on the sixty months she plead out to in her part of the child pornography business she and her brother Tiny Troy were convicted of.

Tiny Troy and his two cousins, Weeta Wee and Keeta Wee, all plead guilty to numerous drug charges, as well as the child pornography charges, and each received a 168-month sentence which was rather good, considering. Fourteen years was light, thought Hot Shot. Luckily, neither of them had any previous criminal history. If they had, then the time they received would have been a lot more.

During the wait in between making their plea deals, Nola felt she had to go stand beside her family through this trying time. Hot Shot, who felt extremely guilty because he knew he was the reason her family was going to jail, knew he couldn't protest her leaving to go be with them in Texas, so he accepted that, even though Nola was pregnant with their child. But after two months of dealing with all of the pressures of things for her family,

Nola suffered a miscarriage and lost their child. Next to losing his mother, father, and little brother by some unknown murderous bastards, this loss was devastating to Hot Shot. What made it even worse is that Nola refused to talk to him after she miscarried. She ended their relationship because she felt everything was all bad in her life and God was punishing her for her wrongs, as well as her family's. She was lucky that she didn't have to go to federal prison along with her family for her part in their illegal businesses. Now with the loss of her firstborn, she was devoted to making sure that her family would be okay while they served their time and that she kept up their ranch-style home that their parents left them when they died. This all seemed so unfair to Hot Shot, but when he thought about it, he knew that he too was being punished for his deception and lies to the only woman he had every really and truly loved.

The ringing of his cell phone snapped him out of his trancelike state. He went to the bed and grabbed his phone without looking at the caller ID to see who it was calling.

"What up?" he asked as he sat down on the end of his bed.

"What's good, boss man? Where you at? I thought you would be out here by now," said Cotton.

"Had a few more things that needed to be taken care of. I should be there in a few days. I'm driving out and stopping in Dallas before I come to Oklahoma City."

"Come on, boss man, don't do yourself like that, man. She is only going to piss you off and play mind games with you. You gotta let her go so she can see what she has lost, and trust me, once that happens, she'll come running back to your arms."

"Since when did you learn Nola so well?"

"It's not about knowing her well, it's about knowing how women—*all* women—get down. Now shake that shit out your brain and get out here so we can get this bread. I've been sitting out here for three months now spending way more than I wanted to because you wanted me out here mixing it up and learning the town. It's some serious paper out here, but these dudes are on some goofy shit."

"What you mean by that?"

"Can't really explain it, but there are some serious hustlers here, and at the same time, most of the dudes getting they paper are kinda like some fiends themselves. They're popping pills, smoking sherm, or playing with they nose."

"Snorting cocaine is big out there?"

"Hell, yeah! For real, that's where I think we're going to make the most money at. Birds out here are going for like twenty-nine, and these fools spend that fast! Not only—"

Hot Shot cut Cotton off by hanging up the phone on him. He couldn't come out of character and let Cotton continue to talk so recklessly on the phone. He set the phone down and two minutes later the phone rang. When he answered it, Cotton said, "My bad, boss man. You need to hurry up and get here."

Hot Shot smiled into the receiver and said, "I'll be there in a few days, like I said. You make sure you get a nice, low-key spot where I can rest my head and feel comfortable."

"Oh, don't trip. I got us a nice condo that's out of the way, yet close enough for us to be in the mix like we need to be."

"*Us?* Since when did we do that roommate-type stuff, Cotton?"

"Kill that shit, boss man. No way in hell you gon' have me out here lying low by myself. We in this together, so come on so we can get this damn money. And don't worry about Nola. I've met a few breezies that I think will be able to keep you busy enough so you won't have to be stressed about your girl."

"I *know* you haven't brought any of these breezies to the place where I'll be staying, Cotton?"

"You know I know better than that shit. Trust this, though, there are some bad females out this way. And they are *definitely* feeling ya boy! I thought I was having a ball in Atlanta and MIA, but these country thangs are live, and I do mean, *all the way live!*"

Shaking his head, Hot Shot couldn't help but smile at the antics of his little helper Cotton. "See you in a few days, clown," he said and ended the call.

He lay down on his bed, and all he could think about was Nola. He missed her so much it hurt. But Cotton was right. There was no need for him to go to Dallas to try to convince her to snap back from whatever she was tripping on. She would have to do that on her own time. He had work to do. A mission to complete. No time to let his emotions override his mental. He sat up and called his handler, JT. As soon as JT answered the phone, Hot Shot told him, "I'm on the move. Driving to Oklahoma tonight. I'll give you a call after I've had a sit-down with Cotton. From what I've been told, powder cocaine, pills, and sherm is what will be needed."

"I'll be waiting for your call and everything will be ready. Be careful, Hot Shot."

"Always," he said and ended the call. It was time to do some good. Though he was ready to do some good and try to bring down as many criminals as he could in Oklahoma, his heart was hurting, and he didn't know how he would be able to deal with this type of pain. "Love is extremely painful," he said to himself as he got off of his bed and started to pack.

Oklahoma, here I come.

Chapter One

"Come on, boss man, you need to dead this dry shit you on. You only move when we got some money to get and that shit is whack. The ends have picked up, and now it's time to play some. Your ass is getting your swag back on tonight, and ya boy ain't taking no for an answer," Cotton said as he stepped to Hot Shot's closet and opened the door. "I'm about to go take a shower and get fresh. I expect for you to be doing the same 'cause an hour from now, we're going to be rolling out in that fly-ass Audi of yours and get our club on. If things go as I think they will, we should be leaving the club with two or more bad bitches with us."

Hot Shot sat at the end of his bed with a grin on his face. It was odd to him how he let Cotton grow on him in such a short time. He looked at Cotton as a little brother, and that thought made him feel good—and sad—at the same time because it made him think of his little brother that was murdered. He quickly shook that thought from his head and said, "All right, Cotton, I'll go out and see what happens, but I am *not* promising you we'll be leaving with any females. Where are we going anyway?"

"We're going to hit this spot called the Purple Martini and see what the crowd is like. Been there a couple of times. It's like a hip-hop club, but the tenders in there are nice. If we don't feel that, then we can hit up the Grenadier, a twenty-five-and-older club where they like to say they get their grown and sexy on. So, pick out something where you can fit in at either."

"No problem. What up with those Crips you told me about?"

"I haven't heard from Sharp Shoota yet, but they're definitely interested in copping a few birds. From what I've learned about his big homeboy, Shoota, he likes to play with his nose as well as gettin' his money with the trap moves on the NW Side."

"And these two are the Hoover dudes you told me about?"

"No way. These are the dudes from Rollin' Sixties."

"Oh. It's amazing how I can go to different states and hear about the same gangs from the West."

"You know how it is, that gangbangin' shit is every-where. It may have started in Cali, but now it's the norm almost everywhere you go, even on the West Coast. I met some East Coast Bloods when I was in Miami. Shit tripped me out. They be yelling that 'Soo Woo' shit like a war chant. Wild for real."

"Never thought it would get like that. Anyway, what about the Hoovers you met?"

"They are more into the pills and said when they need some more they will give me a call and try me out. I told them I would give them some love, so it's basically wait and see."

"Okay."

"Those Bloods in Midwest City been acting shady, so I've basically stayed away from them clowns. They don't seem serious about their money anyway. Would hate to let you loose on them," Cotton said and smiled.

"The Bloods in North Highlands seemed like they are about the money. You haven't heard from them anymore?"

"A few times. They pill popping big, though. They be wanting pills and that water, but nothing worth talking about."

"The money has been decent, but I think we need to turn up a little more."

Nodding his head in agreement, Cotton said, "That's another reason why we're getting out and about tonight, boss man. It's not all about the pussy; it's all about business as well. When we're seen more, more of these nuccas will holla."

Hot Shot smiled. "Nuccas, huh?"

With a smirk on his face, Cotton said, "Yeah, since the N-word puts your panties in a bunch I thought I'd switch it to nucca. You like?"

"Go get dressed, clown, so we can see what we can get popping out there tonight."

"Holla at ya in a few, my nucca!" Cotton was laughing as he left the bedroom.

Hot Shot shook his head as he went to his closet and picked out what he was going to wear. He chose an expensive pair of black jeans with a black silk T-shirt and a pair of black Polo loafers. He thought about his selection, and then stepped back to the closet and grabbed a black blazer. He figured he'd wear the blazer if they went to the grown and sexy club, and if they stayed in the hop-hop club, then he would be good without the blazer.

As he went to take his shower, he thought about what Cotton told him. It was time for him to start enjoying his stay out here in Oklahoma City. But he was still having problems getting Nola off of his mind. *If she doesn't want to be with me, then I can't do anything about it*, he thought as he showered, knowing that he still missed her like crazy. He thought about Cotton's words and laughed aloud while lathering himself.

"I'm telling you, boss man, you can't stay like this. You got to get back in the mix. It's been too long. I know you need to get your nuts outta the sand. The only way to forget about some good pussy is to find some even *better* pussy!"

Though Cotton's words were crude as ever, he was right. *It's time for me to start living my life out here. Plus, I can't be shaded like I've been doing if I want to make more moves. Surprised JT hasn't gotten at me yet about that. Yeah, it's time to turn the mack game back on and see what this city has to offer me,* Hot Shot said to himself as he finished his shower with a smile on his face.

When they pulled into the parking lot of the Purple Martini, Hot Shot knew instantly that this club was just too young for him. But he decided to go in and give it a try. *One drink and we're out of here,* he told himself as he got out of his car and let Cotton lead the way inside the club, bypassing the long line of people waiting to get inside of the hip-hop club. Once they were inside, Cotton headed straight toward the bar and ordered them both a drink. After the bartender gave them their peach Cîrocs, they turned and stared out toward the dance floor. Hot Shot had to admit, there was definitely a lot of high-caliber eye candy walking around the club as well as dancing on the dance floor. The only thing was they were a tad too young for Hot Shot's taste. The club made you show IDs to prove you were over twenty-one, but Hot Shot could tell that some of these sexy, young ladies inside of the club were barely twenty. He shook his head and smiled as a thick and sexy female walked by them and gave her ample ass an extra switch as she passed them.

Cotton sipped his drink and smiled. "You like all that ass, boss man, don't ya? Told you this town had some bad broads."

"Too young for me, Cotton. I'm not trying to catch a case messing with these kids. Half of them look barely older than eighteen."

"You need to stop tripping. What, you wanna ask for their IDs too? Shit, if they in here, they're legal."

"Whatever," Hot Shot said as he sipped his drink.

"I see someone I need to holla at. I'll be right back, boss man. That fool Sharp Shoota and his girl is here."

"Go handle your business then. Like I said, it's time to turn up out here and start making some serious paper."

"I'm all over it," Cotton said as he quickly downed the rest of his drink, set it down on the counter of the bar, and stepped toward the back of the club. He stopped in front of the table where Sharp Shoota and his girlfriend were sitting and said, "What it do, Sharp Shoota? You good?"

Sharp Shoota stood and shook hands with Cotton and said, "I'm always good, loc. How about yourself?"

"I'm straight, getting money and enjoying the scenery all at the same time."

"That's right. You met my girl, huh? Sherry, this is Cotton. Cotton, this is Sherry."

"Hello, Sherry."

"Hello," Sherry said, not really paying attention to Cotton as she bobbed her head to the music of T.I. that was bumping on the club's sound system.

Sharp Shoota stood five foot seven and was considered one of the most dangerous of the Rollin' Sixties Crips in Oklahoma City. Small in stature but deadly with a gun. He got his name from his big homeboy, Shoota. Shoota was known as a ruthless Crip in Oklahoma. He's rumored to have murdered plenty of gang members over the years. Sharp Shoota carried the Shoota name to the next generation, and from what Cotton learned, he lived up to his name exceptionally. He may be small in stature, but he was still a cold-blooded killer. Light skin with long French braids and a thin build, Cotton couldn't help but think, *Yeah, this fool is a killer because he has a little man complex. Most little nuccas like him always do.*

"Tell me, have you thought about handling some business?"

"As a matter of fact, I have. I was going to get with you so we can chop it up some and see if you can give me a cool ticket on a couple of birds. My big homie's connect out in Cali is slow playing us right now, so what's up?"

"What you paying for them now?"

Sharp Shoota smiled and lied. "Twenty-six."

Laughing, Cotton said, "You need to quit that shit, Sharp Shoota. You know damn well unless you copping a load, you ain't paying nothing under twenty-eight. But I ain't tripping. If you trying to fuck with me and my mans, then we can work out something."

"Where your mans at?"

"At the bar."

Sharp Shoota told Sherry, "Say, baby, why don't you go dance or holla at one of your girls for a minute while I take care of some business, all right?"

"Whatever. Gimme some money so I can go buy me a drink."

He reached inside of his jean pocket and pulled out a big wad of cash and peeled off a hundred-dollar bill and gave it to her.

"You want me to get you something and have the waitress bring it over here to you?"

"Yeah, you know what I want," Sharp Shoota said as he sat back down.

Before he sat down, Cotton waved toward Hot Shot and motioned for him to come and join them. He sat down and said, "This is my plug from the West, and he has plugs on whatever you need. And I do mean *whatever*."

"Is that right?"

"Yep. The yay, the bud, the water, the pills, guns, whatever."

"Damn, he like that, huh? Shit, a nigga can always use a plug for more guns."

"I know that's right. Check it out, though, do me a fave and try not to use that N-word. My mans has a problem with people saying that word around him. He feels it's disrespectful, not only to him but to all black men."

Laughing, Sharp Shoota said, "Damn, our mans on some fight-the-power shit, huh?"

"He's a man you *would* want to fuck with, trust me."

"I feel you," Sharp Shoota said as Hot Shot made it to the table and took a seat.

"Shot, this is Sharp Shoota. Sharp Shoota, this is my mans Hot Shot."

"Call me Shot."

"That's what's up. You can call me Shoota. I only go by Sharp Shoota when I'm around my big homeboy, Shoota."

Hot Shot nodded but didn't speak. Cotton took this as his cue. "I was telling Shoota here that we can handle whatever he needs. Right now, he's looking for a cool ticket on a couple of birds."

"What are you paying for your units now?" asked Hot Shot.

With a smile on his face, Sharp Shoota said, "I told your man here the ticket we paying, and he laughed at me."

"I don't laugh when discussing business."

"Damn, cuz, you a serious nig—dude, huh?"

Shot smiled because he knew by the way Shoota stopped himself from using the N-word that Cotton had told him about his dislike for the use of the word. By stopping himself showed Shot that Sharp Shoota respected his get down, and that, in turn, made Shot have some respect for the small man seated across from him. "I'm always serious when it comes to getting this money. Again, what are you paying now?"

"Twenty-six."

Shot gave a nod and said, "And you get two at a time for this price?"

Sharp Shoota shrugged and said, "Sometimes we get more; it depends on how thangs is moving."

"I'll tell you what, you get five or more and we can give it to you for the twenty-six. Anything less than five, and I got to charge you twenty-seven."

"That's straight. When will you want to handle this?"

"Whenever you and your people are ready. Give Cotton a call and we can take it from there."

"That's what's up, cuz. I think we can handle some serious business then."

"One thing, though."

"What's up?"

"If I'm going to give you guys the twenty-six or twenty-seven ticket, I need to meet your big homeboy Shoota."

"And why is that?"

Shot shrugged his shoulders and said, "That's just how I get down. I've done business all over, some deals bigger than these, some smaller. I prefer to deal with men I can look in the eyes and shake their hands. It's good for both of us. That way, we can get a feel for each other and maybe do business continuously."

"Hold on for a sec, cuz, let me hit Big Shoota," Sharp Shoota said as he pulled out his phone and made a call. When Shoota answered the phone, his namesake said, "What's up, cuz? I'm here at the Purple Martini, and I bumped into that nigga Cotton I told you about. He has his people with him, and they talking like they can drop us some thangs for twenty-six if we get five or better. Twenty-seven for anything less than five."

"Yeah, that sounds good. Do they look like they on some grimy shit, cuz, 'cause you already know how we'll get down if they play with the chips."

Staring at Cotton and Shot, Sharp Shoota said, "Nah, I'm feelin' it, cuz. Just wanted to get at you to see if you wanted to move or not."

"If you with it, then I'm with it, li'l homie. Set it up."

"Will do. Check this out, though, cuz. Cotton's man, Hot Shot, wants to meet you before we get down, though."

"What the fuck he want to meet me for?"

Sharp Shoota repeated what Shot had told him, and then waited for a response from his big homeboy.

After a full minute, Big Shoota said, "I'm not feeling that shit, cuz. That sound like some police shit for real."

"That was my first thought too, but I don't feel that shit, cuz. I think everything is straight up and down."

"All right, cuz, tell them we'll get at them tomorrow afternoon, and we want five of them. Can't let that ticket get away from us. Shit, we been getting them for twenty-eight a pop."

Sharp Shoota laughed and said, "I know."

"If this shit works out, we can turn up the North Side and trap like a mothafucka."

"Yeah, and you can have your extras to play in ya nose!"

Laughing, Big Shoota said, "Fuck you, li'l nigga. Handle that shit and get at me in the morning. I'll get the ends ready."

"Six minutes, cuz," Sharp Shoota said as he ended the call. He put his phone back in his shirt pocket and said, "We want to get five of them. I'll get at you tomorrow afternoon, and we can make it happen."

Hot Shot nodded.

Cotton smiled.

"Will your big homie be joining us?" asked Shot.

"Yeah, he'll be there. He's not feeling the meeting him shit, though. He feels that's some police shit. So, tell me, are you the police, Shot?"

With a grin on his face, Hot Shot stared directly at Sharp Shoota and said, "Nope. I don't do police, nor am I one. I'm all about my business, and when you deal with me, you will see that's what's most important to me. I'm a man of action because actions always trump the rhetoric. My word is all I have, and I stand on that at all times."

Sharp Shoota nodded and said, "I feel you, cuz. I don't peep any bullshit in you. I hope I'm correct. Like you said, you're a man of action. I feel that because so are we."

There was no need to respond to the subtle threat Sharp Shoota had just given. It was understood.

"All right, then, hit me when you're ready and we'll pick a time and place and handle that shit," said Cotton.

"That's what's up, cuz," Sharp Shoota said as they all shook hands.

As they were leaving the table, Hot Shot told Cotton, "I've had enough of this spot. Let's try out that grown and sexy club."

Laughing, Cotton said, "Being around all these ronis done got your blood flowing again, huh, boss man?"

With a grin on his face, Hot Shot said, "Yeah, something like that. But I need a grown woman, not no barely legal thing that can get me knocked for statutory."

"I feel you. On to the Grenadier, then," Cotton said as he led the way out of the club.

Chapter Two

The Grenadier Club was located on the Northeast Side of Oklahoma City, a part of town that's considered to be the roughest since it posted a high crime rate. What baffled Hot Shot was that the Governor's Mansion was also located on the Northeast Side. One would think that the place where the governor resided the surrounding area would be relatively crime free.

When he pulled into the parking lot of the Grenadier, his first thought was this couldn't be a club. It looked more like a local lodge building for older people. He saw men and women getting out of Cadillacs and a few Lexuses and thought, *This should be really interesting. Grown and sexy, huh?* He noticed the older women, some looking pretty good and some totally overly made up trying hard to bring their sexy back. He shook his head as they entered the club. He saw a mixture of older people and men and women, whose ages ranged everywhere from twenty-five to their forties. The music was a mixture of old-school rap, R&B, and some newer rap. He laughed aloud as they found a table and sat down because the DJ put on the rapper, Yo Gotti's hit single, "Act Right." For some reason, he liked the atmosphere of the Grenadier. He was comfortable and was able to relax.

Cotton could tell that Hot Shot was feeling the club and that made him smile. "Okay, this is the spot, then, 'cause I see signs of the old Hot Shot coming out."

Hot Shot rolled his eyes and said, "Shut up and get the waitress over here so we can get some drinks." While Cotton did as he was told, Shot let his eyes roam around the dimly lit club and was checking out what the females were really working with. He was somewhat impressed. Somewhat. That changed almost instantly when he noticed how almost every male inside the club basically stopped what they were doing or paused with whatever conversations they were having and stared at two gorgeous sisters as they entered the club and went to a table toward the back of the club. These two sisters knew they were top flight, and they carried themselves as if they were royalty, heads held high as they strolled confidently to their table.

One of them was a light-skinned sister with either really long hair or a very real-looking weave. Her hair hung almost to the middle of her back, a long, luxurious mane mixed with brown and blond hues. She was a slim woman with curves in all the right places and small breasts that fit her frame perfectly.

Her friend was equally attractive; actually, she was incredibly attractive to Hot Shot. He couldn't take his eyes off of her. She had a short haircut with light brown eyes and a large, sumptuous mouth. She was brown skinned and tall, which only added to her attractiveness. Five foot ten barefoot, he guessed with an alluring physique; thick yet not too thick. D-cups that looked nice and firm that Shot was positive would stand firm even without a bra. Sexy as hell and she knew it. They both knew they were showstoppers. As he continued to stare at the two lovely ladies, he noticed they were wearing matching thin platinum chains around their necks with a diamond encrusted "SS" emblem attached to their chains. *Wonder what the SS stands for*, Shot said to himself as he smiled at the waitress who brought their drinks.

He sipped his peach Cîroc, and then asked Cotton, "Okay, champ, since you're up on everyone who's some-body in this city, who are those two bad females that just came into the club and made every male inside become highly aroused?"

With a smile on his face, Cotton said, "Yep, my boss man is *definitely* back. I see you likey, huh? Well, let me tell you this . . . Those broads are *not* to be fucked with. If you watch them, you will see that no man in here will even think about approaching them. I think they're some dykes, for real."

"Why is that?"

Cotton shrugged and said, "I dunno, just a feeling. I've seen them out and about a few times, and every time they enter the spot, they have a few drinks, bob their fine-ass heads to the music for about an hour or so, and then bounce. Any nucca try to holla at them gets shot down or flat-out checked. One time at the Sky Bar I watched them check a nucca so serious that I thought they were going to murk that fool. I'm telling you, boss man, they aren't to be fucked with."

Shot smiled.

"Uh-oh, not again."

"What are you talking about?"

"The last time I tried to warn you about not getting at a broad, you ended up going against my warning."

With a smile playing on his lips, Hot Shot said, "And look what came of that."

"Yeah, look at it. You ended up with your heart broken."

Shot's smile turned to a frown. "That's not what I meant."

"I know. But look, there's all types of broads in here, and if you pay close attention, most of them have been checking us out on the cool. That's fucking crazy too. I've been to this spot several times and came up on some cool breezies, but I've always had to be the one doing the chasing. For some reason, I don't think we're going to have to do any chasing tonight."

"And why do you think that?"

Cotton smiled and said, "Because here comes two nice-looking breezy broads right now."

Shot turned in his seat slightly and grinned as two sisters, who looked to be in their early thirties, approach their table. Each sister was dressed in some sexy attire and looked pretty good he surmised as they stopped and stood in front of their table.

"Now I know you two fine men aren't about to waste this night away by sitting down drinking and listening to the music, are you?" asked the prettier of the two sisters. "My name is Shirin, and this is my sister, Ameedah."

"Hello, Ameedah and Shirin. My name is Cotton, and this is my mans, Hot Shot," said Cotton.

"Hot Shot? Why they call you that?"

Shot smiled, ignored her question, and said, "You can call me Shot for short."

"Okayyy, but that doesn't answer my question."

Cotton stood and asked Shirin, "Would you like to dance, lovely lady?"

"You better say it, sexy chocolate. Let's go!"

Cotton laughed and said, "Sexy chocolate? Mmm, I like that," he said, following Shirin out onto the dance floor.

Since Shot hadn't asked Ameedah to dance, she took it upon herself to sit in Cotton's seat. "Now, can you answer my question and tell me why they call you Hot Shot?"

"I'd rather sit here and get to know you better, and hopefully, if everything works out, you will find out on your own why I have that moniker."

She smiled and said, "Mmm, okay, we can do that, Mr. Hot Shot."

"Call me Shot, please."

"Shot it is. So, tell me, Shot, where are you from because you're definitely not from the city?"

"Born and raised in Inglewood, California."

"What brings you to Sooner land?"

"Business."

"What kind of business?"

"Very profitable business."

She stared at him and noticed the two-carat gold and diamond bezel Ulysse Nardin watch on his wrist and simply said, "Okay, so you're a baller, huh?"

He frowned and said, "That depends on what your definition of a baller is."

"You know, dope boy."

He shook his head and said, "No, I don't know, and I am not a dope boy. I'm a grown man who handles his business." Before she could respond to that, he said, "Tell me a little about yourself."

"Not too much to tell. Born and raised out here, went to school at Douglass High, attended college briefly, got preggo, then married, then preggo again, and then divorced. I work for the Department of Human Services as an adoption specialist, and I love to read and come out and enjoy myself every now and then. That's about it. Nothing really all that exciting. Now, you, can you give me more than you not being a dope boy and being a businessman?"

He shrugged and was about to speak but was shocked to see one of the sexy women with the "SS" emblems around her neck approach their table.

"Excuse me, honey, but I need to borrow this man for a few." She then reached her hand out for Hot Shot's. He stared at her for two heartbeats, and then let her take his hand and pull him out onto the dance floor without saying another word.

"Now, ain't that a bitch!" yelled Ameedah as she watched Shot dancing with the bold and beautiful woman.

As soon as they made it to the dance floor, the DJ switched the fast song to a slow jam by the Isley Brothers. The bold sister slid into his arms and gave him a tight squeeze as she pressed her very impressive pair of breasts against his chest. Shot felt his manhood begin to stir and inhaled deeply to try to gain some control. She felt him as well and whispered, "Something told me you would be impressive, and from what I'm feeling thumping against my thing, looks like I was correct."

"Mmmm," was all he could think to say as they continued to dance. Since she was so tall with her heels on, she was almost standing the same height as Shot, and he was able to stare at her as they danced. He stared into her light brown eyes and felt himself become slowly hypnotized by their intensity. She smiled at him and said, "I know you like what you see, Daddy, so tell me what you gon' do with all of this woman you holding onto."

Before he could respond to her question, Cotton materialized next to them with Shirin in his arms and said, "Only you, boss man, only you, dog!"

Shot ignored him and smiled at his dance partner and whispered in her ear, "I'm going to show you why they call me Hot Shot."

Laughing, she said, "I bet your name is Hot Shot. You *look* like a Hot Shot."

"Oh, best believe I am, love. Now tell me your name."

"Daun."

"Hi, Daun."

"Hi, Hot Shot."

"Call me Shot."

"Gotcha. And I do mean gotcha. When we're finished dancing, I expect for you to return to your table and get rid of the waste-of-your-time broad sitting there trying to give me the evil eye."

"And afterward?"

"Afterward, I want you to tell your friend that your night here at the Grenadier is over."

"Now why would I just up and leave my mans? That would be rude."

She leaned a little closer to his ear and bit the tip of his earlobe hard enough to make him flinch and whispered, "Because I *want* you to be rude. What Daun wants, she always gets. And Daun wants you all night long." She then pulled back from his embrace and went back and joined her friend at their table with a satisfied smile on her face.

Shot went back to his table and took a seat and grabbed his glass and downed the rest of his drink thinking about this very sexy and intriguing woman who had boldly come to him and made him dance with her. Though he had met some aggressive women in his days, this woman topped them all by a mile. He was so caught up thinking about Daun and her actions that he totally ignored Ameedah who was sitting across from him staring at him as if he were a piece of shit.

With a disgusted expression on her face, she said, "Well, I guess you've been snared by one of those nas-ty-ass Sin Sisters, huh? Don't let the high-priced clothes and expensive jewels get you twisted, Hot Shot. Those skanks are no good, I can tell you that."

"Sin Sisters? Is that what they call themselves?"

"Mm-hmm. That's what those SSs on their chains stand for."

"Why do they call themselves the Sin Sisters?"

"Uh-uh, you ain't about to get me caught up with them bitches. Look how they're staring at me." She stood and said, "Bye, Hot Shot. If you're still around, maybe we can get together sometimes." With that, she quickly made her departure from his table.

He turned in his seat and grinned as both of the Sin Sisters smiled and held their glasses in the air in a mock toast toward him. He gave a nod of his head and stood and went to Cotton who was still dancing. He tapped him on the shoulder and told him to follow him. Cotton disengaged himself from Shirin's embrace, telling her that he would be right back, and followed Shot out of the club. Once they were standing in front of Hot Shot's car, Cotton asked, "Okay, what the fuck is going on?"

"I don't have a clue, champ. But I do know what's about to go on. I'm going to go see what that sexy lady is talking about. From what she told me, she's trying to have me all night long, and I'm going to give her exactly what she wants. It's been a long time, and like you crudely told me, it's time for me to get these nuts outta the sand."

"So you're just going to roll out with them broads, and you don't know jack about them? You tripping, boss man."

Shot ignored him and said, "Now you know better than that. Listen, I want you to go back inside of the club and finish enjoying yourself with Shirin. I want you to get all the information you can out of her and her sister about the Sin Sisters."

"The who?"

"That's what they call Daun and the other female. That's what the SS stands for on their chains."

"The Sin Sisters. What kind of shit is that?"

"I don't know, but that's what you're going to find out. I'll hit you up when I know what's what."

Before Cotton could say a word, the Sin Sisters came out of the club and walked confidently to the men. When they were standing in front of Hot Shot's car, Daun said, "I hope you're ready to go because we got some serious fucking to do tonight, mister."

Cotton started laughing and said, "Well, I'll be damn! Only you, boss man, only you!"

"So am I riding with you or are you leaving with me?"

"Yes, you're leaving with me. So give ya man the keys to your whip and come on, Daddy."

"What makes you think this is my whip?"

With a smirk on her face she said, "Come on now, I know that's your man and all, but he doesn't look like the type to rock a new Audi S8. He's more of a SUV type. So come on. We got some fucking to do. That is, unless you're not going with me to have the time of your life."

"Oh, I am with that."

"Then what are we waiting for, Mister Hot Shot?"

Shot turned toward Cotton and said, "Do what I told you and give me a call in the morning." He then tossed his keys to Cotton and turned and faced Daun. "I'm ready to roll, love."

She smiled at him and turned and led the way toward her car. The other Sin Sister smiled a wicked smile and said, "By the way, did Daun tell you that we share everything?"

Hot Shot stood there with a shocked expression on his face as he watched both of the Sin Sisters get inside of their 7 Series BMW, laughing.

Chapter Three

Ten minutes after leaving the Grenadier, Janeen, the other Sin Sister, pulled the BMW in front of a large building right on the outskirts of downtown Oklahoma City. She had a smile on her face as she watched Daun get out of the car. Shot got out of the backseat and looked over his shoulder at Janeen with a questioning expression on his face.

"Don't worry, Hot Shot, I was just teasing you. We don't share everything. My sister is feeling you, so she gets you all to herself. This time. See ya in the morning, sister. Don't hurt him. He's a cutie; he might just be a keeper!" She sped away from the curb laughing.

Daun grabbed Shot by his right hand and led him into the building which actually was a condominium that housed several high-rise condos. They rode an elevator to the twelfth floor and entered Daun's condo. As soon as they were inside, Daun peeled off her form-fitting cocktail dress and unfastened her bra, and just like he assumed, her firm D-cups held fast and did not drop an inch once freed from her bra. Shot's mouth began to water as he stared at her delicious-looking breasts.

She smiled and said, "You like what you see, Shot? That's good, because you're about to *love* how I'm going to make you feel." She then stepped to him and starting taking off his clothes. His blazer, then shirt, then she dropped to her knees and took off his shoes. While on her knees, she looked up into his eyes as she unbuckled his belt and slid his pants down. She laughed when she saw that he wasn't wearing any underwear. "I see you stay ready. I like that." She then put the tip of his semierect penis inside of her mouth. She moaned, and so did he as she began giving some very good head.

He put his right hand behind her head and held on as she took him deep inside of her mouth. It had been too long since he'd had sex. Too damn long, he thought as he felt himself quickly getting ready to explode inside of her mouth. Daun sensed that he was almost there and her sucking intensified, and she was then rewarded with an extreme amount of come inside of her mouth. More than she was ready for as some of it slid out of her mouth. She wiped the excess come on her fingers and stuck them inside of her mouth to make sure she didn't miss a drop.

"Damn, that was a lot, Daddy. Has it been a long time since you got off, or is it me?"

"Both."

"Mmmm, well, let's get to the next level, shall we?"

"Yes, we shall," Hot Shot said as he pulled her to him and tried to kiss her.

She turned her face before their lips could make contact and said, "Uh-uh. Kissing can be dangerous, Daddy. Feelings come from that shit. This is about nothing but some good fucking."

She grabbed his hand and pulled him into her bedroom. He went straight to the bed and watched her as she grabbed a small remote from her dresser and hit a few buttons. Music started playing from some speaker that he didn't see. An old jam by Adina Howard that he vaguely remembered played as they came together like a roaring fire. The intensity had been building since they first laid eyes on each other, and the sex was explosive. They feasted on each other and made sure that their tongues touched every inch of their bodies.

Daun wasn't a loud lover, and that seemed to excite him even more as he drove himself deeper and deeper inside of her, trying his very best to get some verbiage from her sexy lips. No matter how deep he went, all he received for his efforts were small grunts. They switched from the missionary position to Daun on top of him, and he held onto her waist and pulled her down to him with some extra strength so she could feel all of him deeply inside of her. Still, Daun just grunted and continued to ride him and work her hips from side to side, driving him closer and closer to his second orgasm. When she bent forward and let her dark nipples become in reach of his lips, he knew he was a goner. As soon as his mouth had one of her delicious nipples inside of his mouth, his orgasm almost made him see stars. He came so hard he feared that the condom would shoot off of his dick.

Daun continued to ride and pinch her nipples as her orgasm shot through her body. Even while coming, all she did was grunt, and that made Shot even more determined to get more from her verbally. It was on for real now he thought as he quickly flipped her onto her back and raised her legs onto his shoulders. He checked to make sure the condom was still firmly in place, and then eased himself back inside of her soaking wet and steaming hot pussy and began to give it to her like he'd never given it to a woman before, not even Nola. He was ferocious inside of the pussy, and he refused to stop until he got more than some damn grunts from this absolutely gorgeous woman. She drove him mad because it was as if she knew what he was trying to do and refused to give him what he wanted. But by the time her third orgasm rocked through her body, she screamed, "Oh! Shit! What are you doing to me, Shot?" That was a start, but he wanted more—much more.

He pulled out of her right smack in the middle of her orgasm, grabbed her by her hips, and flipped her onto her stomach and raised her to her knees and entered swiftly from the back and started banging her as hard as he could. This seemed to make her orgasm intensify, and she finally gave him what he'd been after for the last forty minutes. "Oh! Oh! Oh my God! This feels so fucking good! Shot! Don't stop, Daddy! Please don't stop serving me this great dick!"

Hot Shot smiled and did exactly as she requested because he was on the verge of his third nut of the night, and the harder he banged inside of her, the closer he came. What took him over the edge was when she told him to turn her back around because she wanted to look at him while he came again. He quickly put her on her back and was back inside of her with her legs wrapped tightly around his waist as he again drove his dick as hard as he could inside of her.

"Come for me, Daddy, come for me!" she screamed, and he exploded and gave her what she asked him for. She surprised him when she pulled him to her and gave him her tongue in a deep, passionate kiss as the last of his sperm filled the condom up.

He rolled off of her and sighed heavily and wiped some sweat from his forehead. After catching his breath, he asked, "I thought kissing was dangerous and could cause feelings?"

"Shhh, no talking, Daddy. You did good, real good. Better than I've ever had in my fucking life! Sleep now, 'K? Sleep," she mumbled as she closed her eyes and drifted off to a deep sleep. He stared at her for a few minutes before sleep overtook him too.

Shot opened his eyes after what seemed like after only a few hours of sleep. He was surprised to see that it was after 11:00 a.m. He got off the bed and stretched, then went into the living room looking for his sexy sex mate. He noticed how expensively furnished her condo was and began to wonder exactly what Daun, the Sin Sister, did to earn her money. His thoughts of her finances abruptly stopped when he turned and saw Daun leaning on the rail on her patio talking to someone on the cell. He smiled because her big ass looked so enticing in the transparent thong she was wearing. He tiptoed back into the bedroom and quickly grabbed a condom and eased back into the living room hoping Daun was still on the patio. She was. As he approached her, he stared at her big backside and began to get erect as he tore open the condom package.

Daun heard him coming behind her and turned around to see him slowly putting the condom on his dick. He then put his index finger to his lips, signaling for her to be quiet and to keep talking. She shook her head no, but he knew she didn't mean it because she was smiling while staring at his now very hard, condom-wrapped dick. She turned back around and continued with her conversation on the phone. She sighed heavily when she felt Shot's hand on her. He pulled her thong down, and she stepped out of it and spread her legs while holding onto the rail. He eased his dick inside of her wet pussy, and she moaned as he slowly stroked her deep.

Janeen heard her and asked, "What's wrong with you, sister? You feel all right?"

"Mm-hmm, I'm good."

"You don't sound good all of a sudden. You sure you're straight?" Janeen asked, worried.

"Yessss, I'm fine."

"Damn, girl, you sound like you got a dick in the butt. What the hell is going on over there?"

"I'm. Getting. Fucked. Right. Now. And. It's. Soooo. Goood. Call. You. Back. 'K?" she said as she pressed END to terminate the call. She looked over her shoulder and said, "You wrong for that, Shot."

He smiled at her and continued to serve her his early-morning hard dick. "You want me to stop?"

"You bet not stop! Slap my ass, Daddy. Slap my ass hard!"

He slapped her hard on her big, firm ass, and she moaned, then grunted. His pace picked up every time she grunted, and that told her that grunting would not be tolerated. "Give me what I want to hear and dead that damn grunting," he said as he pounded harder into her while slapping her ass at the same time.

"It's good, Daddy! It's so damn good!" she screamed. She couldn't believe how good this man was making her feel. As he went deeper inside of her, she stared out toward the downtown area and felt as if she were in heaven. "Never thought a dick could feel this damn good! Give it to me, Daddy! I'm about to come!"

He slapped her once more, and then grabbed her hips and pulled her into him as he felt his orgasm mounting as well. They came at the same time, both screaming how good their sex was.

After they finished, he scooped her into his arms, much to her delight. She was a big woman, and for a man to be able to pick her up so easily made her feel as if she was being handled like a smaller chick. She loved how this man made her feel. He was definitely all-man. He carried her into the bathroom, and they got into the shower and took a long, lingering shower together. She couldn't believe that she was breaking rules. Never had she let a man kiss her, and here she was kissing this man she just met as if she'd known him all her life. *This is scary,* she thought as she continued to stick her tongue deep inside of Shot's mouth. *So damn crazy, but it feels so damn right.* When they finished showering, they went back into the bedroom and got dressed.

Sitting on the bed applying lotion to her legs, Daun asked, "Are you hungry, Shot?"

"Starving."

"Hate to disappoint, but I don't cook. Let me hit Janeen and tell her to come get us, and we can go have some lunch somewhere. Cool?"

"Fine with me. I need to hit my mans and check on him," he said as he watched her leave the room to go get her phone that she left on the patio. As she walked by in her boy shorts, he reached out and slapped her on her ass. She smiled as she left the room. He grabbed his phone and called Cotton. "What's up, champ, you good?"

"Am *I* good? I should be asking you if *you're* good, boss man."

"What you mean, I'm straight."

"I did what you told me, and man, them Sin Sisters ain't to be fucked with."

"What's up with them?"

"They on some serious gangsta shit, boss man. Don't know exactly what they're into, but it's some serious money involved, and they are known for putting the smash down on fools."

"Come on, that sounds real extra, Cotton."

"It can sound extra, but I can tell you that Shirin and Ameedah wasn't bullshitting when they told me how they saw the Sin Sisters eat up some bitches who got in their way at a park one summer. Then when the broads went and got their nuccas, the Sin Sisters switched from the razors to the guns and shot the park up. No one dared speak on it, so they walked away as if shit didn't happen. Did you pay attention to the ice them broads were rocking?"

"A little bit, but my focus was on something else."

"Dig that. Those broads are some high-caliber bitches, boss man. The rumors fluctuate from being some high-priced hoes, to some big-time-balling bitches, to some straight-up killers."

"Interesting."

"So, how was the pussy?"

Shot smiled and answered honestly. "Fantastic!"

Before he could speak more, Daun came into the room. "Excuse me, Daddy."

"Hold on, Cotton," Hot Shot said as he set his phone on his lap. "What's up, love?"

"Janeen is on her way. She wants some breakfast, so we're going to go to Jimmy's Eggs. Is that all right with you?"

"Yes, that's perfect."

"She also asked me to ask you if your friend who was at the Grenadier with you could join us."

Shot smiled as he put his phone back to his ear and said, "Say, do you want to meet me at Jimmy's Eggs to eat?"

"I already ate. What's up?"

"Daun said her sister wants you to join us for breakfast, but since you've already eaten, I'll tell her you said maybe another time."

"Are you fucking kidding me! Come on with that shit, boss man! Which Jimmy's Eggs? I'm on my way right now!"

After Daun told him which Jimmy's Eggs restaurant they were going to eat at, Shot told Cotton, and then said, "But what about what you just told me? 'Dangerous,' remember?"

"I ain't worried about them broads if you're not!"

Laughing, Hot Shot said, "Whatever. See you in a little bit." He ended the call and stood and walked to

Daun as she slipped into some slacks that hugged her ass perfectly. He turned her to face him and asked, "What made your sister want to meet my mans Cotton?"

She smiled and said, "After I told her about how you put it down on me last night and this morning, she said she wanted to see if your mans had some of that in him too."

"I thought you two shared everything?"

She looked him directly in his eyes and gave him a kiss. "We do, but I'm not sharing you, Shot. You're all mine, Daddy."

He kissed her back and for the first time in months, Nola was no longer on his mind.

Chapter Four

Cotton was leaning against Shot's Audi in the parking lot of Jimmy's Eggs restaurant when Janeen pulled into the parking space next to where he was parked. He smiled as he watched as the sexy ladies exited the BMW. *My God, if I can crack this bad broad, I am definitely in the game,* he said to himself as he watched as Janeen approach him with a bright smile on her face. Definitely a good sign. "What's good with you, sexy chocolate?" asked Janeen as she stood directly in front of Cotton.

"Everything is good if I've done something to attract your attention, ma."

"Is that right?"

"Yep."

"Well, let's go get our eat on and see what we can make of this afternoon."

Cotton reached out his hand as Janeen placed her right hand in his and they led the others inside of the restaurant. After they were seated and made their orders, Shot watched with an amused expression on his face as Cotton and Janeen openly flirted back and forth. He wondered about what Cotton had told him about the Sin Sisters and was trying to think of a nonchalant way to start a conversation to see if he could get the two gorgeous sisters talking about how they got their money. Cotton, ever the one to not mince words, gave him the opening he was looking for.

"So, tell me, are you two really sisters?"

"Yeah, same mother, different fathers," answered Daun.

"So, it's safe to say we can blame all that sexiness you two possess on your mama."

Laughing, Janeen said, "If you're talking about all this ass we're packing, then, yeah, blame it on moms."

"In that case, I think it's only right that we have a toast to your mom because she definitely blessed both of you," Cotton said and laughed.

Shaking his head, Shot smiled and raised his glass of orange juice as they all clinked their glasses. "I truly hope that this will be the start of something good for all of us," Shot said as he sipped some more juice.

"Daddy, you've already made sure that this *is* the start of something good," Daun said as she stared directly into his brown eyes.

"Damn, Shot, what you do to my sister?"

He grinned and said, "A gentleman never brags on his discreet actions. Let's just say I tried my best to please."

"From the way you got my sister all goof acting and calling you 'Daddy' and shit, I'd say you did some hell of a pleasing!"

They all laughed.

"I aim to please! I have a question for you two."

The sisters waited for him to ask and remained silent.

"What do those SS emblems mean? Neither of your names begins with an S, so you have me curious."

"How long have you been in Oklahoma City, Shot?" asked Daun.

"About three months now."

"What brought you to our city?"

"Business."

"Do you mind telling us what kind of business?"

"Very profitable business. I am a man that gives people what they want or need; depends on how you look at it."

"Drugs?"

He didn't answer her.

"Guns?"

"Whatever is needed I get, for a price."

"When I first laid on you, I could tell you're about getting your money. You have a look about you that shows it. You're not too flashy, yet you dress classy enough to be a businessman on either side of the law."

"Compliments will get us back to your place doing more of what we did last night, or should I say, this morning?"

"Both!" They started laughing. "But for real, talk to me, Daddy, what's your business out this way? We might be able to assist your some."

"I'm not accustomed to speaking on my business, love. And I believe I asked a question first before you started with yours. You first, and then we can proceed."

"Oh, our SS emblems. They stand for the Sin Sisters."

"Sin Sisters? Mmm, so you're both sisters in sin?"

"Something like that. Something we came up with when we were good little Catholic girls. We've always been naughty, and now that we've grown up, we've become even naughtier."

"Damn, that shit sounds hot," said Cotton.

Janeen placed her hand on top of his and said, "Keep on looking so edible, sexy chocolate, and you're going to see how naughty I *really* am."

Cotton sighed, raised his hand, and said, "Check, please!"

Everyone started laughing.

"Now come on, Daddy, talk to me. What's your business?" asked Daun.

He stared at her for a moment, and then said, "I make money by selling whatever is needed. Drugs, guns, whatever. Whatever kind of drug and whatever kind of weapon. There's nothing I cannot get my hands on."

"Damn, that sound like you have a monster plug somewhere."

"I have business associates all over the place, and if I don't have direct access to what's asked of me to deliver, it won't take me more than forty-eight hours to get whatever is asked of me."

"Where are you from originally?"

"California."

"What part?"

"Inglewood."

"Don't we have some cousins who live out there, sister?"

"Yeah, but they stay in Oakland, I think," answered Janeen.

"So, if I needed, say, a couple of kilos of cocaine, could you get that for me, Daddy?"

"Yes."

"What if I needed an order for, say, fifty brand-new 9 mm SIG Sauers?"

"I can handle that as well."

"Pills, can you handle a few bundles of Ecstasy and Oxy?"

"Yes. Before you continue, please understand that there is nothing I cannot get as long as you have the funds necessary."

"I feel that."

"Now, can you answer some questions for me since you've gotten all my business?"

"Ask away."

"The drug trade, is that you and your sister's business?"

Daun stared at her sister for a moment, and Hot Shot watched Janeen give Daun a subtle nod. She said, "Kinda-sorta, in a way. We have some people we deal with who dip and dab with the drugs. We've had certain issues with finding someone who can be consistent with meeting our needs. This may become even more special than either of us ever imagined."

"Maybe, but right now, I'm ready to eat. I worked up quite an appetite from our adventure," he said as he noticed the waitress coming their way with their food.

When they were all finished eating, they sat back full and content. Their conversations switched back and forth from business stuff to sexual flirting. Shot was definitely feeling Daun, and he could tell that Cotton was ready to jump Janeen's bones just as soon as he could. Cotton received a call on his cell and after one look at his caller ID, he frowned and said, "Excuse me, ladies, but I need to take this call." They nodded and became silent as he answered the phone. "What's good, Sharp Shoota?"

Upon hearing the name Sharp Shoota, both of the sisters shot each other a look. Neither paid attention that Shot saw the look they gave to each other. "So, they know Sharp Shoota, huh?" he said to himself.

"Yeah, it's all good. When do you want to hook up?"

"Whenever you ready. You with your mans?"

"Yep."

"Okay, give me a holla at this number, and we can link up and make it happen."

"All right, I'll hit you back in a minute," Cotton said and hung up the phone.

"They're ready?" asked Shot.

"Yep."

"I hate to have to bring this to an abrupt end, ladies, but duty calls. What's the game plan for this Saturday night?"

"Since we did the Grenadier last night, I thought we might pop in at City Walk and see what that crowd is like. Either that or Club Social. That is, unless you guys have something else in mind for us?" said Daun.

"Now you already know we got some plans for y'all, so don't you dare think any different," Cotton said, staring directly at Janeen.

"Mmmm, don't you make any promises you can't keep, sexy chocolate," Janeen said and gave him a kiss on the cheek.

"How about this, me and my mans will go handle this business, and then hook up with you two ladies for a nice meal somewhere, and then we hit those clubs up together?"

"And after the clubs?" asked Daun with a smile on her face, knowing what he was going to say.

"Afterward, we do what we did last night, but this time, longer and much better."

"Better? Oh, Lord! It gets better?"

"Trust me, love, it's really better."

She fanned herself and said, "Damn, Daddy."

Shot noticed how Daun's smile quickly turned to a frown and asked, "Something wrong, Daun?"

Daun ignored his question and told her sister, "It's SS time, Janeen. Look who just came into this mothafucka."

Janeen looked toward the door, and once she focused on the two men and one female who entered the restaurant, she too frowned and reached inside of her purse. Before either Shot or Cotton could react, both of the sisters were out of their seats and damn near running toward the front of the restaurant.

"What the fuck?" asked Cotton.

"Come on!" Shot said as he too jumped up and followed the sisters, hoping he could stop them from doing something extremely stupid in the restaurant in the middle of the afternoon. He made it to Daun's side just as she was about to raise the pistol she had in her right hand. "Don't, love, not here. You'll be in the back of a squad car before we can make it out of Edmond."

"This is my business, Shot, not yours. I suggest you and your mans beat it. This is how we get down when a bitch-ass chump tries to play us for our money."

Shot noticed how the Daddy thing disappeared and also how Daun's pretty face was distorted in anger. "I respect your get down, love, but I would appreciate it if you let me assist you." Before she could respond, he turned toward the man Daun was about to pull her pistol on and said, "I suggest we step outside so we can address this properly, my man, because my lady friend here really wants to do you something."

Shaking his head no nervously, the man said, "Nah, man, fuck that! I'm safer staying in here."

Janeen eased by Shot and slapped the shit out of the man with her pistol and yelled, "You bitch-ass nigga, you ain't safe nowhere! You think we give a fuck about going to jail? You better bring your punk ass outside right mothafucking now or get shot up in this bitch! Now, move, nigga! You mothafuckas too! Move it!"

Shot and Cotton stood there amazed at what they were witnessing. Not only did the group of three do as they were told, but no one in the restaurant seemed to be paying any attention to the ladies and their antics. *JT would have a fit if I went to jail behind this crap,* he said to himself as he quickly followed the group out of the restaurant while Cotton went and paid the bill for their breakfast.

Once they were outside, Daun was yelling at the guy who she was on the verge of shooting. "It's been a month since we cleaned up your shit, bitch. What, you think we do this shit for nothing? Where is our fucking money?"

"Come on, Daun, you know I told you it was slow for me. The ends are good. Ain't no need for you to be going ape shit on me like this. I ain't trying to play y'all."

"Yeah, you know Bubba is going to pay you. Why you tripping, Daun? Damn," said the female who was with Bubba.

Janeen slapped the shit out of her so fast Cotton jumped damn near two feet in the air. "Bitch, who the fuck you think you talking to? You got to be out of your fucking mind to think you can speak to a Sin Sister like that. You better stay in your fucking place or get your entire look rearranged." She then turned toward Bubba and said, "You got your credit good and was supposed to get the loans you needed to handle the business. It's been two months. *Two months,* bitch! You have seven days to get that money. *Seven fucking days.* Do you hear me, Bubba?"

"Yeah, I hear you, Janeen. I hear you."

"But do you fucking *understand?*" asked Daun through gritted teeth.

Bubba gave her a fucked-up look and sarcastically said, "Yeah, I fucking understand."

Bad move, Bubba. Before either Cotton or Shot could react, Daun slapped Bubba in the face so hard, Shot could have sworn she broke his jaw. "Don't! You! Ever! Get! Slippery! At! The! Lips! With! Me! Bitch! I'll! Fucking! Kill! You! You! Ho! Ass! Bitch! Do you understand me?"

Holding the side of his face with tears streaming down his cheek, Bubba cried, "I hear you, Daun, I hear you. Seven days I will have your ends. I swear to God!"

Ignoring him, Daun turned toward Shot, smiled with all traces of her anger gone in an instant, and said, "Okay, Daddy, y'all go on and handle your business and give me a call so we can hook up for dinner." She then reached and grabbed Shot's phone out of his pocket and put her number in his phone, gave him a kiss, and said, "See ya later, Daddy." Shot watched her, stunned and speechless as she went and got inside of Janeen's BMW.

Janeen was staring at Bubba, his friend, and the female that she'd slapped the shit out of with a look as if she was debating whether she should shoot them. Cotton touched her on her shoulder, and she seemed to snap out of her murderous mood and smiled at him. "Damn, sorry you had to see us get down like that, sexy chocolate. Let me get out of here. I'll see you later too, right?"

Cotton smiled at her and said, "You just make sure you can get my dick as hard as it is now later with your deadly fine ass!"

She smiled and gave him a quick kiss on the lips and ran and jumped inside of her car and sped out of the parking lot, leaving both men watching them as they left totally fucked up at what they had just witnessed.

"Damn, boss man, do you believe that shit?"

"I believe it because I saw it with my own two eyes, Cotton."

"What have we gotten ourselves into with those broads?"

"Your guess is as good as mines, champ. Come on, we got some bread to get," Shot said as he led the way toward his car.

Chapter Five

The meeting location was arranged at Kevin Durant's new restaurant. Cotton was mad because Shot didn't want him to come to the meeting. If it would have been just Sharp Shoota they were meeting, then Shot would have let Cotton do the deal alone, but since both Big Shoota and Sharp Shoota would be there, Shot wanted Cotton out of the way. He didn't want Cotton caught up with this too heavy because he knew sooner or later that JT may want to pull Cotton in, and he would then become a victim of Operation Cleanup. Cotton had become like a brother to Shot, and he realized that he was going to have to find a way to get him immunity for all of the crimes he had committed, all in the name of Operation Cleanup. The thing was, he didn't know if JT or the director would go for that.

He put Cotton to the back of his mind as he headed toward KD's restaurant. He was still flabbergasted with the actions of Daun and Janeen. The Sin Sisters were no joke. He had to make sure he kept his feelings in check when it came to Daun because it looked like they too would become victims of Operation Cleanup. *Man, this is getting wild,* he thought as he pulled into the parking lot of the restaurant and entered it. By the time he was seated, Big Shoota and Sharp Shoota entered the restaurant and came and joined Shot at his table. After they were seated, Shot said, "Good afternoon, gentlemen."

"What's up, cuz? So, you're Hot Shot, huh?" asked Big Shoota. Big Shoota looked to be around five foot ten and was basically a taller version of Sharp Shoota. Both wore their hair in long braids and were dressed almost identically in all-blue Crip attire.

"Yes, I am him. And you're Big Shoota?"

"The one and only, cuz."

"Perhaps after this transaction, I hope we can continue on and do more good business."

"If your work is right, then I don't see why not. But before we proceed with this, I wanna know something."

"What's up?"

"Why was it so important for me to come and meet with you?"

"When I do business on any level, I prefer to meet the men I deal with. I like to look the men I deal with in the eyes. Just a preference of mine."

"That shit sounds like some police shit, for real. No dis, cuz, but I got to ask even though my li'l homie here told me he asked you already. Are you working for the police of any form? That's a law enforcement agency?" Shoota asked as he stared directly at Hot Shot.

Shot returned his stare with a poker player's intensity and said, "No way. I am not a police officer, nor do I work for any form of law enforcement agency."

Shoota stared at him for a full minute before smiling and said, "Well, now that's outta the way, how you wanna handle this business, cuz?"

"I'm not really hungry since I just ate a couple of hours ago, so I thought we could have a few drinks and chop it up some, and while we chop it up, Sharp Shoota here can go outside to my car and retrieve the small duffel bag that's sitting on the front passenger's seat and check it out in your vehicle. Once he's satisfied with the quality of my product, he can put the money inside of my car and come back and join us."

"Damn, like that, cuz? Like *that?* You trust us and you just meeting us? That's some wild shit."

"I don't think you're the type of men that would play with my product. I mean, is $130,000 worth going to war for? Because if you try to do anything shady, you *will* have a war on your hands."

Big Shoota started laughing and said, "I like that shit. I respect your get down, cuz. That's some real shit right there."

Shot nodded as he saw the waitress approaching their table. He ordered a peach Cîroc while both Crips ordered double shots of Crown Royal on the rocks. "I've been to plenty of states getting paper, and I've always believed in being as straight up as I can when it comes to the business. That way, there will never be any misunderstanding on how I move."

"*That's* what's up, cuz. My li'l homie tells me your man said you're from Cali."

"Yes, born and raised in Inglewood."

"You affiliated?"

"No. Never had time for the gang thing. Too much paper for that. Money has always been my motivation in life."

"Inglewood, huh? I heard it's nothing but Bloods out there. That true?" asked Sharp Shoota.

"Yes. Inglewood is mostly a Blood city, but there are several Crip sets as well. I grew up in a Blood neighborhood and went to school with plenty of Crips. Around my way, they all know that's not my lane, and we get along just fine," Hot Shot said as the waitress returned with their drinks and asked if they were ready to order anything to eat. After they declined and told her they were just having drinks and enjoying the scenery, she seemed somewhat agitated. Shot made a mental note to make sure he tipped her well. "From what I heard, the bang thing out here is serious."

"Yeah, but the beef with the Bloods isn't as rough as it is with the other Crips in the town. The Hoover fools be trying to get at us something serious so we're constantly going at it."

"That's wild because that's a serious beef back home; been big beef as long as I can remember. I've met some original Hoovers as well as some original Sixties, and they have both told me that they would rather beef and kill a Hoover or a Sixty before they killed a Blood. That's something that confused me greatly."

"That's how serious the beef is, cuz. It's us or them since they deep, and we're deep. It is what it is," said Sharp Shoota.

"So, do you have any problems with killing other Crips?"

"Nope. It's them or us. We're keeping with the beef like it is back in Cali, and we're holding our own quite well."

"But doesn't that beef interfere with the money?"

"Sometimes, but fuck it. We can't let those fools get too aggressive without being more aggressive. It's the law of the land," said Big Shoota.

"Killing other brothers in the name of a color or a set . . . That is something I've never understood, and I've been around that way of life my entire existence."

"When you're not a part of it, it's hard to understand. When it comes to this gangsta shit, cuz, it's about loyalty to your set and representing it with all you got. Kill or be killed."

"And that doesn't bother you that you're killing other black men?"

"Like the homie said, it's either them or us. I'm unfeeling, uncaring, and remorseless when it comes to slaying my enemies. I don't know words like 'compassion' or 'empathy.' My name ain't Big Shoota for nothing, Shot. I'm a killer, plain and simple."

"You kill for your set and ready to die for it as well?"

"Yeah. Honor in death. You die for your hood, you died doing what real Crips is supposed to do. Crip hard. The death of honored warriors. Read that somewhere when I was in the pen. But for real, in my eyes, ain't no honor in being dead. When you gone, you gone. The homies will get your name tatted and will honor you with parties or visits at the grave site, but once a nigga gone, he gone."

Sharp Shoota remembered what Cotton had told him about how Shot didn't care for the use of the word "nigga" and said, "Cuz, I forgot to tell you that Shot here would prefer if we didn't use the word 'nigga.'"

Big Shoota sipped his drink and laughed. "My bad, Hot Shot, no dis intended. I can respect that, a man of principles."

"We have to stand for something in this life. I feel somewhat like a hypocrite at times being a black man doing the business I do, but it is what it is. That's how I was raised. Thank you for respecting that."

"No problem, cuz. All right, Sharp, go on and handle that business. We need to go get thangs ready for the party later on."

"I'm driving the white Audi out there. Here's the keys. Hit the alarm and it will unlock," Shot said as he gave Sharp Shoota his keys for his car.

After Sharp Shoota left, Big Shoota asked, "Have you dealt with any of them Hoover fools out here."

"Not directly, no. My mans Cotton has had some dealings with them for smaller transactions."

"When and if you do, you need to watch out for those fools. They are some shady suckas for real, cuz."

"Are you telling me this to warn me of them or because of your dislike for them?"

Big Shoota smiled and said, "Both. Fuck them ni— excuse me, fuck them bitches."

"Duly noted."

"The homie tells me you can get your hands on some heat too. Is that right?"

"Yes."

"Any type of heat?"

"Whatever you want, I can get it."

"Hmm, I might want to get some serious heat since it's about to be summertime. Shit will get to cracking, and I need to make sure the homies are working with some shit heavier than pistols."

"What do you have in mind?"

"I do a lot of reading. I know I don't look like a reader, but I love that CIA espionage shit. You know, that terrorist killer shit. I read this book by Vince Flynn and his main character, Mitch Rapp be having some serious firepower. There was this one gun he used called a Galil SAR. I want to get my hands on a few of those bad boys and put some serious work in on them Hoovers."

The Galil SAR is an Israeli-made assault rifle. SAR standing for Short Assault Rifle. The Israelis developed that particular assault rifle after the war in 1967 because they felt they needed a smaller, lighter combat rifle. "It's a very precise and deadly weapon. Comes with a stand thirty-round magazine and can be flipped from semi- to fully automatic. You are very serious about putting in the work."

"Yep. Like I said, they don't call me Shoota for nothing. Damn, you know your weapons, I see."

"It's necessary that I know what I'm distributing. Some of my buyers like to know that I am knowledgeable about what I'm selling them."

"That's what's up, cuz. So, can you get your hands on some of those SARs for me?"

"How many?"

"How much?"

"Depends on how many. The normal price for those run around $2,500. If you bought more than ten, I would drop the price to about $2,000 apiece."

"Damn, more than ten?"

"Yes."

"Can I ask what you're getting them for?"

"Seventeen hundred."

"So, you would make three hundred off each one if I bought more than ten? But, if I got less than ten, I would have to spend $2,500 for each?"

"Yes."

"I appreciate your honesty, Shot. I think I'm going to like fucking with you, cuz. Ain't no lying in you. I like that shit."

Before Shot could respond, Sharp Shoota returned to the table and said, "I bust them open, cuz, and they're straight fish scale. Strong as fuck too. We good."

"That's what's up, cuz."

"The money is on the floor of the front seat, Shot. It's all there, cuz."

"I'm sure it is, Sharp Shoota."

"Give me a week or so to get this work crackin', and I'm going to get at you with the ends for ten of those SARs, cuz."

"Shall I make the order so I can have them on deck, or would you prefer for me to wait until you get at me?"

"My word is my word, Shot. You can go on and order them. I'll snatch up fifteen to be exact so I can get the 2-G ticket."

"I'll be ready when you call."

"That's the business. All right, then, cuz, we got some parting to do. It's my broad's sister's birthday, and we're going to the club and do it big Six-O style. You might want to come through. There's going to be some nice broads at the club."

"What club are you going to?"

"Club One 15. If you ain't doing shit, slide through, cuz. Drinks on the Sixties."

"I'm going out with some female friends. We might just come through."

"Trust me, cuz, if you do come through, you might not want to bring any female friends with you. When I tell you there will be some bad broads there, there are going to be some *superbad* broads there," Big Shoota said and laughed.

"I believe you, but the female friends I'm talking about bringing are bad in their own right." Hot Shot thought about it and figured he'd try to see if he could learn a little something about the Sin Sisters from the two Crips and asked, "You ever hear of the females that call themselves the Sin Sisters?"

Both of the Crips responded in unison, "Hell, yeah! Them bitches are crazy as fuck!"

"Don't tell me you fucking with one of them bitches, Shot," said Sharp Shoota.

"Afraid so. I had the pleasure of spending time with them, and I do agree with you about them being crazy. I watched them act a fool earlier today at Jimmy's Eggs out in Edmond. A fool who owed them money came into the restaurant, and they went ballistic on him and a female what was with the dude."

"Did they cut the female?" asked Sharp Shoota.

"No."

"Did they shoot the dude?" asked Sharp Shoota.

"No."

"Then you ain't seen shit, Shot. When them broads get down, they don't play. Normally, someone either gets shot or cut. I'm a fool about mines, but I stay clear of them broads. They on some goofy shit, for real," said Sharp Shoota.

"What are they into?"

Both of the Crips shrugged.

"From what I've been told, they get down with a little bit of everything. But their main goal is something to do with credit cards or clearing people's credit. Some shit like that," said Shoota.

Shot thought back to what Janeen had told the guy Bubba about getting his credit right for some loan or something like that, and he realized Shoota had given him some vital information. "Well, I've just met them, and like I said, they may be with me if I do go to your party. Will that be a problem?"

Shoota laughed and said, "Nope, it's all good. Tell me, which one are you getting at?"

Shot smiled and said, "Daun."

Shoota groaned and said, "Damn, she is *fine,* cuz!"

They all started laughing.

"She *is* bad, but if I had the chance to fuck with them, I would holla at Janeen's bad ass," said Sharp Shoota.

"My mans Cotton is currently trying his luck that way."

"No shit. Damn, cuz, you two fools done came up! But be careful, cuz. Those bitches ain't no joke when crossed."

"Not worried about that at all. I don't cross people," Shot said seriously.

"*That's* what's up. You try to come through, cuz. I want to see you with them bad, crazy-ass bitches," laughed Big Shoota.

"I'll see if they're with it. If not, I'm sure you will see us out and about sooner or later."

"All right, cuz, let us get on. You stay safe, Shot," Big Shoota said as he reached across the table and shook hands with Shot.

After shaking both of the Crips' hands, Shot told them, "Stay safe yourselves, gentlemen. Hopefully, this will be the start of some good business."

"No doubt. We'll holla, cuz," Sharp Shoota said as the stood and left the restaurant.

Hot Shot sipped some more of his drink, pulled out his phone, and called JT. When JT answered, he told him he needed fifteen SARs sent to him within the next two weeks and to make sure he had them ready and rigged with the transformers so they could be tracked when the time came to bring down Shoota and some of the Rolling Sixty Crips of Oklahoma City. Operation Cleanup had just got turned up in Oklahoma City. After he ended the call with JT, he thought about Daun and her sister. Looks like the Sin Sisters will be his next victims. "Better enjoy them while I can," he said to himself as he downed the rest of his drink. He stood and left a fifty-dollar tip for the waitress who gave him a mean look when he walked by her leaving the restaurant.

Chapter Six

Daun called Shot and informed him that they would not be able to meet them for dinner because something important had come up, so they agreed to meet at the City Walk Club at 11:00 p.m. He told her that he had been invited to a party at Club One 15 and asked her if they wanted to join him and Cotton. She was cool with that, so they flirted back and forth a bit, and then ended their call. After he hung up the phone with Daun, he went in his room and took a nap. He woke up a few hours later feeling refreshed and ready for another long night with the sexy Sin Sister.

He heard Cotton in the other room talking loud to someone on the phone, so he got up to see what the problem was. When he came into the living room, Cotton was yelling at someone, obviously a female because he kept calling her "baby" and telling her to calm down. Shot shook his head and went into the kitchen and grabbed a bottle of water. As he returned to the living room, he head Cotton scream several obscenities and watched as he hung up on whomever he was speaking to.

"What's up, champ? Problems in playboy land?"

"Ha-ha. Funny. Nah, man, that was that chick Shirin. She had the nerve to go off on me because I haven't called her yet. I mean, damn, it's not like I fucked or some shit. Glad I got hooked up with Janeen. She doesn't seem like she's going to be a headache like that other broad."

"You never know. Once you put that wood on her, she may get crazy with it too."

"God, I hope not. You seen how her and her sister gets down. That would *not* be a good look. So, everything went cool with those Sixty nuccas?"

"Yes, everything went fine." Shot turned and went back into the bedroom and returned with several stacks of hundred-dollar bills and tossed them to Cotton. "Here's fifteen grand for you, three thousand off every bird I sold them."

"*That's* what's up! Do you know where we're taking the Sin Sisters out to eat?"

"Change of plans. Daun hit me and told me that they had to take care of something important, so we're going to meet them at the City Walk Club and proceed from there. Big Shoota is giving a birthday party for his girl's sister, and he invited us to swing through Club One 15. I asked Daun if they would be with it, and she said yes, so that's the plan. We meet them at City Walk and chill for a bit, then move it to Club One 15 and see what's going down at Shoota's party."

"*That's* what's up. I've never been to Club One 15. It's over there off Sheridan. I heard it was cool, though."

"I learned a little more about the Sin Sisters and how they are rocking out here. They make moves with some credit scam; not sure what exactly, but it sounds interesting."

"I thought they was lightweight into the work. I mean, they did ask about some guns, but they seemed more focused on if you could help them with the drugs."

"I thought the same thing until Big Shoota told me he had heard all types of rumors over the years, but the word was their main hustle was something to do with credit and loans or what have you. I remembered hearing Janeen tell that dude they served at Jimmy's Eggs how they fixed his credit, and he was supposed to get the loans to pay them back, and it seemed to match up."

"What you wanna do? Do some business with them on the credit tip?"

Laughing, Shot said, "I've never had any credit problems in my life, champ. I have over an 800 score on my credit."

"Shit, I don't. My credit screwed all the way up."

"Maybe you can get at Janeen and see if she can fix that for you. Never know, she might do it for free . . . that is, if you can give her that wood properly. Something tells me she's going to give you more than you can handle, champ."

"Not worried at all. I plan on serving her real decentlike. She will love my get down and enjoy herself thoroughly, trust that. I'm not going to give her the normal ejaculatory inevitability, which translates to me just getting mines. You know my rule, come before I do or come when I come back!"

Shaking his head, Shot said, "Crude as ever. Do you really take the time to think about the things you say? I mean, you come up with some of the craziest stuff."

Cotton shrugged and said, "It is what it is. I speak it how I see it. I keeps it real, though. Janeen obviously wants it, so she will get my A-game."

"I sure hope so. You disappoint, and she might slap you with a pistol."

"Then there's going to be one less Sin Sister."

Laughing, Hot Shot said, "Yeah, whatever, tough guy. Anyway, what we looking like businesswise? We straight?"

"Yeah, we're good. No one has hit me up today, but odds are I'll be getting some hits later. If so, then they will be put off because Janeen gets all my attention tonight."

With a frown on his face, Shot said, "That depends on what type of hits you get. We don't turn down any serious money, champ, always remember that."

"Oh, for sure. If the digits are big, then Janeen will have to hold up while I go get that bread."

"I feel you. We might as well go and get dressed. I want to go have dinner at Kevin Durant's restaurant."

"Damn, the food was that good that you want to eat there twice in one day?"

"No, I didn't eat when I met with Shoota and Sharp Shoota. We had a drink and chopped it up some. I checked out the menu while I was there and some of the choices looked pretty good So, like I said, let's go on and get dressed and go have dinner there. On you, of course," Hot Shot said and smiled at his little helper.

"On me my ass! It's on *you*, boss man. I paid the last two times we went out to eat."

"Whatever. Go get yourself together. Looks like we're in for a very interesting evening."

"And I plan to make it one of the best nights of my life."

"I'm sure you will, Cotton, I'm sure you will."

The Sin Sisters were sitting down in Janeen's living room having a serious discussion about their business. They were undecided on how they were going to make their next move.

"I'm telling you, sister, we should go on and make the call and have that bitch-ass Bubba laid down. He's going to keep shaking us. Let's chalk it up as a loss and go on and do that bitch," said Daun.

"We do that then we lose all the way around. The money we spent to have that punk-ass bitch's credit hooked up—gone. The money we paid our people at Equifax—gone. The money we sent to our people at both Transunion and Experian—gone. That's too much money to be coming up off on. If we pay to have him done, then that's even *more* money out our pocket. We don't have it like that to just chalk this one up as a loss right now. Shit ain't been coming in like it's supposed to."

"I feel you, sister, but at the same time, I don't like how that bitch can think he can play us like that. Word gets out that we let him make it, then we look weak, and that's *not* a good look."

"You right. So, we need to make sure we set an example, but at the same time, stay dead on that coward's ass so we can get what's owed to us."

Daun smiled and said, "What you got on your mind for his soft ass?"

Janeen returned her sister's smile and said, "Gimme a minute to let things marinate and I'm sure I'll come up with something wicked enough to make a strong enough statement for us."

"Okay, now, what about Shot and Cotton? Should we get at them about that scandalous-ass-fool Shoota? You know he's no good, and sooner or later, he will try to make a grimy move against them."

Janeen didn't speak; instead, she just stared at her sister.

"Why are you staring at me like that?"

"You're really feeling that guy, sister, and I'm wondering whether that's a good thing. You don't normally meet a man and fall so easily for him. The sex was great, I get that, but damn!"

"The sex wasn't great, sister, it was fanfuckingtastic! But there's more to it than that. There's something about how he carries himself that I'm feeling. Plus, with our finances taking these hits, he may just be able to help us out. You heard him at the restaurant. He said there's nothing he can't get his hands on for us. We can make some side moves and make some nice change with the pistol thing if he gives us a cool ticket. That, plus the Oxy and Ecstasy."

"You right. Shit, we can even twist up some change if we cop a few kilos from him."

Daun frowned at her sister's comment.

"Don't frown at me like that. I know you don't like fucking with Prophet, but he spends a grip when it comes to his business. If Shot can plug us decent with the cocaine, we can get at Prophet and make a killing. That fool buys shit by the hundreds."

"I know, but you already know I ain't fucking with him. I'm not going anywhere near him, sister. If we deal with him, it will be *you* that gets at his ass, *not* me."

"Stop it. As soon as I give his ass a call, he's going to ask about you before he even says hi to my ass. He has a weakness for you, Daun."

Shaking her head vehemently, Daun said, "Weakness, my ass. That man is dangerous, and I swore once I stopped fucking with him that I would never go near his ass again. So like I said, if we get at him, it will be you. I don't give a fuck what he asks about, I'm not going nowhere near his sadistic ass."

"I understand. Let's wait and see what we can come up with on the other stuff with Shot. We might not need to go the cocaine route. Tomorrow, I'll hit Todd in Tulsa and see if he and his bank-robbing crew need any weapons. You just get with Shot in the morning after you finish fucking his brains out and see if he can give us the love we need for the guns."

Smiling brightly, she said, "Now, you know I don't have a problem with that. What about you? You're planning on having a good time with Cotton, right?"

"Mm-hmm. I'm going to give him the opportunity to blow my back out. But he's just Shot's boy. I like his black ass, though. He's cute. You know I have a soft spot for dark-skinned men."

"Yeah, I know. But back to my original question, should we get at them about Shoota and his snake ways?"

"Definitely. I'll talk to Cotton and you get at Shot. We'll let them know about Shoota's scandalous exploits of the past so they can remain on point. That should give us a good standing with Shot, so hopefully, when we get at him on the business tip, he will show some love."

"He's going to show us that regardless. Trust me, he's feeling me just as much as I'm feeling his sexy, fine ass."

"Don't be so cocky, sister. That man strikes me as a straight-up businessman. He doesn't seem like the type that would let his sex life interfere or sway him when it comes to business."

"You know what? You're right. So when I get at him, it will be on some strictly business approach."

"Good. Now, you might as well take your ass on home and get dressed. I'll be by there to scoop you up in a few hours. Right now, I'm about to take me a long, hot bath and trim the coochie so Cotton will be able to have some fun eating her out real good."

"TMI, sister, TMI."

"I didn't say that when you told me how good Shot was serving your ass when you were on your patio talking with me." They both laughed.

By the time Shot and Cotton finished their meals at Kevin Durant's restaurant, they were feeling real good. Full from a great meal and a little tipsy from a few glasses of peach Cîroc, they left the restaurant and headed to the City Walk Club where they were going to meet with the Sin Sisters. When they arrived at the club, the parking lot was packed, and there was a large crowd of people standing in front of someone's brand-new Ferrari. As they strolled toward the entrance of the club, they saw that the Ferrari belonged to none other than Russel Westbrook of the Oklahoma City Thunder.

"Look, boss man, there's Russel Westbrook," Cotton said as they got in line to enter the club.

"Yeah, I guess since the Spurs ended their season last week, he needs to unwind and get his club on."

"Yeah, that was a cold defeat right there. I really thought once Ibaka came back, they were going to look at the Spurs."

Shaking his head, Shot said, "No way. The Spurs are playing like a well-oiled machine right now. You see what they did to the Heat in game one."

"I don't know about that, boss man. If LeBron wouldn't have cramped up, they might have lost that game."

"We'll see what happens in game two," Shot said as he paid for their entrance into the club. They made a beeline straight toward the bar and ordered a couple of glasses of Cîroc and checked out the scenery. They were enjoying the view of lovely ladies who were inside the club. There were a variety of women to choose from, and Shot had to admit that some of the white females were putting the sisters to shame. That struck him as odd because he wasn't one to be turned on by white women. Cotton, on the other hand, loved him some snow bunnies.

"Damn! Look at all those badass white broads walking around this bitch. Janeen better hurry her ass up and get here before I snatch me one of those beckys and be gone for the night."

Shaking his head, Shot laughed and sipped his drink. His phone buzzed in his pocket, and when he pulled it out, he saw that he'd received a text from Daun informing him that they had just pulled into the parking lot of the club. "Well, looks like the Sin Sisters are here, so you're going to have to put your white-girl fetish on hold for the time being."

"That's cool, but I will definitely be back at this spot next week!"

Though there were plenty of sexy women inside of the club, when the Sin Sisters entered, it seemed as if everyone inside of the club had their eyes locked on the two badass sisters as they stepped to the bar and stood next to Cotton and Shot. Shot could tell that some men were totally shocked when they saw Daun come to him and give him a kiss on the lips, then grab a napkin and wipe her lip gloss gently off of his lips. Cotton wore a shit-eating grin as Janeen too gave him a kiss. Both men were feeling themselves because, without a doubt, they had the two baddest women inside of the City Walk.

Shot stared at Daun's attire and said, "I like, love. You're looking quite edible tonight."

With a grin on her face, she asked, "Does that mean you're going to eat me up later on tonight, Daddy?"

"Definitely."

"Mmmm."

Not to be outdone, Cotton told Janeen, "Not only are you gangsta with your get down, you are one classy-looking woman, babe. It's truly an honor to have you by my side this evening."

She gave him another kiss, but this time, she slipped him a little tongue and said, "Compliments like that will get you all the pussy you can handle, sexy chocolate."

Laughing, Cotton said, "Well, please let me tell you how good you're making that dress and those Red Bottoms and—"

Laughing, Janeen said, "Okay, okay! I get it, baby. This pussy is all yours tonight."

Cotton frowned.

"What's wrong?"

"Just for tonight?"

She smiled and said, "That all depends on how you perform, baby. You please this kitty, then you will have full access to her whenever you want. Cool?"

The frown vanished just as quickly as it appeared as Cotton said, "You damn skippy! Now, what are you two lovely ladies of sin drinking this evening?"

"I want to pop a bottle. How about some Rosé?" said Daun.

Shot turned and ordered a bottle of Rosé from the bartender. Once he had the bottle along with four flutes, he led the ladies toward a vacant table he spotted. They sat down, and Shot popped the bubbly and poured the ladies a drink. After pouring some for himself and Cotton, they made a small toast and clinked their flutes together. "To a great evening with two great-looking women."

"Cheers!" they all said in unison.

Daun downed her drink and stood and told Shot she wanted to dance. They went out on the dance floor and started bumping and grinding to Beyoncé's hit, "Drunk in Love." While they were dancing and enjoying themselves, Janeen took this opportunity to talk with Cotton and give him the warning about Big Shoota from Sixty.

"When we were eating earlier, we heard you when you were talking to Shoota. I assume that's Big Shoota from the Rollin' Sixties?"

"Yeah, that's him."

"How did everything go with your business? I ask because that dude is known to be coldhearted as well as a snake when it comes to the streets."

"Is that right?"

"For certain. He is no good, sexy chocolate. You and Shot need to be careful dealing with him. It will start out all good, then right when you think he is good peeps, he'll come with the shady shit and get at you. If he thinks you two are strong, then when he moves, he will make sure that neither of you are breathing once he's done."

"That's good looking out, babe, but we don't slip, and though I wasn't at the get down earlier, I'm positive

Big Shoota understands that me and my mans ain't to be fucked with."

"That's good to know, baby. I had to make sure you knew how he gets down."

"Right. Now, since we're speaking on things that happened earlier, can you put me up on something?" Cotton asked.

"What's up?"

"I heard you when you told that dude y'all were getting at that y'all did something for his credit or loan or something to that effect."

"Yeah."

"What's up with that? Y'all be on some credit moves? If so, I'm trying to do some business with you."

"That can be arranged. As a matter of fact, we're trying to do some business with you two as well. But later for that. Let's enjoy the evening and discuss business in the morning after I serve you breakfast in bed."

"Damn, sexy, fine. Classy as fuck, gangsta with it, plus you cook. I am *definitely* winning right about now."

Laughing, Janeen said, "Where did you get cooking from, sexy chocolate? I wasn't talking about serving your fine, dark ass no food for breakfast in the morning. I was talking about this sweet pussy I'm going to feed you!"

They both started laughing.

Janeen stopped abruptly and said, "Oh shit!"

"What's wrong?" asked Cotton.

"Shit is about to get real ugly. Come on!" she yelled as she jumped out of her seat and headed out to the dance floor where Shot and Daun were dancing. When they made it to where the two were, they saw Daun standing in between a man who was saying something slick to Shot. The man was huge, at least six foot four, and weighed close to 275 pounds. He had another man standing next to him who was just as big. Janeen stepped on the side of her sister and said, "Come on with this shit, Herc. Why you out here tripping the fuck out?"

"We come into the club and see this nigga dancing with Daun and holding onto her ass like she's his woman or something. You know we don't play that shit, Janeen."

Looking past Herc, Daun said, "Would you please tell your henchman to get the fuck away from me and my friend, Prophet?"

Prophet smiled lovingly at Daun and said, "Now, you know how Herc is when he thinks I've been disrespected, baby. Your friend needs to keep his hands to himself."

Daun rolled her eyes at him and said, "*Really,* Prophet? You aren't my man, and Herc is dead wrong for coming out here acting like an asshole. So, you need to call him the fuck off."

"Yeah, Prophet, chill with this silly shit," added Janeen.

Prophet shrugged his broad shoulders and said, "I don't care to see another man's hands all over that big ass, Janeen. That ass still belongs to me."

"I've heard enough of this rhetoric. If you feel I've disrespected you, my man, then why not tell your boy here to go and make his move? After I've finished handling him, then you can gladly get some," Hot Shot said in a tone that shocked the shit out of both men *and* the Sin Sisters as well. The only one who wasn't shocked was Cotton.

"Oh-oh, shit is about to get real."

Prophet and Herc started laughing.

"Did you hear what this nigga just said, cuz?" asked Herc. "On Hoover Crip, cuz, I'm about to beat the fuck out of your punk-ass nigga."

"If you call me that N-word one more time, I'm going to take it to you first. I feel you've disrespected Daun enough, but by calling me that word, I take serious offense. So, it's best you step or get ready to get served," Shot said as he gently moved Daun out of his way.

Daun tried to stand her ground and said, "Come on, Daddy, you don't know these guys. They're serious."

Shot stared at Daun with such intensity in his eyes that she actually could see his eyes transform into something seriously dangerous. It was like they were speaking to her telling her that he was about to hurt Herc *and* Prophet. She nodded as if she had been told something and stepped aside.

"Your punk ass sure you want this, cuz?" asked Herc.

With a smirk on his face, Shot said, "You talk all that smack, and now you're asking me if I'm sure I want what you think you can give me? That really makes you seem like a chum. Make your move if you're going to make one. You're boring me."

Herc turned around and gave his boss Prophet a look as if saying, "Do you want me to handle this nigga?" Prophet gave a slight nod of his head. Herc turned back and faced Shot and said, "I'm about to fuck your ass up, cuz. You got me fucked up, nigga, this is—" Herc didn't get to finish the sentence he was saying because Shot hit him with a tightly closed fist right in his throat. He followed that punch with a series of others to Herc's kidney, nose, and jaw, breaking both before dropping the big man with a powerful right uppercut. He did all of this so effortlessly that it looked somewhat choreographed. Big Herc was laid out on the dance floor, knocked out cold. There were several *"oohs"* and *"ahhs"* from the other clubbers as well as the security who came just as Shot delivered his knockout punch.

Shot wasn't even breathing hard when he turned and stared at Prophet and asked, "Are you ready for your turn, Prophet?"

Both of the Sin Sisters stared at Herc out cold on the floor and were completely shocked at what they had just witnessed.

"I told y'all it was about to get real," laughed Cotton.

Prophet gave his fallen homeboy/security man a look of disdain, then gave Shot a nod of admiration. He then glared at Daun with a look of total disgust and said, "'Daddy'? You called that man 'Daddy'?" With that said, he turned and walked off of the dance floor, and Daun knew that Shot had just brought a whole lot of drama into both of their lives.

Fuck!

Chapter Seven

The three extra large security guards who witnessed Shot's superb fighting skills approached him slowly and very politely asked him if he would leave the club because fighting was not tolerated there. Daun tried to intervene on his behalf saying that he hadn't started anything.

"Calm down, love, the man is just doing his job." He faced the security and gave him a nod and said, "No problem, I have another engagement to attend." He smiled at Cotton and told him to go get their bottle of Rosé so they could move on with their evening. Once they were out of the club, Shot smiled and said, "Well, ladies, since that got cut short, hopefully, we'll be able to enjoy ourselves at Club One 15."

Shaking her head, smiling, Daun said, "You are something else, Daddy."

Shot ignored her comment and told Cotton, "You ride with Janeen; Daun will ride with me. I'll follow you 'cause you know I don't know my way around this city yet."

"Gotcha," Cotton said as he grabbed Janeen's hand and led her toward her car that he saw was parked right next to Shot's Audi. When they were in front of the BWM, she tossed him the keys, and he smiled as he hit the key fob to unlock the car and opened the door for her. When she was inside, he closed the door and walked around the car to the other side pumping his fist. "Yes!"

Both Daun and Shot saw Cotton's antics and laughed as they got inside of the Audi. Once they were underway,

Shot sighed and said, "I really hate it when fools try me. It seems like this has become some sort of pattern."

"You didn't do anything wrong, Daddy. That's how Herc is. He does whatever Prophet tells him to do. I swear, I can't stand that prick."

He gave her a glance, then said, "Care to give me the history on you and this Prophet fella?"

She sighed heavily and said, "I wish there wasn't any history between me and that sick fuck, but sadly, there is."

She then went on to tell Shot about how they were in a relationship for about a year, and it ended because she found out that his taste went from being slightly rough sexually to damn near brutal. She went into vivid detail on how Prophet would tie her up and beat her. Bruise her entire body. He even went as far as to burn her with candles. When Shot asked her why she messed with a creep like that, she explained that he wasn't like that when they first met. He was the perfect gentleman. Wined and dined her and made her feel special.

"Where'd you meet him at?"

"I've always heard of him. He's one of the original 107 Hoover Crips out here in the city. He has been getting plenty of money out here since the late '90s when his big homeboys, Killa and Weasel, got kicked by the feds back in late '98. Our paths finally crossed when he heard about me and my sister's connect on cleaning up people's credit. He sent word to Janeen through a common friend, and we all met up to discuss business. We did what we do for him, and he was satisfied and paid us handsomely. He also hooked us up with some more people, and it was all good. Then he slid in how he was feeling me. He wasn't bad on the eyes, and it had been a good minute since I'd been with a man, so I was like, why not. I'll see what he's working with. Like I said, in the beginning, it was all good.

"Then one night he asked me if I was his woman. I hesitated and was like, 'I don't know if I want a man.' He actually broke down in tears and told me how much he loved me and wanted me to be his forever. That shit hit me hard, and I fell for it, hook, line, and sinker. I told him I would be his woman, and from there, shit went straight to hell, and I mean that literally. I was so afraid of his ass that I would hide from my sister for weeks until my body was healed because I didn't want her to know what I was letting that fuck do to me."

"How did you finally end that situation?" Shot asked, wishing he had beaten the crap out of Prophet.

"My sister. She figured out that something wasn't right, and when I tried to avoid her, she came over to his house, and when he wouldn't let her inside, she pulled her pistol out and told him if he didn't let her see me, he was going to die that day. She then barged inside and saw me and went nuts. It took all my strength to stop her from killing Prophet. She made me pack my shit and got me out of there. I was so bruised up and in pain that I could barely move.

"She took me home, and I stayed with her until I got right. Prophet would call and call and beg forgiveness and tell me to come back and he would never hurt me again, but by that time, I was back to my damn senses, and I told him it was a wrap. He swore that I was his forever and he would never let another man have me. That's been over a year now, and I've stayed clear of him and anywhere I think he may be. He's not the clubgoing type. That's why I was so shocked to see his ass tonight at the damn club. I'm telling you, Shot, that man is sick. He's also one of the coldest fools out here. He is about his business, and he will kill or have people killed. You're most likely number one on his hit list right about now. So, you're going to have to watch your back at all times, Daddy."

He grinned at her and said, "I don't like looking back like I'm nervous or something. I prefer to look straight ahead and move forward confidently, love."

"I'm serious, Daddy, that man is dangerous. He has a lot of beef out here in the city. The Bloods can't stand him, and the Neighborhood Crips want his head as well. And neither of them has even come close to getting at him."

"There's something you need to know about me. I have no conscience. I've been known to be ultracool under pressure and quite ruthless when called for. Don't worry about me, I'm good. Now, tell me, what's his hustle?"

"Drugs. He's one of the biggest dope boys in the state. It's a miracle he hasn't got knocked out yet. The main reason why is the fools who do the snitching know better than to tell on him because Prophet will slay their entire family if it ever happens."

"Mmmm."

"I would never forgive myself if something happened to you behind me, Daddy."

Ignoring that statement, Shot said, "So, you and your sister make moves with the credit thing, huh?"

"Yeah. But thangs have gotten kinda slow for us, so we're looking at making some other moves."

"Like what?"

"Was hoping you could hook us up with some pills and cocaine so we can get at some of our people we know that's into that and keep the flow coming in decent until things pick back up with our other moves."

"Exactly what *are* your other moves, if you don't mind me asking?"

She then broke down how they have connects inside all the major creditors and have inside people who can adjust people's credit scores. Equifax, Transunion, Experian, and the top one, myfico.com. Shot was really interested because that could definitely be a good bust for

Operation Cleanup. The mere thought of busting Daun and her sister made him think of what he did to Nola and her family, what ultimately led to him losing their unborn child. He knew that he had to make sure that he kept his feelings for Daun in check.

"You seem like a highly intelligent woman, what's up wit' the street life? Why not go to school and make a better, safer way for yourself?"

"I could ask you the same question, Daddy. You know how it is. I like living like a boss bitch. Boss living it up is the way my sister has to have it. When you come from nothing and get a hold of a little something, you want more and more and more."

Nodding in understanding, he said, "Yeah, I can relate."

"Lavish luxuries excite me. Money gives me power and an added sense of security. After dealing with that prick Prophet, I never thought I'd want a man for anything other than sex."

They were stopped at a red light, and he turned toward her and asked, "What changed?"

She looked him straight in the eyes and said, "You. You make me feel secure. You make me feel like I've never felt in my life. You are a special man, Daddy, and I hope we can make more of what we've started here."

The light turned green, and he sighed as he drove on. "I've recently gone through a bad breakup, Daun. I don't want to mislead you in any way, but jumping right back into something deep would not be productive for either of us. Let's take it slow and see what comes from it."

She smiled and said, "Damn."

"What?"

"You are a real one, Daddy. No games or lying in you. Most men would have said the exact opposite. They would have lied and told me they want the same thing as I want to get me all goofy and in love. I respect your honesty, Daddy. Thanks."

"It's how I was raised."

"Care to share your heartbreak with me since I've given you some very embarrassing personal info on my crazy life?"

He then told her all about Nola and how she lost their child by miscarrying. Of course, he skipped the part he played in getting her twin sister, brother, and two cousins locked up in federal prison. He told her how he had never loved a woman until he met Nola. He shared how much he hurts at night when he thinks about her, how he tosses and turns all night long, almost every single night since she refused to speak to him.

"That's some cold shit right there, for real. She is wrong for that. She's trying to remain loyal to her family. I admire that, but she is denying herself happiness all because of what happened to her family, and that's not fair to you or her."

"I feel that way, but I can't get her to see that type of reason."

"You said you haven't slept peacefully because you toss and turn every night since Nola stopped talking to you."

"Yes, this is true."

Shaking her head, Daun smiled and said, "That's not true, Daddy. You were sleeping soundly last night. When I got up this morning to use the bathroom, my cell phone rang, and you were out good. You didn't move when I answered it. You were sleeping so soundly, I chose to go into the living room so I wouldn't disturb you."

He smiled and asked, "What are you trying to say, Daun?"

"Maybe—just maybe—you've started to move on."

"Because of you?"

She shrugged and said, "Maybe. Me, combined with some supergood, exhilarating, and draining sex helped you have the first good night's sleep you've had in a long time."

"This is true," he admitted.

"Let's see if we can have a repeat performance later on, shall we?"

"Definitely," he answered with a smile on his face as he pulled into the parking lot of Club One 15.

As soon as the two couples entered the club, Sharp Shoota spotted them and made his way to them with a huge smile on his face as if they were the best of friends. "Damn, look at my dudes all fly and shit. You in here, cuz! Welcome to Club One 15! It's the night the Six-Os are turned all the way up! I see you brought your sand to the beach, huh? That's cool. The more lovely ladies in the building, the more this little shindig will be talked about around the city. Come on, let me take you to a table so you can get right. Drinks on me and the big homie tonight, cuz."

"Appreciate that, Sharp Shoota," Cotton said as he followed the young Crip toward a table in the back of the club. When Janeen saw Big Shoota a few tables away, she gave him a slight nod, and he returned one of his own. He raised his fist at Shot and stuck out his thumb, index, and middle finger, throwing up the Neighborhood Crip sign. Shot nodded and sat down at the table.

A waitress appeared just as they were seated and asked what they were drinking. Since they had already started on some Rosé, Shot felt they should stick with that and ordered another bottle of the expensive champagne. Sharp Shoota asked Cotton if he could have a quick word with him. They stepped away from the table and Sharp Shoota told him, "Cuz, that work was cavi, and we doing real good dumping it. We may need to get with you again soon."

"*That's* what's up. Now that your mans Shoota has met my mans Shot, we can hook up from now on, and it will be all good."

"That's what's up. Cuz, you two fools doing it right. The damn Sin Sisters. Wow, cuz. Do you know that dark-skinned one used to mess with that Hoover nigga Prophet?"

Cotton laughed and said, "Yeah, I heard about it. As a matter of fact, my mans Shot just got into it with Prophet's homeboy, Herc. Knocked him out cold on the dance floor at the City Walk Club."

"Stop that lying, cuz! Say that shit is a lie, Cotton, loc."

Cotton raised his right hand and said, "My right hand to God." He then gave him a play-by-play of what happened. When he finished, he said, "I'm sure Prophet didn't prophecy that one coming!"

Sharp Shoota stared at Cotton and said seriously, "Cuz, that snake Prophet is the enemy, but I have to give props where props are due. He ain't to be taken lightly. If your mans handled his mans Herc like that, then odds are, they gon' try to get at y'all."

"Not tripping. If they want drama, they'll get all they can handle. Shot ain't for the weak shit; he's more focused on the business. But if they want to see how he gets down, then we ain't ducking no extracurricular activities. Anyway, let's get back to this party and have some fun. Tell the birthday girl that Cotton and Shot wishes her a happy birthday," Cotton said and pulled out a few crisp, one-hundred-dollar bills and gave them to Sharp Shoota to go give the guest of honor. When Cotton returned to the table, he told everyone what Sharp Shoota had told him about Prophet. Daun gave Shot an "I told you so" type of look.

He shrugged and his expression was like, "So what."

Janeen sighed and said, "I was thinking about that shit. I think you need to move back in with me for a little while, sister."

"Yeah, I was thinking that too," Daun said dejectedly.

Shaking his head, Shot said, "Why don't I move in with you, love? No need for you to move from your comfort zone. I'm sure I can give you adequate protection if this Prophet feels the need to come see you. It's the least I can do. That is, if you don't mind having me as a roommate?"

Daun looked from her sister to Shot and back at her sister and laughed. "Sorry, sister, I think I'll take Daddy here on his offer!"

"I bet your nasty ass will! Shit, I may need some protection too." She turned and faced Cotton and said, "So, you gon' come and stay with me to keep me safe, sexy chocolate?"

"It would be my honor to keep you safe and sound, babe."

"Okay, let's work it like this, for you have to pass a couple of tests for me. You pass, then you can become my personal protector as well as my lover/homie/friend."

"You mean, homie/lover/friend, don't you?" asked Cotton.

Shaking her head, she said, "Nope. I meant it just how I said it. My security comes first, then the lover part and last, the friendship. So, are you ready for test number one?"

"Yep."

"How big is your dick?"

"Janeen! You need to quit that!" laughed Daun.

"Quiet, sister, we have tests going on here."

Cotton leaned forward and whispered his answer in Janeen's ear. Her light complexion turned beet red when she said, "Are you fucking *serious?*"

"Yep," Cotton answered proudly.

"Okay. You passed that one, and your ass better not be lying!"

"I speak the truth, babe, and I can't wait to show you."

"Okay, next test. Is your tongue game wicked enough to keep me squirting for a long time?"

"Ugh! That's enough! Let's go hit the dance floor, Daddy, and pick up where we left off at the other spot so these two nasty fuckers can have the rest of these test questions in private."

"I'm with you, love," Shot said as he stood and grabbed Daun's hand and led her onto the dance floor where they danced and enjoyed the rest of their evening.

Outside in the parking lot of Club One 15, Prophet was sitting in his car sending multiple texts to his secret lover. Though he knew she was inside of the club with her man and her sister, he wasn't in the mood to be told no. Seeing Daun with that nigga inside of the club pissed him off, and he needed to vent and release some of this frustration.

When Lynette finally got a chance to return his text, she told him that there was no way possible that she could get out of the club and speak with him, no matter how fast they were. He texted her that if he had to come in and snatch her ass out of there, then tonight would be when their dirty secrets were revealed. He waited for about three minutes, then she texted him back saying give her five minutes and she would be there, but for no longer than five minutes. *Yeah, right,* he thought and smiled as he waited for her to come to him.

Prophet always got his way when it came to women. The only exception was Daun, and he was determined to change that shit. She actually called that nigga Daddy! *Now ain't that some shit,* he fumed as he waited impatiently for Lynette. Fucking her gave him extreme pleasure. What made it so good was she loved that shit. She loved the pain he made her feel. She was a true submissive, but when it came to her man, she was the dominate one. Shit, she ran the show for real, and no one would have ever guessed that OG Big Shoota from Sixties' girlfriend actually belonged to none other than Prophet, Shoota's sworn enemy. Every time he thought about that, his dick became extra hard. He stuck his hand inside of his slacks and began stroking himself as he waited for his bitch. When she finally came, she hopped inside of the car, and he told her what had happened at the club.

"You got to be bullshitting, baby. Herc got knocked out? By who?"

"Some fool Daun fucks with."

Damn, uh-oh, this damn sure isn't the time for him to be giving me what I deserve. I got to calm his ass down before he gets too fired up, Lynette said to herself as she removed his hand from his slacks and undid his belt and released his healthy erection. She dropped her head into his lap without saying a word and began to give him the best head she could give. She knew she was putting in the best work ever because he was squeezing the back of her neck so hard she knew he would be coming inside of her mouth any minute. She was sucking his dick as if her life was on the line—which it actually was because if Shoota ever found out she was fucking with Prophet, she was as good as dead. She couldn't believe she had let this situation get so out of hand. But the way Prophet dominated her turned her on in ways she couldn't even describe. And all because Shoota had the fucking nerve to cheat on her with his little dick ass. For his indiscretions, she chose to do him back but upped the ante by fucking the same man he hated most in the world. Never did she expect to be turned out and become this sexy man's submissive. *Come on, Prophet, come for me, baby, I'm running out of time,* she thought as she moaned on his dick, hoping to ignite his orgasm. She reached and grabbed his balls and gave them a soft squeeze and that seemed to do the trick. She tasted some of his precome and started taking him even deeper inside of her mouth. He moaned loudly and squeezed her neck harder. She groaned, and he said,

"Yeah, bitch, just like that! Just like that!" he panted as he exploded in her mouth. She knew better than to stop. She kept right on sucking him as he filled her mouth with his semen. Once she had swallowed every last drop, she stopped and rose from his lap and smiled at him.

"You good for now, baby? I got to get back in there, okay?"

"Call me tomorrow as soon as you can get away. I need to get dead in that ass and give you what you deserve. Understood?"

She dropped her eyes and said, "Yes, Master Prophet."

He smiled because he loved the power he had over her. Though he didn't give a fuck about controlling her, she drove him mad with lust for her pretty ass. But she wasn't Daun, and that pissed him off. "Get the fuck back to that sissy-ass nigga. Now!"

Lynette didn't say a word as she cautiously got out of the car and went back inside the club to continue celebrating her sister's birthday with her and the rest of the Rollin' Sixty Crips of Oklahoma City.

Chapter Eight

Daun opened her eyes a little after 8:00 a.m. and smiled when she saw Shot sound asleep looking totally content. *Nola, my ass*, she thought as she gently put her warm hand on his semihard dick. She eased her naked body to the middle of the bed and made sure she didn't wake him. She made her lips and mouth really wet and slowly grabbed his dick so it was sticking upward. She then put the tip of her wet tongue on the head of his dick and began to gently lick it, getting it really wet. Shot started moving and moaning in a dazed sleepy manner because he didn't realize just yet what was actually happening. She took his tool and put him all the way inside of her wet and hot mouth, sucking him long and hard from the top to the bottom. When she reached the top, she started sucking the head medium hard, and this feeling was so good to Shot that his eyes popped open. Instinctively, he put his hand on the back of her head and let out a serious moan. "Mmmmmmmm!" She stayed with her mouth directly on the head of his dick sucking it harder now that she knew he was with her. He pushed her head down hard, and she inhaled deeply so she could take all of him in her, passing her uvula. This caused her to gag, and he did it again, and she gagged again. Her mouth seemed to become wetter as she continued to suck his dick long and hard until he finally came inside of her mouth. She pulled away from him so he could quirt his come on her lips, chin, and chest. After he let all his juices loose, she started rubbing his dick, getting him hard again instantly.

Once he was saluting her, she smiled and thought she could never get enough of this man. She climbed on top of him backward and slipped his dick inside of her wet, throbbing pussy. She was so hot and yearning for that dick that as soon as she slid him inside of her, she had an orgasm simply because sucking his dick made her so damn hot! She rode him hard with all she had, bouncing her big ass on his dick harder and harder. He put his large hands around her waist to try to control how much dick she was getting because he didn't want to hurt her. She was beyond feeling any pain, though. She wanted all of him and was determined to get as much of his big dick inside of her as she could.

He smiled as he stared at her big ass and watched as his dick slid in and out of her wet pussy. It was as if they were playing a game of tug-of-war. She would push, and he would pull. Push, pull, push, and pull. She was making sure that he knew she could handle him and would do whatever it took to please him.

Top this, Nola! she thought as she bounced her ass on his erection even harder. The harder she bounced on his dick, the louder their moans became.

"Come for me, Daddy! Come for me!"

Her cries for him to come took him over the edge, and he started coming, realizing what he wasn't wearing, and he didn't give a damn because it was feeling too damn good to stop. But Daun was aware, and she hopped right off him in the midst of his orgasm and started sucking his dick again, swallowing his come.

When she was done, she slid on top of his chest and eased toward his face. She watched as he smiled as she covered his lips with her pussy. She squirmed a little and started screaming when he began working his tongue on her pussy lips and clit, bringing her to one of the most explosive orgasms she ever had in her life. She slid on his now-shiny face and eased to his face and began kissing him passionately, tasting her juices from his tongue and lips. Neither realized when they had stopped kissing and fell back into a deep sleep.

When they woke up, neither could believe that it was almost one in the afternoon. Shot got out of the bed and went into the bathroom to relieve himself. When he came back into the bedroom, Daun was lying on top of the covers with a satisfied smile on her face and her legs spread wide open. She stuck her middle finger inside of her sex and moaned, "You want some more of this, Daddy?" she asked as she pulled her finger out of herself and stuck it inside of her mouth. "Mmmm, I taste so good."

Shot held up his hands and closed his eyes and said, "Please, I beg you, Daun, please stop. I'm done for a while, and on top of that, I'm starving. I have to get some substance inside of my body before I pass out."

She pouted her sexy lips and said, "Spoiled sport. But I do agree, I need me some grub bad. Let's take a shower, and then we can go get something to eat."

He shook his head and said, "No. *You* take a shower, and then I'll take one after you're finished. You are not about to get me like that, love. Plus, I need to make some important business calls."

"Spoiled sport," she teased again as she got off of the bed and walked naked into the bathroom. As she passed him he slapped her on her firm bottom. "Ouch! Daddy, that hurt."

"Good. Now go!" he said pointing toward the bathroom. Once the door closed behind her, he went to the bed and slipped on his boxer briefs and grabbed his phone. He saw four missed calls. Two from JT, one from Cotton, and one from a 214 area code that made him pause.

Nola. She would pick this time to call me. A woman's intuition, he thought as he dialed her number first. He took a deep breath and waited as the phone rang. When Nola answered the phone, he said, "Hello, there, Nola. Is everything okay?"

"Yes, Shot, everything is great. Just wanted to give you a call to see how you were doing. I know I'm not on your favorite persons list right now."

"Not true. You will forever be one of my favorite people."

"That's sweet. Are you in Oklahoma City?"

"Yes. I've been here for about three months now. So close and you haven't called or tried to come and see me. What, you gave up?"

"Look, if you called me to tease me I want you to know that I don't appreciate that, and I don't really deserve to be treated that way."

"Calm down, I was just playing. Seriously, I miss you. And I just wanted to make sure you are okay out there."

"I'm fine. Miss me?"

He sighed and answered her honestly. "Yes. Very much so."

"So you haven't found someone else to replace me yet?"

Again he gave her total honesty. "You're irreplaceable, Nola."

That statement gave her a pause. "I—um, okay. Glad to hear that from you and know that you're good. Bye, Hot Shot," she said quickly and hung up the phone.

He refused to let her get into his head, though just hearing her voice made him feel as if his heart rate increased all of a sudden. He shook his head, and then called JT in California. When JT answered the phone, Shot said, "What's good, champ?"

"All is well on my end. What about you?"

"Everything is going slowly but going. Made a few new meets and got some serious players lined up."

"That's good, son, real good. The director wanted a brief report so I need you to send me something in the next week or so, so I can let him know how things are progressing out there."

"Will do. I may have an order for some S&Rs soon."

"S&Rs? That's some serious firepower there."

"I know. These young gangbangers out here take their gang banging seriously. I may have some other orders as well. I'll let you know in a day or so."

"No problem. Anything else you need to tell me?"

"No. Do you have anything to tell me?"

JT knew Hot Shot was referring to any information on the people who murdered his mother, father, and little brother execution style in their home almost two years ago.

"Nothing. That case is cold, son. I know this bothers you greatly, but we have absolutely nothing. I put all the feelers and snitches we know out there, and zilch came from it."

Hot Shot was silent for a moment, and then sighed. "All right, let me go. I'll get at you in a few days or sooner."

"Stay safe."

"I always do," he said and ended the call. He then called Cotton. When Cotton answered the phone he was breathing extremely hard. "What's wrong with you, Cotton? You okay?"

"Boss man, this lady is insatiable! I haven't been to sleep all damn night! Come get me please before she kills me!"

Shot started laughing and said, "Trust me, it must run in the family."

Before Cotton could respond, Shot heard Janeen in the background yelling, "Don't you dare come get him, Shot! This black, sexy mothafucka is mines! All mines! So if y'all got some business to take care of, you better put it off or handle it yourself!"

"Please, please, boss man, if you have any love for me, come get me so we can go handle that thing."

"What thing?"

"I don't know! Whatever thing you need me to handle! Help me!"

Laughing again, Shot said, "Sorry, pal, you're on your own. I'm sure a strong stud like yourself can handle a strong woman. I'll hit you later if something comes up. Talk to you later, champ," Shot said as he ended the call laughing just as Daun came out of the bathroom with a towel wrapped around her voluptuous body. He smiled and sidestepped her and quickly went into the bathroom so he could shower—alone.

When he was finished, they got dressed and had lunch at The Outback Steakhouse. They were both famished and had very little conversation as they devoured two healthy-sized T-bone steaks. When they were finished eating, they sat back in their seats content and sipped their drinks.

"So, what's on the schedule for the rest of the day, Daddy?"

"Not much. I need to get to my place and grab some clothes and a few other things since I'm going to be your roommate for a little while."

She gave him a wicked smile and said, "It may turn out to be longer than a little while. I'm feeling you more, Daddy, and it's not just about the sex. You're a good man, and you make me feel safe."

"I will not lie because that's not my way. I'm feeling you as was well, love. But I don't want it to seem as if I'm using you to get over my past situation with Nola. She is still very much heavy in my heart and on my mind."

"I respect that, and that's totally understandable. But can I ask you a question?"

"Yes."

"Was she on your mind during out sexing?"

"No. Not one bit."

"What about after we were finished, did you dream about her?"

"No. I was too tired to dream. You knocked me out, love."

"Has she been on your mind any time today?"

"Yes. While you were showering I had some calls to make. I had four missed calls and one of them was from her. That totally shocked me and freaked me out at the same time. That was the first time we had spoken since I'd left L.A. Before that, she was refusing to talk to me, or when we did talk, all she would say is for me to leave her alone and move on with my life."

"What did she have to say today?"

"Not much, actually. She was playing with me, teasing me, like asking me if I missed her and stuff like that. That's what freaked me out some. Wondering where that came from all of a sudden. I mean, it's been over three months since we last spoke."

"A woman has instincts that a man will never under-stand. I'm willing to bet you she feels as if you've met someone else and have started to get over her. That was the reason for the call."

"I was thinking the same thing."

"I think you should go see her."

Shaking his head, he said, "I have business to take care of, and right now, my business comes before Nola. I don't let women control my movements or how I get down," he stated firmly.

"I can respect that. But tell me, how will you staying with me and being my protector from Prophet affect your business?"

"It won't."

"What if you have to go handle some B.I.? What you gon' do? Take me with you?"

"If I feel that's necessary, yes, I will."

She stared at him and smiled. "Damn, you *are* special, you know that?"

"After you told me your story with that dude, I don't feel special. I feel like I should have given him some pain so he can understand that you are not to be bothered by him ever again."

"Shot, I don't want you to get hurt behind me. I couldn't take that. I'm a big girl, and I can deal with him if need be."

"I'm sure you can. But don't forget I put hands on his people, so now, *I'm* in this, whether you want me to be or not."

Daun's eyes grew wide when she whispered, "Damn, we done spoke that fool into existence, and he just came into the restaurant and is headed to the far right corner followed by a female. Oh snap! That's Shoota's woman! Now ain't that a bitch! What the hell is she doing here with Prophet? That's a definite violation of their codes. No woman affiliated or in a relationship with a Neighborhood Crip can ever be around or with a Hoover and vice versa."

"Mmm, that's interesting. I think we should use this opportunity to our advantage. This may give us some leverage over that joker."

Daun smiled and said, "What you got planned, Daddy?"

Shot said, "Follow my lead and you'll see." He rose from his chair and grabbed Daun's hand and led her toward where Prophet and Lynette were seated. Once they were standing in front of them, both Prophet and Lynette looked up at them with shocked expressions on their faces.

"I'm sorry to disturb you two, but I saw you enter the restaurant, Prophet, and I wanted to come over here to speak with you."

Prophet quickly regained his composure and said, "About what?"

"About the incident last night at the club. I've heard a lot about you, and I don't want no drama. Your mans pushed the issue, and you did nothing about it. I understand you thought your man could get at me, but now that we know different, and he took that loss, I don't want or need this to escalate into anything further. It's a dead issue as far as I'm concerned. I'm out here all about my business. I have no time for senseless issues that aren't putting money in my pockets."

Prophet was listening to Shot but was glaring at Daun. He couldn't believe she had the audacity to be standing in front of him with this nigga. He inhaled deeply and said, "Cuz, I haven't given last night a thought since that shit happened. Now my mans Herc, that's a different story. He's laid up right now with a broken jaw sipping Ensure, mad as fuck at you, and I'm quite certain he will be trying to see you again. And that will solely be his decision to make, not mine."

Shot shrugged and said, "Understood. Please do me a favor and let Herc know that if he tries to get at me again, the next time will be worse than a broken nose and jaw. Much worse."

"Cuz, you're standing in front of me and giving a threat to another 107 Hoover Crip. Don't you know who I am?"

"Yes, you're Prophet."

Before Prophet could speak again, Shot turned his attention to Lynette and said, "I saw you last night at Club One 15, didn't I?"

"That's not your business, cuz," answered Prophet.

"Yeah, I saw you too. You're Big Shoota from the Sixties' woman, aren't you? Lynette, right?" Daun asked with an innocent look on her face.

Lynette was so scared she couldn't speak. She could only give a subtle nod of her head.

Shot smiled and said, "Like I was saying, Prophet. I'm out here to make money not enemies. You have your business, and I have mine. I will mind my own business if you stay away from me."

"That goes for me too, Prophet," said Daun. "I will mind my business and stay all the way out of yours as long as you leave me the fuck alone." Before a furious Prophet could say another word, Daun grabbed Shot's hand again and said, "Come on, Daddy, I'm sure Prophet would like to be alone with Big Shoota's woman." They turned and left the restaurant laughing loudly, further infuriating Prophet and scaring the hell out of Lynette.

Chapter Nine

It had been two weeks since the incident at the club and Shot had to admit that he was falling for Daun more and more each day. They were spending so much time together since he moved in with her that it felt as if they were in a relationship. They went everywhere together—shopping, to the movies, out to eat. Even when Shot had to go handle business, he took her along and felt totally at ease with her by his side while he conducted his business. It felt as if he had a partner watching his back other than Cotton out there in these streets of Oklahoma City. Daun was a positive addiction to him businesswise, because she introduced him to more and more people who were wanting guns or drugs. Business had picked up dramatically since she'd become somewhat of a teammate for him. Little did she know that every person she was introducing him to would soon become a victim of Operation Cleanup. He felt bad, but at the same time, he had a job to do, and he couldn't let his feelings interfere with him doing some good.

Cotton and Janeen hit it off equally as well as she too helped him while he was out there making moves in the city, so all was good. They all had become inseparable. They went out together and did the club thing regularly. Shot even took the time to take them all to the gun range to show them how to shoot properly. He was shocked at how quickly both of the Sin Sisters picked up handling weapons and shooting them with deadly confidence.

If someone ever got at them in a precarious way, they would be in store for a huge surprise.

Daun even started working out with Shot every morning when they woke up. She loved his discipline, and the fact that no matter what, he stayed true to the man he was. She loved everything about him. She loved how he made her feel when they made love. She loved how he looked at her whenever they were out and about. He made her feel as if no one existed in the entire world other than her. Plain and simple, she was in love with Shot. She knew without a doubt that she loved him, yet she refused to get into all of that with him. She didn't want to ruin their time together. She didn't want it to end because she caught true feelings for him. She knew all she had to do was bide her time and not put any pressure on him. He was a man that wouldn't be forced to do anything he didn't want to do. She respected that also. Every day they spent together was special, and she would enjoy it for as long as it lasted. If they were meant to be, they would be, and she was taking it day by day.

Shot, on the other hand, was seriously confused. He felt strongly for Daun, there was no questioning that. But at the same time, he couldn't get Nola out of his mind. Since her last phone call to him, she had begun sending him a text at least once a day, saying little things like Hi, how are you? or Just checking on you. Lately, the texts had become more and more intimate. I miss you, you do know that, right? I miss how you feel inside of me. The last text he received from her blew his mind and made him dizzy with confusion. I want you. Tell me you still want me, Hot Shot. He refused to respond to any of her texts, yet she continued to send them every single day.

Now, here he was spending all his time with a wonderful woman, a woman he genuinely cared for, but at the same time, a woman that would soon be in federal custody for defrauding the top creditors in the United States. He had gotten Daun and Janeen to hook Cotton's credit up so he could have an 800 credit score. Daun explained to them that the main come up to what they did was to get their people top credit so they could take out loans and get credit cards and charge up all types of expensive things and sell them off for a monster profit. Cotton wanted to get some loans so he could make some serious moves with them, but Shot told him no, that wasn't their lane, and left it at that. He made sure that Cotton understood he was not playing, and he threatened to cut him off completely if he went against what he told him not to do. He couldn't let Cotton get caught up in any of that. It was going to be hard enough as it was to keep him a free man and not an additional victim of Operation Cleanup, so he prayed Cotton wouldn't be hardheaded and greedy and go against his wishes. If he did, then their time would be up as well, and that thought saddened him.

Though he knew he was doing some good with this operation, he felt sad at times because his life, his entire existence, was a lie. All he had in this world other than JT was this life he was leading. He had Cotton as a friend, and their friendship meant more to him every day. He shook his head to try to get focused on the business at hand.

Though it had been two weeks since he had the most talked about beat down in Oklahoma City with Herc, he had a gut feeling that sooner, rather than later, he would have to get at Prophet and the Hoover Crips. His gut feeling never gave him false warnings. He had learned on the battlefield in the desert in the Middle East to always trust his gut. Right now, his gut was sending him warning signals like crazy as he listened to Daun replaying a conversation she'd just had with Prophet.

She sighed heavily as she set her phone on the dining-room table and said, "He wants to have a meeting with you, Shot."

"About what?"

"Business. He says he's heard about you and how you're moving, and he wants to talk shop. Nothing else. Strictly business. But that's bullshit. It may start out as that, but just as sure as my name is Daun Buckner, he will either try to get at you right then or sometime afterward. He can't stand the fact that we're together, and he has absolutely no chance of being with me ever again. Seeing us together, along with me calling you 'Daddy' hit him real hard and has made it crystal clear that it's all over between me and him. I know his warped mind thinks if he removes you from the equation, he will be able to have me again. And he is so damn wrong."

"When does he want to meet?"

"Daddy! Didn't you hear *anything* I just said?"

"I heard everything you said, love, and I understand completely. But I'm a businessman out here to handle my business. If he wants to meet with me to discuss business, then I will give him the opportunity to do just that. You have to understand that no one, and I mean absolutely no one, intimidates me. I'm the one known to intimidate, love."

"Ugh! Men and all that macho shit! Drives me fucking crazy," she fumed, clearly frustrated by his comment.

"That's where you're wrong, Daun. There is nothing macho in my words or actions. Like I said, I'm all about the business, and I will give him the chance to do some business with me. If he has any ulterior motives, then I will deal with him accordingly, trust and believe me on that. Show no pity. Take a life for a life, an eye for an eye, a tooth for a tooth, a hand for a hand, and a foot for a foot. I'm an Old Testament-type of man."

She stared at him for a moment, and then said, "Deuteronomy 19:21."

He nodded. "Again, when does he want to meet with me, love?"

"I don't know. He told me to give you his number and for you to give him a call."

Shot smiled at his lover and said, "When are you going to give me the number? Or should I ask, *are* you going to give me his number?"

"Before I do, I want you to know something, and before I tell you, there is no way I'll accept no for an answer."

"If you are going to tell me that you are going to join me when I meet with Prophet, then you shouldn't waste your time because that's not happening. You will cause more problems if you are there. He won't be able to focus on the business because he will be upset and feeling as if I'm throwing our relationship in his face. So, no."

She smiled and said, "Our relationship? I like how that sounds."

"Stop."

"Okay. But I still want to go. If I can't join you for the actual meeting, I want to be close enough to be able to watch your back. Can I at least do that?"

Shot thought about that for a few minutes, and then said, "Maybe."

"Ugh!"

He smiled and relented, the optimist in him made him hopeful, but the pessimist in him made him start to prepare for the worst. A true battle within. Having Daun watching his back would be an added plus. He was no fool. If he was going to have her watch his six, he might as well have Cotton and Janeen join the show as well.

"Okay, you can watch my back, but I want you with your sister on this. I'll meet with him and have Cotton join me. We'll be armed, and we'll let it be known that if we even *think* any shadiness is in play, we're shooting first and asking questions later."

"Best believe if you start shooting, we're coming in hard and killing every Hoover in sight," she said in a deadly tone, and he believed every word spoken from her lovely lips.

"Now, may I have the number so we can put this in play?" After she gave him the number, he grabbed his phone and called Prophet. When Prophet answered, Shot got right to the point.

"This is Hot Shot. I received your message, and I'm good with meeting you. If you want to talk some business I'm always with that. Like I told you at the restaurant, that's all that interests me. But, if you're on some other moves, then we should not even waste our time, because I have no time for messiness. Please don't take my words as weakness because you should know from my previous actions there is nothing weak about me."

"Calm down, loc. If I wanted to get wild and wicked with it, cuz, I would have already been to Daun's condo tearing that bitch up. That's not what I'm on. Don't get it twisted, though, you being with her and sharing her bed drives me fucking nuts. But I too am a businessman. When it comes to my business, I play no games. My money means more to me than a bitch."

"Can you kill that type of language about her, please?"

Laughing, Prophet said, "My bad, you got that, loc. Now on some real nigga shit, I—"

"Hold up a sec. Before we go any further, you have to understand something about me. I don't care for the N-word. Hearing that is a form of disrespect to me, so I would appreciate it if you refrained from using that word when talking to me."

"Damn, cuz, you pushing shit for real. Do you want to make some money with me or what?"

"I said what I said, and I meant that. As long as you understand what I said, then, yes, I don't have a problem doing business with you."

"Like I was saying on some real shit, I've heard about you and how you rocking out here in the city. And if what I've heard is real, then we need to meet up fast so we can make some thangs crack, cuz."

"When and where?"

"Tomorrow afternoon at Remington Park Casino. We can hit up the buffet and have a nice lunch and maybe gamble after we've finished discussing the business. I figured public places like that would make you feel comfortable while meeting with me."

"Appreciated. What time exactly?"

"Whatever is good for you."

"Noon is fine."

"See you then, cuz. Oh, and can you please leave Daun's fine ass at home? I don't think I would be able to focus on business with her there."

"She won't be there. She won't be at home either."

Laughing again, Prophet said, "I didn't mean anything like that, cuz. See you tomorrow."

"You sure will," Shot said and ended the call. Then he told Daun what was said. "Now that that is over with, are we going out tonight or what, love?"

Shaking her head with a smile on her face, Daun said, "You are too damn cool, you know that, Daddy?"

He returned her smile and answered her. "Yes, I do know that."

After Prophet hung up the phone with Shot, he smiled and said, "See, I told you that fool would get at me, cuz. Them Cali niggas are greedy. They don't turn down a chance at getting no money."

"That's good, real good. We've been hearing way too much about this Hot Shot out here. It's time for him to go down, and you, my man, Prophet, are going to be the man to help us lock this guy up for a very long time." Prophet smiled at Narcotics Detective Bishop and said, "It will be my pleasure."

The two couples met up at the Purple Martini Club and were enjoying the hip-hop music dancing and drinking until Shot stopped dancing right in the middle of a Kanye West jam and stared straight at the one and only woman he ever loved in his entire life. Nola. Daun stopped dancing and turned and saw the light-skinned woman dressed in a pair of tight skinny jeans with some black Jimmy Choo pumps on her feet, giving off plenty of cleavage with a black sheer blouse on her small frame. She knew instantly by the look on Shot's face that this was none other than Nola. *Damn.* Shot whispered in her ear that he would be back and stepped toward Nola. Once he was standing in front of her, he smiled and said, "Hello, Nola."

She frowned and said, "Why won't you return any of my texts, Shot?"

Something about the way she said his name didn't sound right to him. It was as if she was not the same Nola he remembered. He ignored her question and said, "You started this not talking stuff, and now that I refuse to fall right back into your hands, I'm wrong?"

Her eyes softened when she spoke, "Do you miss me, honey?"

Hearing her call him honey brought back a flood of memories, and he couldn't help himself. He smiled and answered her honestly. "Yes. Yes, I've missed you terribly, Nola."

"I've got a room at the Skirvin. Come. Come with me so you can come inside of me over and over tonight, honey."

Her words were mesmerizing, like sweet music to his ears. It had been so long. All he wanted to do right then was leave with her and give her exactly when she was asking for. But that would be classless. And being classless was not Hot Shot's style at all. He shook his head and said, "Tonight is not a good time for that. I'm here with someone, and I'm leaving with her."

"Damn, you couldn't even try to lie about it. You just want to crush my fucking heart, don't you? You want to punish me for losing our child! Fuck you then. Fuck you, Hot Shot!" she screamed and marched out of the club.

"Great! Fucking great!" he said to himself as he turned and went to the table he was sharing with Daun, Janeen, and Cotton. Once he was seated, he signed heavily and said, "Order another bottle of Rosé, Cotton. I need to get wasted." Cotton smiled but didn't say a word. He wasn't the only person at the table with a smile on their face. Daun was smiling brightly as she grabbed Shot's right hand and gave it a soft squeeze.

Chapter Ten

After another long session of sexing with Daun, Shot woke up the next morning feeling more confused than ever. Something was terribly wrong with Nola, and he didn't know if he was to blame for it. What he did know was that he would never stand for her disrespecting him. He didn't blame her one bit for having that miscarriage. That was ridiculous of her to say it. He told her over and over that's one of God's mysteries and that if it was meant to be they would make another child. She refused to listen to him then, and now it was him trying to punish her for the miscarriage. That didn't make any sense at all. Women, go figure.

He slipped on his workout clothes and went into the living room and began stretching. He needed his workout more than ever this morning so he could be fully focused on meeting Prophet. He knew he needed all of his wits for this one. He also knew he had to make sure that he was extra cautious. He refused to slip and let that man get the best of him. Losing wasn't an option. He shook his head to clear the perilous thoughts invading his mind. Daun slept soundly as he worked out furiously. After 500 push-ups, sit-ups, crunches, and jumping jacks, he went into the bedroom to see Daun sitting up on the bed. "Hey, love, sleep well?"

She stretched, yawned loudly, and said, "Mm-hmm. Why didn't you wake me so I could work out with you, Daddy?"

"I felt you worked out good enough last night so I let you get your rest. Besides, I needed to go a li'l extra hard to get my blood pumped right."

"I feel you." She looked at the clock and saw that it was a little after 10:00 a.m. "It's about that time for us to get ready, right?"

"Yes. You go on and shower first. I need to call Cotton and speak with him and Janeen. I want them to come over here before we leave. It's going to be a team effort today to make sure everything goes smoothly."

She got off the bed and stepped to him, gave him a kiss, and smiled. "You do know I love being on your team, right, Daddy?"

He returned her smile and said, "As I love having you on the team. Now go," he ordered as he tried to slap her on her bare bottom; however, she was prepared for his action this time and blocked the blow and laughed as she went into the bathroom to shower. Shot grabbed his phone and called Janeen and Cotton and told them to come over to Daun's place as soon as possible. After he hung up with them, he called JT and told him everything concerning Prophet, along with the meeting he was about to have with him.

"Do you think he's going to try to do you dirty, son?"

"Not today, no, but I'll be ready for anything. I just wanted you to know the business just in case it got crazy. I need my ace in the hole on deck for precautionary reasons. Don't need the director having a coronary on us if I have to get wicked."

"Ain't that the truth. People who are multi-degreed professionals are often known to be perfectionists. Trust me, son, the director is a perfectionist of the highest order. So don't get trigger happy out there in the OK Corral."

"I'm using my gun only if I have to, JT."

"Understood. Anything else?"

"For now, no. But if things go good, then I may have an order for you."

"Guns or drugs?"

"From what I've learned about this guy, most likely both."

"All righty, then. The transformers are working well, and looks like those SARs you ordered are sitting still. We have the location locked in. So when it's time, everything will be set up just right."

"Cool. Let me go. I'll give you a call after I finish up with this meeting."

"Stay safe, son."

"Affirmative," he said as he ended the call.

Shot went into the bathroom just as Daun was getting out of the shower. He couldn't help himself as his hands moved like they had of mind of their own. He grabbed her and pulled her into his arms. They shared a warm, passionate kiss. Before either of them knew realized it, Daun was bent over the bathroom sink as he slid deep inside of her from behind. He pumped into her furiously as he held onto her waist. Just as he felt the first signs of his orgasm, he pulled out of her, and she turned around, dropped to her knees, and put him inside of her mouth and sucked him until he exploded.

Then she stood and smacked her lips. "Mmm, nothing like some early-morning protein." She laughed as she turned and got back into the shower and they showered successfully without having any more impromptu sex. By the time they finished showering and got dressed, Janeen and Cotton arrived. Shot went into the kitchen and got some juice and returned to the living room so he could tell them what he needed them to do.

"Okay, listen up and pay close attention," Shot said, all businesslike. "This is how we're going to do this. I'm meeting Prophet at noon at Remington Park Casino.

We're going to have lunch at some buffet so what I want is for Janeen and Cotton to be there before I arrive. I want you to be posted up and make sure that you keep a lookout for any of his homeboys. Cotton, you've dealt with some of them, and I'm sure Janeen here will be able to spot some of them in case you don't know them. If you're watching me, then it should be easy for you to spot them because they'll be watching us as well. If either of you see something suspicious, I want you to text me and tell me if the threat's on my right or left. I'll take it from there."

Both Cotton and Janeen gave him a nod of under-standing.

"What about me, Daddy?"

"I don't want to take the chance of Prophet seeing you or Janeen, so I want you to watch the outside of the casino. I want you to get a parking spot close as you can to the entrance of the casino. You see anyone you recognize that can be affiliated with Prophet or the Hoover Crips, then I want you to text Janeen and let her know who's entering the casino and they will be able to look out for them from there. Any questions?"

"Weapons?" Cotton asked.

Shot went into the bedroom and returned with a duffel bag. He opened it and gave each of them a 9-mm berretta. "Each weapon is locked and loaded. The chamber is empty so if it has to go down, rack in a live round and don't hesitate to handle your business. I highly doubt we will need to shoot our way out of the casino, though. This is purely for the exit. When the business has been handled and you two see me stand, proceed to the exit, and I'll be watching your six. Daun, I'll text you to let you know when we're headed out so you can pull up right in front and scoop me, and we're outta there." He checked the time on his watch and saw that it was 11:15 a.m. "Okay, let's do this.

It's time." The ladies put each of their guns inside of their purses while Cotton put his inside of his pants on his right hip, and Shot in the small of his back. It was time to go see what Prophet was talking about.

Janeen and Cotton made it to the casino about fifteen minutes before Shot arrived. They were posted by the slot machines sliding quarters inside of a machine while looking toward the buffet that was a few feet away from where they were. Cotton spotted Shot as he entered and was met by Prophet. He watched as they shook hands and entered the restaurant. Janeen stood from the slot machine and began to let her eyes roam all over the casino floor, looking for any of Prophet's homeboys. Cotton was doing the same thing, letting his eyes scan all around them, looking for any threats to his boss man. After a few minutes, they both felt pretty sure there were no threats around. Cotton texted Shot and told him everything was looking good, and they were still on point.

Inside of the restaurant after they were seated with their food, Shot told Prophet, "I'm glad we could get together on this business. I've heard you're a serious dude when it comes to getting money."

"I'm a serious dude, period. But, yeah, it's time to put the other shit aside and get this bread. From what I've been told, you got plugs on everything, and right about now, that's the type of plug I need in my life."

Shot gave a nod and kept on eating some of his shrimp platter.

"So tell me, what's some of your prices?"

After swallowing, Shot said, "It depends on what you want and how much of it you request."

"I need a solid line on some birds. They're charging way too much for that shit now. What ticket you got for, say, twenty bricks?"

"I can get them for you for twenty-six. As long as you get more than ten, that ticket will stay the same."

Prophet gave a nod of his head and said, "I'm feeling that. What about weapons?"

"What about them?"

"I need some heavy shit. You know, them Rambo-like guns and shit. Fully auto and able to tear shit up. Shit is wicked out here with my enemies, and I need to stay on top of my game."

"I can get you whatever you want. But you have to tell me precisely what kind of assault rifle or weapon you want. Then I can give you a price."

"Anything . . . any kind?"

"Yes."

"Damn, Shot, you a serious dude, huh?"

Shot stared directly into his eyes and answered, "Yes."

"All right, then, when do you want to make this happen?"

"When you tell me exactly what it is you want."

"Let's start off with the fifteen birds at the twenty-six ticket. How much will you charge me for ten fully automatic assault rifles? I don't care what kind. I just want them fully loaded and powerful."

"I can get you some AK-47s or some fully auto AR-15s for 2,000 bucks apiece since you want ten."

"New?"

Shot gave him a look as if to say, "Are you serious?" "Of course new, still inside of the box."

"Okay, now that you know what I want, when can we make this happen? I'm ready whenever you are."

"I need a couple of days to get everything out here. I'll call you when I'm ready. One thing, though."

"What up?"

"When we do the deal it's you and one man who meets me where I choose. Any funny business, I mean *any at all,* then we will have serious problems. And I do mean right then and there."

"Are you threatening me again, Shot?"

Shaking his head, Shot said, "No. I am giving you my word. If you get shady, I will kill you."

"Like that, huh?"

"Yes, exactly like that."

"I don't play shady games when I do business. You don't have to worry about me."

"I'm not worried at all, Prophet. I'm clearly letting you know how it's going to be. Like I said, I'll give you a call when I have what you've ordered."

"Cool, cuz. Now, with that out of the way, can we have a discussion somewhat personal to me?"

Shot wiped his mouth and said, "No. I don't do personal. Whether it's your business or not, I will not discuss Daun or our relationship with you. I will say this, though, she is a friend of mine, and I always look out for my friends." Shot felt that his point had been made and that the meeting was concluded. He stood and said, "You'll be hearing from me in two to three days." He then left the restaurant. As he left, he saw Janeen and Cotton walking a few feet in front of him leading the way out of the casino. When they made it to the outside, everything seemed clear as they went into their cars to leave. When Shot was inside of the car he smiled at Daun and said, "All is good, love."

Daun had a puzzled expression on her face and said, "Maybe. Then again, maybe not. Look, stay here and wait for me, 'K? I have to go check something out."

"What's up, Daun?"

"I'm not sure; just give me a sec. I'll be right back," she said as she hopped out of the car and quickly entered the casino. She strolled toward the restaurant where Shot had met with Prophet and started inside to see if what her gut was telling her was happening. When she saw the narcotics officer that they call "Big Bishop" sit down with Prophet, she knew her gut had been right.

"You fucking coward-ass snitch bitch. You can't fade Shot head up in the streets so you're trying to get him out of the way by setting him up. Ain't that a bitch," she said aloud as she watched Prophet and the narcotics detective talk and laugh inside of the buffet. She spun on her heels and returned to the car. When she was inside of the car she sighed and told Shot to drive.

"Talk to me, love," Shot said as he pulled the car out of the parking lot of the casino.

"You first. What was the meeting about?"

"He wants fifteen birds and some fully automatic assault weapons. I gave him my ticket for them, and he agreed to the prices. I told him we would meet up in two to three days once I had everything ordered. Now, what's up with you?"

Shaking her head, she said, "You're not going to do any business with that bitch. He's a snitch, Shot. He's trying to set you up with the police."

"What? Explain that, please."

And explain she did. She told him how while she was outside surveying the parking lot for any Hoovers or shady people, she saw the narcotics detective they call "Big Bishop" enter the casino just before they came outside. She had a feeling that he was there for a reason and wanted to check and make sure that his reason for being there had nothing to do with Prophet. She was correct because she saw Prophet and the detective sitting down in the restaurant laughing and talking about something, and she was pretty positive the "something" they were discussing was Hot Shot. "I wonder if that bitch wore a wire," Shot said after she finished telling him what she saw.

Then Shot smiled and shrugged as if it didn't matter. "It's all good, love. I'll take care of this with a phone call to the West."

"What? You got it like that—that you can get the police off your ass when you got a bitch snitch trying to get you knocked?"

Shot smiled at her as he turned onto the highway and said, "Yes, I got it even better than that."

"Damn, you are a boss for real."

Still smiling, he turned on the radio and said, "Yes, love, I am that."

Chapter Eleven

When Shot and Daun made it back to her place, he told her he had to make a call so he could deal with the situation of Prophet trying to set him up. This puzzled the hell out of Daun, but the confidence in Shot's tone told her not to be nosy and let him handle his business. She sat down on the couch and slipped off her Nike running shoes and sat back and relaxed while Shot made a phone call.

Shot called JT and gave him a play-by-play of what had taken place at the casino. When he finished, JT said, "So, this joker is trying to get you popped, huh?"

"Seems like it. I need you to make this go away, JT. I don't need people on me like that. Bad for business, you know what I'm saying?"

"Exactly. It shouldn't be a problem for the director to handle this situation. Since it's Sunday, I'll have to take care of this first thing in the morning. So, in the meantime, you fall back and relax. Those locals may be all over you."

"Those were my exact same thoughts." Shot stared at Daun with hunger in his eyes and said, "I think I can find something else better to do with my team than getting out there in the streets until you get back at me. But make it happen soon, champ."

"Like I said, son, first thing in the morning."

"Talk to you tomorrow then," Shot said and ended the call. He stared at Daun and said, "My people in the West told me they'll take care of everything first thing in the morning and for me not to get out and about and handle any business."

She smiled and said, "So, I guess that means I will be able to have all of your attention then?"

Nodding, he said, "This is true. What do you want to do?"

She stood and slipped out of her Capri pants and took off her tee shirt and asked, "What do you think, Daddy?"

The next morning when JT woke up, he checked the time and saw that it was ten minutes after eight in the morning, so that meant it was after 11:00 a.m. on the East Coast. He made the call to the director in D.C. He then explained everything to the director, and he told him that it was imperative to their operation that he make the necessary calls to get the situation rectified so the local police in Oklahoma City would back off of Hot Shot. The director agreed and told him he would call him back after he had confirmation that everything was taken care of. He hung up the phone with JT and buzzed his ever-efficient secretary and told her to get him the number to the U.S. assistant attorney of Oklahoma City. Within two minutes after his request, his secretary buzzed him back and told him that she had the U.S. assistant attorney of Oklahoma City, Helen Hollier, on the line. He thanked her and said, "Good morning, Mrs. Hollier, this is Director Denver Johnson."

"Good morning to you, sir. How can I be of assistance?"

He then explained to her that there was a very important operation underway in her city, and that it was very important to him, as well as the president of the United States, that things continue to run smoothly. He told her what JT had told him about Detective Bishop using one of his informants to help set up their operative. After he finished, he gave her an added incentive to do what he needed her to do.

"I don't know if you're aware of what took place in Dallas, Texas, last year with the major busts that the U.S. Assistant Attorney Walter Long Jr. was a part of."

"Actually, sir, I am."

"Good. Then you should be willing to take care of this little problem for me. You do this favor for me, and I'll make sure once this operation concludes, you will be the prosecuting attorney on all cases involved. A nice boost to your conviction rate and record."

She smiled into the receiver and said, "Sir, it would be my pleasure to take care of this problem for you. Give me a couple of hours to get everything underway, and I'm positive I can have everything taken care of."

"Thank you, Mrs. Hollier. I'll be waiting for your call so we can get our operative back in play."

"No problem, sir, I'm all over it."

"I'm sure you are. I'll be waiting," he said and hung up the phone.

After she hung up with the director of the FBI, she called the chief of police of the Oklahoma City Police Department. Once he was on the line, she explained to him what she needed and why. He didn't give her any resistance. He was in no way trying to piss off the director of the FBI—or the president of the United States of America.

"I'll need no more than an hour to have this problem taken care of, Helen."

"Thanks, Chief. Give me a call so I can get right back at the director. And lunch is on me next week."

The chief of police smiled into the receiver and said, "That's great. I've been waiting to try out KD's new restaurant, and I'm sure I'm going to enjoy myself on your dime."

She laughed as well and said, "I'm sure you will. I'll be waiting for your call."

"One hour," he said and hung up the phone. He picked up the receiver again, and then set if back down and decided that this needed to be handled in person. He stood and grabbed his suit jacket and walked out of his office. Fifteen minutes later, he was walking into the downtown police headquarters where Detective Bishop worked. He went directly into captain's office without knocking.

When Captain James Crais saw his boss enter his office, he quickly ended the call he was on and said, "Hello, Chief. I hope to hell I'm not in any trouble with this surprise visit," he laughed nervously.

After taking a seat on the other side of the captain's desk, the chief told him what he needed and why. He finished with, "We don't need any issue with the FBI, and I sure don't want the director of the FBI calling the president telling him we weren't cooperative with their operation."

"Neither do I, Chief. I'll get right on this for you."

Chief of Police Curtis Williams smiled and said, "If you don't mind, I want to be present when you speak with Detective Bishop."

"No problem, sir," said the captain as he buzzed his secretary and had her get the detective on the line and tell him to be in his office within the next ten minutes. He then shared a few golfing stories with his boss until Bishop arrived. Detective Bishop made it to his office in less than the ten minutes that the captain requested. When he entered the office and saw the chief of police sitting at the captain's desk, his first thoughts were, *Oh, shit! What the fuck have I done now?* He smiled at both of his superiors and stood there waiting for them to speak.

"Detective Bishop, I'm sure you know who this is?"

"Yes sir. How are you, Chief?"

The chief gave a nod in greeting but remained silent.

Captain Crais then told him that the current investigation he was handling concerning a certain CI named Prophet needed to come to a halt immediately. He then went into detail how it was interfering with a federal operation, and that couldn't happen. He saw the look of disdain on Bishop's face, and his voice grew stern. "Is there a problem with the order I've just given you, Detective?"

"No, sir. It's just this guy we're targeting is a big fish out of the Los Angeles area, and I hate that I have to back off because of the feds."

"I understand, and I respect your position on this, but this is bigger than us. Your target is indeed a big fish, but he's the fed's big fish, not ours. So let it go. Get your CI to back off. Am I understood?"

"Yes, sir."

"And you are not to bother or put any pressure whatsoever on the target."

"Yes, sir."

"You're dismissed."

Bishop left the office with a lot of questions swirling around inside of his head, but he was more pissed than anything. He shrugged it off and decided to get Prophet to focus his attention elsewhere and leave that guy Hot Shot alone and let the feds do what they do.

After Detective Bishop left the office, the chief asked him if he could use his phone. He then called the U.S. assistant attorney and gave her the news she was waiting to hear. She hung up from him with a smile on her face, and then called the director back and gave him the news. Satisfied immensely, the director thanked the attorney and promised that he would be giving her a call once everything was ready for her.

"If, by chance, you do not hear from me, you will be hearing from a John Tackett on my behalf. I promise you, you will have some dead bolt locked convictions from this, Mrs. Hollier."

"Thank you, sir, I really appreciate this."

"I appreciate the solid you just did for me, and so does the president. Talk to you soon." The director hung up, leaving the attorney with a huge smile on her face. He then called JT back and told him that everything had been taken care of and that he can tell Hot Shot that he is good to get back to work.

"That's great news, sir. He's been making significant progress out there, and we didn't need this in our way."

"I understand. What's the time table on this one?"

"Give or take another six months top and we'll be ready to bring down just as many as we did in Texas, if not more."

"Good, really good. I'm sure the president will love hearing about this in our briefing tomorrow. Make sure you tell Agent Gaines that I said keep up the good work, and be careful."

"Yes, sir." JT hung up the phone and quickly called Shot in Oklahoma. When Shot answered the phone, JT said, "It's done. You're good to go. They're off your back, and you shouldn't have any problems. If you do, don't hesitate to get right back at me."

Shot smiled and said, "Cool."

"Do you have anything you need from me?"

"No, because what I was going to order was for that rat. Now that that's a wrap, I'm cool with what I got. I'll hit you when I need a load."

"Be safe, Hot Shot."

"Always," Shot said as he ended the call and smiled at Daun who was cuddled next to him.

"I guess since you're smiling, your people on the West handled that situation for you then, huh?"

"Yes."

"How?"

He shrugged and said, "Who knows. That man has people in high places, and there's basically nothing he can't handle for me. That's why I've lasted so long in this business. It's not what you know, it's *who* you know."

"Mmmm, well, I'm sure glad I know you, 'cause as long as I'm with you, I'm safe and good. On top of that, I get all the fringe benefits of you being around me so much."

"Fringe benefits? Like what?"

She smiled and pointed toward his crotch area and said, "Like all of that meat you packing, Daddy!"

Shot laughed and said, "You're insatiable, you know that?"

She smiled at him and said, "Yep." She then reached for and started to stroke his big man and got the response she was looking for as she slid down his chest and put him inside of her mouth.

"What the fuck you talking about, Bishop!" screamed Prophet.

"You heard me. Everything is dead with that asshole Hot Shot. The feds are all over him, and they pulled some strings to get my superiors to back the fuck off. So we back the fuck off. You are *not* to get at him anymore. You do, then I won't be able to help your ass because you'll have a fucking fed case and looking at a million years."

"That's some fucked-up shit."

"It is. In the meantime, you need to get me something. Your get-out-of-jail-free card is close to expiring."

"Man, I gave you a nigga. That should have given me all types of room from your ass. Come on with that bullshit, Bishop. It's not my fault the fucking feds got in this shit and deaded that situation. Cut me some fucking slack."

"You're right, it's not your fault, Prophet. But I'm not cutting you shit. Get to work or prepare yourself to get knocked on all the shit I got on your ass!" He hung up the phone, and Prophet was extremely pissed off. Bishop smiled because he loved having Prophet by the balls. He knew he would give him something soon and that made him feel better about losing the Hot Shot bust.

Prophet sat back on his bed and grabbed Lynette by her hair roughly and forced her to start giving him some head. As he was enjoying oral ministrations, he thought about what Bishop told him and smiled. *At least that cocky fuck is about to get knocked. Fuck it, jail is jail. Whether it's the state or the feds, that bitch nigga will be outta my way so I can get Daun's fine ass back. Yeah, it's all good,* he thought as he erupted inside of Lynette's mouth. He stared down at her while she continued to suck him and wondered when he was going to go on and get rid of her ass. She was cool, but she wasn't Daun. He knew he got more of a thrill from her only because she was Big Shoota's bitch. Sooner or later, this shit would backfire on him. Yeah, it's about time to dump the broad, but for now, he was about to give her some pain and enjoy the pussy a little longer. He pulled her off his dick by her hair and slapped her so hard she got dizzy. Before she realized what was happening, he had her bent over and was ramming his dick as hard as he could inside of her asshole. She screamed, and he laughed.

The pain had only just begun.

Chapter Twelve

Thanks to JT and some of his connections, Shot, Daun, Cotton, and Janeen got to watch history when the San Antonio Spurs beat the defending NBA champions, Miami Heat, 104-87 in the fifth and deciding game. Now they were on the highway on their way to Dallas to spend the night before heading back to Oklahoma City.

"Damn, dog, I never thought that the Spurs would do the Heat like that," said Cotton as he cuddled close to Janeen in the backseat while Shot drove with Daun's head resting in his lap, closer and closer to his man meat.

"I knew it. Once Coach Popovich made the switch in game 3 by starting Boris Diaw, it was a wrap. The Heat were outmatched. LeBron may be the greatest basketball player on the planet, but one man can't beat a solid team like the Spurs," said Shot as he lightly smacked Daun's hand.

She frowned at him and pouted. "I'm happy for Tim Duncan. He's so mild mannered and polite; he's a true great."

"I know. He should go on and retire and leave the game on top," said Janeen.

"Nah, they have to keep that team together and come back and defend their title," said Cotton.

"I agree. But the West is loaded, and it may not be easy for them next year. Free agency can change things quickly. You got Melo opting out of his contract in New York. If he goes, to say, someone like Houston, things can change."

"I feel that, boss man, but them Spurs is good."

"I like that guy that won the MVP. That youngster is ready for the big-time money," said Janeen.

"Yes, Kawhi Leonard is definitely ready." Changing the subject, Shot said, "When we hit Cotton's place, I need to go take care of some things, love."

"Nola?"

"Yes. It's time to bring this to a head. I'm tired of the game she's playing with me. The hate texts one minute, then the love texts the next. I'm tired of it, and I need closure one way or the other."

"I'm telling you, Shot, your ex piece of game is on some straight goofy shit. Never thought she would get down like that," said Cotton.

He shrugged and cut his eyes toward Daun and said, "I will never fully understand her, but I care for her, and I will not let my feelings for her keep me off balance. I have business to take care of, and I intend to handle this tonight," he said as he turned off the highway and headed to Cotton's place in North Dallas. When he pulled in front of the building, Cotton and Janeen got out and went inside while Daun waited until they were out of the car.

"I won't front, I'm scared to death of losing you, Shot. You've been so good to me. You've made me realize that life is too short to be alone. I'm no clingy type of woman, but you . . . You do something to me inside and out. Not just the sex either. You're considerate, polite, respectful, and caring. I've fallen in love with you over and over. I had to say that and not because you're about to go see her but to let you know that even if you choose to get back with Nola, my love for you will not lessen one bit. I appreciate your honesty the most. It shows you respect me. Thank you for that, Daddy," Daun said sincerely.

Shot faced her and said, "If I told you I didn't love you, I would be lying to you, Daun. There is no way humanly possible that I could control my feelings for you. Every day they have grown stronger and stronger. That's the main reason why I'm going to bring closure to this situation."

"Closure in what way, Daddy?" she asked holding her breath, waiting for his answer, praying he would tell her that he wanted to be with her.

And that's exactly what he told her, knowing that he would have to find a way to extradite her from the crimes she's committed. He would have to either lie to JT or tell him the truth and be able to find a way use her and her sister as he had Cotton, to keep them from being charged federally. *Love is not only painful, it's greatly confusing,* he thought to himself as he stared at Daun.

"I not only love you, I'm in love with you, and I'm about to let Nola know it. It's over for me and her. She did it. I tried to be as patient as I could, but she pushed and pushed, and she is no longer appealing to me. Nor do I feel as if I'm in love with her. I do love her, though. I doubt that will ever change. But loving her and being in love with her are two totally different things. A man can only be in love with one woman, and I'm in love with just one. You. I love you, Daun, and I hope we can make something special together."

With tears sliding down her face, Daun smiled and reached across the seat and gave him the most tender kiss he ever had in his life. He moaned, and the kiss went from tender to passionate in a nanosecond. Daun pulled from their embrace and said, "You need to go get that closure stuff out of the way, Daddy, and hurry up and get back to me. We gon' make some noise up in here tonight," she said as she nodded her head toward Cotton's home.

He laughed and said, "Maybe I'll stop and get us a suite somewhere. That way, we can have the privacy we'll need.

Because only God knows what those two will be up to tonight."

"I think that's a great idea."

"Be back as soon as I can, love."

"Okay, Daddy. Don't you give her one for the road either. That there man meat belongs to me, and only me, now."

He smiled and said, "Affirmative, love," as he watched her get out of his car and go inside of Cotton's home feeling giddy like a teenage girl after her first date.

Twenty minutes later, Shot pulled into the driveway of Nola's ranch-style home in the city of Rowlett. He called her when he was en route to Rowlett and told her that it was very important that they talked, and since he was in Dallas, he was on his way over, and he wasn't taking no for an answer.

Telling him no was the furthest thing on her mind, however. Nola quickly began to prepare for his arrival. She wanted him so bad it hurt. She went and took a quick shower, and then stood in front of the mirror in the bathroom. She lifted her well toned arms and ran her fingers through her hair, inhaling the scent of Chanel 19 rising from her firm breasts. She was wearing a sexy red negligee that she bought from Victoria's Secret, especially for her reunion with Shot. The negligee fit her curves like a lover's embrace. She smiled at herself and closed her eyes for a moment, wondering how it was going to feel to have Hot Shot.

She sighed and composed herself for what was about to be one beautiful Sunday evening—but, boy, was she in for a rude awakening. She went to the door just as Shot was about to knock on it. When she opened the door and he saw what she had on, he sighed and thought, *Crap! This isn't going to be as easy as I hoped it would be.*

He stepped in and dodged her attempt to hug and said, "I'm not here for the lovey stuff, Nola. You've played a mean game with me mentally for too long, and I can't deal with it any longer. I'm here to tell you that I've moved on. I wanted you more than anything in this world, and you shut me out. When you lost our child, you shut me out. That was wrong. Yet, I understood because only you and God understand what you went through mentally after that terrible ordeal. I tried to be as patient as I could with you. Then you started playing games with me, and you should have known that I'm not a man that takes being toyed with. I had to come tell you to your face that we're done. I'm with someone else, and we're happy."

She frowned; then her frown turned to a scowl, and suddenly, she looked like a woman possessed. "You ain't shit! Just another baller who thinks he can do whatever he wants with women. I should have never blessed you with this good pussy! Fuck you, Hot Shot, fuck you and that Sin Sister bitch Daun you fucking with out there in Oklahoma!"

He stared at her, shocked that she knew about Daun.

She smiled at his facial expression and said, "Yeah, I know all about your little sexcapade with that bitch. I know how you beat up that Crip at the club for her, and you've been shacked up with that bitch for the last few months. You forgot I got family out there in Oklahoma City. I was willing to let you make shit right with us, but you come here with that high-and-mighty shit. You think I can't get me a good nigga out here, Hot Shot?"

"Watch your mouth, Nola. Don't you dare disrespect me talking to me with those type of words," he said in a deadly serious tone. No one would ever disrespect him and get away with it. No one. Not even a female.

"What you gon' do to me, nigga? Hit me? Fuck you! You ain't shit. I should have never fucked with your ass.

My brother told me not to trust your ass, and look what happened. My baby's dead, and now you're leaving me for a stupid bitch. Fuck you!"

"I'm leaving *you*? Are you *serious*? Come on, you need to take responsibility for your part in this! If you would have let me remain a part of your life during that trying time, we would have made it through that together! So don't you get at me like this. And I swear if you call me that N-word one more time I'm going to do something that will make my dead mother do flips in her grave. So be careful."

"You put your hands on me and that will be the last you ever tough anyone else! Fuck you!"

"You're right, it's over. I came to say what I had to say, and now that I've said it, I'm out of here. Good-bye, Nola. If you ever need me for anything, I give you my word I'll be there for you. I wish you well, and I mean that with all my heart."

"You think I need shit from you? You think I'm wanting you because I need something from you? I don't need you! I don't want *nothing* from you. All I wanted you here for tonight was for some dick. You don't want to fuck, then cool. I'll go find me some dick and live happy ever after! My life will go on strong without you. My sister will be home in another 24 months, and we'll be fine. Get the fuck out of my sight!" she screamed with tears sliding down her face, making him feel like dirt.

He didn't want to leave her in that state so he calmed himself down by taking a few deep breaths and said, "Look, I'm going to be gone tomorrow after I take care of my business with JT. After I send him some money for some of my business, I think maybe we can have lunch and try to talk in a more calm and mature manner."

"What do you mean send JT some money? Who the fuck is JT, and what does that have to do with us talking?"

"So you've forgotten who JT is now, huh? Come on, Nola. You can meet me after I go to the post office and handle my business, then we can go somewhere and eat and talk."

"Post office? What the fuck you going to the post office for?"

"You're really tripping. You know that's how I send the ends to JT in the West. Anyways, do you want to have lunch with me tomorrow or not?"

Shaking her head she said, "No, I want you out of my house. The faster you do that, the faster I can start forgetting I ever met your ass. I hate you. I hate you, Jason Gaines! Fuck you!" she screamed as she marched to the front door and yanked it open. He walked past her without saying a word. "And tell JT's black ass I said fuck him too!" she screamed as she slammed the front door.

Hot Shot left the city of Rowlett truly baffled. Something *was* off with her, and he realized that Nola was really twisted. He felt sad as he drove toward North Dallas. All he thought about was the conversation he'd just had with her. By the time he pulled back in front of Cotton's home, he realized that Nola was still highly traumatized from the loss of their baby and the loss of her brother, sister, and cousins. That gave him a monster crash of the guilt. After all, it was all his fault they lost their child. The stress from her family's situation caused her to miscarry, and that was something he would have to live with for the rest of his days. He tapped the horn twice and waited for Daun to come outside. Once she was inside the car, she saw his face and knew he was in pain. She grabbed his hand and gave it a tight squeeze.

"No sexing tonight, Daddy. I'm going to hold you real tight all night long, 'K?"

He smiled sadly at her and started the car, heading toward the nearest hotel because the thought of being held all night long sounded so damn appealing to him. As he drove toward downtown Dallas, he still couldn't shake from his mind the conversation he had with Nola. He would make another attempt at talking to her. He had to. He owed her that much. *Love is painful for real,* he thought as he pulled into the parking lot of the W Hotel, eagerly looking forward to being held all night long by his woman, Daun.

Chapter Thirteen

With the summer heat comes drama in the streets. Oklahoma City was turned up with violence galore. The Crips were beefing heavily with the Bloods, as well as with one another. In the last month alone, there had been over twelve gang-related shootings. Clubs were being heavily surveyed by OCPD and gang task forces, yet the violence continued.

Businesswise, however, things were booming for Shot. He put a halt on the sale of all guns because there was no way he was going to supply guns to all those trigger-happy gangbangers so they could continue to harm one another. It was bad enough that he heard the Six-Os had been highly active with the assault rifles he sold them.

It had been a few weeks since the meeting with Prophet, and Shot knew when all the calls abruptly stopped, that Prophet had received the news to fall back off of him. That made him wonder how Prophet had become so heavy in the streets.

A highly respected leader of the Hoover Crips was an informant for the locals. Interesting. Shot knew that sooner or later he would be able to use that to his advantage, but for now, he was busy getting everything ready to close this operation. He figured by the end of the summer, he would be able to give JT his report and the information needed to lock up a large percentage of OKC's heavyweights in the streets. That thought put a smile on his face. Doing some good. He may not stop all of the crime, but he could put a nice dent in things, and that's what Operation Cleanup was all about.

Now that things had become serious with him and Daun, Shot knew that he had to come up with a way for JT to approve him letting Daun and her sister make it. He wished he hadn't told JT about their credit scam. That way, he would have been able to just not mention it and all would be well. He loved Daun, and the more time they were together, the deeper his love became. He refused to hurt her like he did Nola, and if he went through with his job, he would definitely hurt her. He shook those thoughts from his mind as Daun came into the living room with a smile on her face.

"Hey, Daddy, what ya doing?" she asked as she sat down next to him on the couch.

"Thinking and trying to get some things worked out in my head about the business. These gangbangers are making it difficult to move around, and that's making me want to pull Cotton back some so we can look at it. Can't be having him out there making moves, putting him at more risk than he already is."

"You really care for him, don't you?"

"Yes. He's become like a little brother to me, but it's not really as much about him as it is the money. My business must continue to run smoothly, or it'll be time for me to depart Oklahoma City."

Daun knew that one day Shot would be ready to leave the city and hearing him speak on that gave her pause. She stared at him and wondered if he would consider staying there with her if she asked him to. Better yet, she hoped that if and when he decided to leave, he would be willing to let her go with him. She loved her sister to death, but she knew she wasn't feeling Cotton as much as she was feeling Shot. They were having fun sexing each other and making some money together, but that was it.

Janeen was sticking to their script to the fullest. No love, only the love for the money so they could continue to be female bosses living it up the way they choose too.

As if reading her mind, Shot smiled and said, "You're thinking about leaving, hmm?"

"Am I that transparent, Daddy?"

He nodded but remained silent.

"If I leave, can I go with you?"

"You'd do that?"

This time she nodded and waited for him to say more, praying he would say that he would take her with him when he was ready to leave Oklahoma.

"My life is nonstop hustle, Daun. When I leave here, I most likely will go back to the West, regroup for a minute, then hit another state and get right back on the grind. Could you handle something like that?"

"As long as I was able to be with you, I'd handle whatever you needed me to handle."

"What about your sister? I don't get the love vibe from her with Cotton, only the lust vibe."

"You're right. And I can't answer that, but I know she knows how I feel, and she'll go with me if I asked her to. But then, that would also be something you will have to be cool with. I don't want to make things too heavy for you. We carry our own weight, but still, that would be asking too much of you and that's not how I am."

"I understand. Let's cross that bridge when we get to it, love. Right now, there's still plenty more money to get out of here in your fine city," Shot said just as his phone rang. He pulled it out of his pocket, checked the number on the caller ID, and said, "See what I mean?" He then said to Big Shoota, "What up, champ?"

"I need to holla at you, cuz. Need more of them big thangs."

"That can't happen right now. Things on hold for a minute on that issue."

"Damn, that's fucked up, loc. These fools out here are acting for real. I ain't seen this kind of beef since like back in '03. I'm good, though. I guess I gotta make do with what I'm working with. Been losing weapons at an alarming rate, though, so let me know when I can get at you for a big order."

"Will do."

"What about the order?"

"That's a go."

"Cool. Gimme a few hours and I'll hit up Cotton."

"I'll let him know, so he'll be waiting for your call."

"All right, then, Shot, I'll holla at you," Big Shoota said as he ended the call and turned and faced Lynette on the bed they shared. "Looks like I got to tell the li'l homies to slow it down some out there. The connect for the straps is on hold. Fuck."

"Maybe that's a good thing, baby. You know them Hoover niggas ain't playing. If you fall back some, they will too."

"Fuck them niggas! Whose side is you on talking shit like that to me, cuz?"

She stared directly into his brown eyes and lied convincingly. "I'm always on your side. Forever that, Shoota."

"Act like that shit, then. Don't be telling me who ain't playing out there in them damn streets. Don't be confused. The Sixties ain't playing, and I will make sure we smash all them Snoover bitch-ass niggas, as well as them slobs. I still got plenty heat to take it to them niggas. I'm just trying to make sure we stay ahead of the game so we can remain well prepared for anything that comes our way."

"I understand. No worry, baby; no fear either. And damn sure no confusion on my part. I'm your ride or die, Shoota. Never forget that."

He smiled at his lover and said, "That's the talk I need and expect from your fine ass all the time, you hear me?"

"Mm-hmm," she said as she moved her naked hip against him and moaned as he made love to her slowly, with great affection, in the way lovers who have been with each other for a long time do. Though his lovemaking was good, it no longer excited her. He brought her to several orgasms every time they had sex, but it missed that spark, that fire. She didn't know for certain what it was, but Prophet brought out the true freak inside of her. The mere thought of him slapping her ass real hard or choking the life out of her while driving his dick extremely hard and deep inside of her asshole made her pussy get wetter right at that moment, while Shoota was making love to her. He thought her extra wetness came from being so turned on by him, and, boy, was he ever wrong.

Cotton and Janeen came over to Daun's place, and they were trying to decide what they were going to do for the evening. Shot wasn't in the mood to do any clubbing, so he deaded that before they even brought it up because he knew that would be Cotton and Janeen's first choice.

"I really don't care what we do, just no clubs. There has to be more to do out here than going to the club every weekend."

The Sin Sisters laughed.

"For as long as we can remember, that's been the one thing we have done almost every weekend, Shot," said Janeen.

"For real, I don't have a problem with it. I like getting my club on. Especially when I can enter a club with a badass female on my side," Cotton said with a bright smile on his face.

"Aww, keep on with the compliments and you're going to get fucked real great later on," laughed Janeen.

Cotton frowned and asked, "What? I wasn't going to get fucked great later anyway?"

Shot and Daun just shook their heads and laughed.

"Let's go out to Riverwind Casino and get our gamble on. We can eat and see if they have a show or something tonight. If they don't, we can gamble and have some fun. At least we can have a variety to choose from. No clubs for my daddy tonight," Daun said and smiled.

Shot gave a nod yes and said, "We can do that. Where is Riverwind?"

"Out south by Norman," said Janeen.

"Okay, then, let's do that and see if we can win some money and have some fun."

The sisters both stood and excused themselves so they could go freshen up before they left. This gave Cotton a chance to talk shop with Shot.

"Things are hot out there, boss man. I had to shake a few nuccas because the law is like every-fucking-where."

"Glad you're using your head and being cautious. I was thinking about telling you to fall back for a minute until we could see if this heat would cool down."

"They banging too damn hard out there. The Bloods have gotten into this mix all of a sudden, and they putting it down on nuccas. They getting at the Sixties, the Hoovers, the Shotguns—everybody. But the Hoovers are catching it the most from them. They getting it from both ends hard because Big Shoota's boys are putting in that work."

"It's strange. How could things go from being so smooth to an all-out war all of a sudden out here? Don't they know the more violence they have the more heat will come? These fools don't understand crap about business," Shot said clearly frustrated.

"From what I've learned, as far as the Bloods are concerned, the beef started with the Hoovers because some heavyweight old-school Blood recently came home from the feds after doing a big stretch and found out that one of the Hoovers were fucking his wife in his pad when he was down."

"So he used *that* as a reason to start a war with the Hoovers? That has to be one of the stupidest reasons I've ever heard to start a war."

"I agree. What I heard was the Blood nigga wasn't really tripping. He was in the mall with his wife and that Hoover big homie saw them and walked up to dude's wife and said hello. The wife gets nervous because she knows her husband is peeping this out, so she tries to play it off like it's nothing and speaks to big homie. The fool says some fly shit, and before he realizes what happened, the Blood dude knocks big homie out right there in front of the Foot Locker in Penn Square Mall."

"What? Are you serious?"

"Yep. But it gets better. The Blood dude then calls his wife a crab-loving bitch, and then fires on her and knocks her out too! He walks out of the mall with both his wife and his wife's ex-lover lying side by side in front of the Foot Locker knocked the fuck out."

"Crazy," Shot said, shaking his head.

"Nah, what's crazy is the Blood nigga gets knocked for a violation for assault because big homie turns out he is not a hard nucca at all. He straight pressed charges on the Blood dude. Not only did he press charges, but he sent word that now that the Blood was back in jail, he was going to start back fucking his wife. That's the reason why the Bloods are on one. The Blood gave the green light, and they went berserk, starting with the Hoovers, then just getting at every Crip. The Bloods—all of them— Inglewood Families, 456 Pirus, Robinson Street Boys,

Lime Street Pirus, Skyline Pirus, Bounty Hunters, and the Outlaws—are altogether tearing shit up out there behind the OG who made the call. Supposedly, he's chipped up still even after doing all of that time. He's highly respected, and those Bloods are going real hard right now."

"I see. Okay, this is what we do. We fall back for a week or so. If we get some calls for serious paper, then we'll move together. I do not want you moving solo for nothing. We move as a unit. That way, we can watch each other's backs and still get that money."

"I feel that. Tell me, though, what we gon' do with these sisters? I mean, it's cool and all, but you know I ain't with the relationship thang. After what happened with Meosha and her death, I just can't be with one woman. I don't think I'll ever fall in love again, boss man, and that's real," Cotton said seriously as he thought about how his girlfriend was raped, and how she killed herself after they had been kidnapped by some Bloods in Dallas. Hot Shot knew that scar on his heart was deep, and he wished he could say some words that could ease his man's pain, but there was nothing he could say that would ever erase that type of pain. Instead, he smiled and joked, "You need to kill that noise, Cotton. You know you love Janeen."

Before Cotton could speak, the sisters came back into the living room. Janeen heard Shot and said, "He damn well *better* be loving me!" They all laughed as they left the condo and headed to the casino for a night of gambling and fun. Shot caught a glimpse of Cotton giving him the evil, and he smiled. Daun saw them both and smiled as well. *Things may just be all right after all*, she said to herself as they all entered the elevator.

Chapter Fourteen

As soon as they entered the Riverwind Casino, Daun instantly regretted their decision to go to that particular casino. Prophet was holding court at the craps table with all of his Hoover homebodies crowded around him, cheering him on. He was obviously on a roll because the crowd around him kept cheering loudly every time he rolled the dice.

Shot grabbed Daun's hand and gave it a soft squeeze as they were walking past the craps tables toward the bar. He wasn't worried about Prophet one bit. If he chose to act, then he would be exposed for the snitch he was. *Wonder what his homeboys will think when they find out that their leader is a snitch,* Shot thought as they walked hand in hand right past the craps table and the large Hoover entourage. One of Prophet's homeboys gave him a nudge in the side, and he turned and saw Daun, Shot, Cotton, and Janeen just as they were passing them.

This shit has to stop. I cannot let this nigga keep flossing around the town with my bitch, Prophet fumed silently as he turned back and smiled at the crowd and sent the dice flying back down the craps table.

"Snakes! Sorry, sir. Would you like to roll again?" asked the craps dealer.

"Nah, I'm done. Nothing lasts forever," Prophet said as he turned and followed the path that Daun and her group had taken. When he saw that they had stopped in front of the slots, he turned and gave a nod toward a few of his homeboys to follow him. Once he was standing in front of Daun, who was standing next to Shot, who was sitting down at the slot machine feeding it quarters, he said, "Damn, Daun, you're just going to keep it disrespectful, I see."

Daun rolled her eyes and rested her hand on Shot's right shoulder, making sure she kept him calm. "Would you please give it a break, Prophet? Why can't you get it in your head that it's a wrap? I'm done, and done for good. This is my man, and you already know how he rocks, so don't push this."

"Or what? What you gon' do to stop me from doing whatever the fuck I want to do?"

Daun felt Shot start to rise up out of his seat, and she gave his shoulder a squeeze, signaling that she had this. "You really want to know what I'll do, Prophet? I mean, *really?* After who I saw you with at the Outback that day, you *really* want to push me like that?"

Prophet laughed loudly and said, "Do you really think I give a fuck about that bitch? You can tell the world, for all I care. That's nothing to me. It is what it is, and you already know me and her man aren't on the best of terms!" he laughed loud in her face, which infuriated her to no end.

With a nod she said, "Okay, then, I'll just have to get a tad more creative with it."

"Meaning?"

Shot had heard enough. He stood and faced Prophet and said, "Meaning she will expose you for the fake you are. You say you're a gangster and about your work, but are you really? Where I'm from, gangsters keep it gangster at all times. That means they ride or die, they do what has to be done in the name of their gangsterism, whether it be within a set or solo. Real gangsters do gangster stuff at all times, and, you, my man, need to ask yourself, are you *really* a real gangster? The Crips I've come across over the years would be really disappointed in you if they knew how you *really* got down."

With a tone full of false bravado, Prophet laughed and said, "Cuz, you're tripping. You need to ask around about how Prophet from 107 Hoover Crip has done it all in this city. Ain't no playing with my gangster, cuz, and for you even speaking like it is, is reason for me to take the chains off my riders and let them get at your ass."

Shot smiled and said, "When you mean the chains off your riders, are you talking about your homeboys that are considered killers or Detective Bishop of the Oklahoma City Police Department?"

Janeen and Cotton started laughing. Daun smiled. The look on Prophet's face was priceless.

Prophet knew he had just been given a flooring blow, but he couldn't think of anything to say, so he chose to ignore the powerful jab as if it brushed easily off him. "Cuz, there ain't nothing but gangster in me. You must fear my get down since you easily shook me from that business we discussed the last time we were face-to-face."

"Fear you? *Really?* Why would I fear you? Because you're a 107 Hoover Crip? Or that you're a gangster who poses as a dope boy, among other things? No, Prophet, I don't fear you. I fear God only. I'm a businessman, and I do good business not bad business. Dealing with you would have been bad business for me, so I chose not to deal with you. Let's just leave it at that. That is, unless you want to get 'gangster' with it here in this casino, 'gangster,'" Shot said sarcastically. Before Prophet could respond, Shot continued, "Look, like my girl said, it's a wrap. What you had with her is old news. Done. Over. The next time you approach her with any foolishness, it will be the last time."

"Are you threatening me, cuz?"

Shaking his head, Shot said, "I don't do threats. I'm giving you my word. Not only will I expose you for the fraud you are, I will do way more than break your jaw and nose like I did your man Herc. I don't play games. You are dealing with a more powerful man than you can ever imagine. Let it go, Prophet, and take this L, champ. If not, you will take another L that will totally destroy everything you've worked so hard to achieve." Shot then stepped closer to Prophet and whispered in his ear. "For now, your secret is safe with us. Keep pushing, though, and I will have to let the entire city know you are a working confidential informant for Bishop. You know I'm not bluffing, so calm down and take this L, you peon."

Prophet stiffened and couldn't believe what he had just been told. But Shot was right, there was nothing he could do or say. He had to take this L because it would get worse if he tried to save face right now. He would have to find another way to get at Daun and Shot, and with God as his witness, he was going to get they ass for this.

"You got the best hand, cuz—for now," Prophet said as he smiled at Daun and said, "I see you when I see you, Daun."

Daun laughed and said, "You are amazing. Even in defeat, you got to keep your front game on full blast. I am so damn ashamed of myself for not spotting you as the phony, weak man you are," she said with obvious disgust in her voice.

When Prophet was walking away, his homeboy Squirt asked him, "Damn, cuz, you just gon' let them dis you like that? Want me to get the homies so we can get at they ass and twist them up real tight?"

"Nah, loc, we came out here to get away from the madness in the city. We don't need that shit right now. All we'd end up doing is going to jail in Cleveland County.

Ain't no time for that. Don't worry about them. I got them, and that's on 107 Hoover Crip," Prophet said gritting his teeth, still wondering how in the fuck they found out that he was working with Bishop. *Fuck! They let that out, then I will have some serious fucking problems. I got to get that bitch. When I get her, that bitch-ass nigga Shot gots to get it too. Yeah, it's time to send the riders at the nigga,* Prophet thought to himself as he rejoined the rest of his homeboys at the craps tables. "Come on, cuz, it's time for me to get hot again!" he screamed and asked the craps dealer for the dice, placing his bet before rolling them.

"Twelve! A loser! Sorry, sir, would you like to try again?" asked the stickman.

"Yeah, my luck has to change sooner or later," Prophet said, thinking about Daun and her man Shot. *Fuck!*

Neither of the two couples let the run-in with Prophet stop them from having a good time at the casino. They played the slots for a couple of hours and even won a little money. They then went and caught a comedy show by the comedian Kevin Hart. He kept them in tears with his hilarious antics. Afterward, they went and enjoyed a nice dinner at an all-you-can-eat seafood buffet restaurant inside the casino. By the time they finished eating, they still had the gambling fever so they went back into the casino and split up. The females wanted to go back to the slots where they felt they were most lucky at, and the men went and tried their luck with some blackjack. After a few hours of gambling, they were all tired. Daun ended up losing her winnings while Janeen won close to four thousand dollars. Cotton lost at blackjack, and Shot broke even. They were all laughing as they left the casino and headed home. By the time they pulled in front of Daun's place, everyone inside of Shot's car was fast asleep. He woke them and asked if they wanted to come on up and sleep over. Janeen told him she wanted to sleep in her own bed so when she woke up, she could hop on that early-morning hard dick of Cotton's. They laughed as they said their good-byes. Hot Shot scooped Daun's sleepy frame up in his arms and carried her to the elevator. She smiled and told him that no man she had ever been with had done that for her.

"You know I'm no small woman there, Daddy. You might of hurt yourself."

"I'm not the average man either, love. You're a relatively lightweight to me."

"Is that right?"

"Yes."

"Well, come on, then. Let's take a hot shower so I can show you that there's nothing lightweight about my sexing."

He smiled as he followed her inside of the condo. Fifteen minutes after entering, they were going hard at it under the hot spray from the shower. The sex with Daun was explosive, yet tender every time, and Shot was truly enjoying having her as his woman. Though Nola never left his thoughts, he felt comfortable with Daun and was well prepared to move on with his life without Nola.

Daun was in heaven. She'd finally met a man who cared for her and only her. A man that was respectful and protective. Shot didn't overdo it, but he let it be known that no one was to ever threaten her, and that made her feel safe. She was in love with this man, and she wasn't going to let him get away from her. If she had to follow him to hell and back, she would in order to be with him. Love felt good for once, and she prayed that she never lost Shot.

The next morning, Daun was still sleeping soundly with her legs spread wide open. Shot opened his eyes and got out of the bed to go use the bathroom. When he returned, his intentions were to do his morning ritual by working out, but when he saw Daun's legs spread wide open on top of the sheets, his early-morning hard dick made him head right back to bed. He slid between her legs and put his face between them. The smell of clean pussy and lemon burst rose from between the sheets as he began to feast, putting his finger between her outer lips to separate her wetness. Though still asleep, she tightened her legs because his tongue tickled. He took his other hand and pulled her closer to his face. He then stuck one finger in, and she pushed forward toward it, and he then slid in another finger and looked up because her moaning began to make his mouth salivate. He licked his lips and tasted her. He wanted more of her now and stuck his tongue in her throbbing pussy, causing her to secrete her juices onto his tongue. He swallowed, licked, and sucked. He used his thumb to lift the top portion of her pussy to get to her clit. It bulged out as he gently sucked and licked her love button. He increased his speed because her legs and ass were pushing toward his face, loving his tongue ministrations.

He went deeper inside of her with his finger and sucked her clit even faster and steadily swallowed a healthy dose of her juices. This had taken awhile because he wasn't full or tired yet. Her taste was so sweet he could not get enough of her, but his dick was so hard that he was starting to feel uncomfortable. His body was twitching, and so was Daun's. She could not hold out any longer. She came so hard that he stopped sucking and swallowed everything that she gave him.

Then she turned toward him when she finished and climbed on top of his very hard dick. He easily guided her down his long shaft. She was so wet and hot and he moaned so loud that she felt as if every last inch of his body was inside of her. He held onto her ample hips and set the pace for them as he went deep inside of her pussy.

She was trying her best to get all of him inside of her, but he controlled how much she received with his hands. Once he had her body moving at the pace he wanted, he let her take control, and she began riding that dick and stroking him. With every muscle in her legs, knees bent, and ass cheeks tight, she made sure she gave him all that pussy just right.

He began moaning again even louder than before from the sensation of pleasure he was feeling from her every stroke. He slapped her ass, his legs stiffened, and his toes curled. Her titties were bouncing up and down in rhythm with her pussy. Up, down, up, down. Then he sat partway up, arms bent behind her. She leaned forward holding onto his broad shoulders, taking as much of his dick as she could, giving it all that she could because she wanted that dick deep inside her when he came. She wanted to feel his juices splash deep inside of her. She wanted this so bad. This would be their first time they had unprotected sex, and she wanted it to be the most memorable sex either of them ever had in their lives.

He let out another loud moan and came fast and hard. She didn't slow the pace as his come filled her. Her pussy was vibrating as she continued to give him the ride of his life. Two more seconds later, she came equally as hard and increased her pace and rode him even harder, totally impaling herself on his love stick. She let out a low moan as if it came from deep within her guts to complete her utter satisfaction. Then she slid off of him, her body now limp and sweaty from exhaustion.

Breathing heavily and holding onto each other, with him holding her from behind, naked and satisfied, he kissed her neck. She squeezed his hand. They both knew that their lovemaking had just been incredible. No words had been spoken, no need for any *I love yous*.

They both felt the love during the most incredible twenty minutes of their lives. At that time, that exact moment, everything was right in the world. Their world. They were one, and everything was good. And if Shot had anything to say about it, things would always remain that way. He was in love again, and it felt damn good.

Nola who?

Chapter Fifteen

"Cuz, I'm on the corner of Twenty-third and MLK and you won't believe who is in the car right in front of me!" screamed Sharp Shoota.

"I'm in the middle of taking care of some serious shit. I ain't got no damn time for guessing games. Who the fuck is it?" Big Shoota said and sniffed loudly.

Shaking his head, Sharp Shoota thought, *Some serious shit, my ass. Nigga, you playing with your fucking nose.* But to Big Shoota he said, "Cuz, it's Lynette in that black Benz that nigga Prophet rolls in."

Big Shoota dropped the cut of straw he held in his hands and said, "You better be positive you telling me the real right now, cuz."

"I'm positive, cuz. I'm about to roll past them when the light turns green. She won't know who it is because I got the tint, and this ain't my whip. What you want me to do, cuz?"

"Follow they ass, li'l nigga! What you think? Is that nigga Prophet driving the car?"

As Sharp Shoota passed the black Mercedes, he took a look to his left and saw that Prophet was indeed the driver of the vehicle. "Yeah, cuz, that's him. This is some real fucked-up shit, loc. This is straight-up treason. I know you love this broad, but she has to—"

"Don't tell me what has to be done, cuz. I already know. You make sure my ride-or-die-ass bitch stays in your sight. Today is the day she loses her life. Her and Prophet.

I'm about to jump in my shit and head your way. Don't you lose them, cuz."

"I won't, big homie, just hurry your ass up. Wait! Don't hang, cuz. They pulling into that Waffle House on the corner of Eastern right before you get to the highway. I'm about to go across the street and pull into that barbeque spot and wait for you."

"Play it like this, cuz, soon as I hit you back, pull into the Waffle House and park right behind that nigga whip. Keep his ass blocked in 'cause when I come in, I'm coming hard, loc."

"I got you. Hurry your ass up!"

Inside the Waffle House restaurant, Lynette and Prophet sat down in a booth in the back of the small fast-food diner. Lynette was a nervous wreck when she asked, "Why are we so close to the neighborhood, Prophet? You know this ain't cool. Any one of Shoota's homeboys could come in here."

"Would you shut the fuck up, bitch! I'm tired of these fucking games you been playing. It's time for you to leave that nigga and move in with Daddy. You ready for that shit, bitch? You ready to be mines totally? No more fucking that sissy nigga. You Hoover property, right?"

Shaking her head she said, "No, I'm your property. I don't belong to no damn Hoovers. If that's what you think, then we might as well end this shit 'cause if you think I'm going to be some toss for you and your Hoover homeboys, you got me all the way fucked up, Prophet. Nothing—and I mean nothing—will ever make me get down like that shit."

He smiled and said, "You know damn well I didn't mean it like that, bitch. So calm the fuck down. Are you ready to be all mine or what?"

She smiled as she thought about being with Prophet exclusively. She was scared and excited to no end. She wanted him, but she feared if she left Shoota, he would come after her real hard, and that meant death. She shrugged and said, "You know this will get ugly. I mean, *real* ugly. Shoota will not take this lightly."

"Fuck that sissy nigga! Bitch, you been fucking me for the last fifteen months, and *now* you on some scared shit? I should leave your ass here and say fuck it. So what is it? You my bitch or what?"

Before she could answer, she saw a dark blue sedan pull directly behind Prophet's car. She thought that was strange how they blocked his car in, but before she could speak her thoughts, her eyes grew large when she saw Sharp Shoota get out of the sedan with a big-ass gun in his hand. She put her hand over her mouth when she saw Shoota's car come flying into the parking lot. "Oh! My! God! We're about to die, Prophet!" she screamed at the top of her lungs.

Prophet was already in defense mode with his gun in his right hand. He stood and walked calmly toward the glass door, ready to confront his enemies head-on with no fear at all on his face. If he was going to die, he was going down fighting. He stopped in the doorway of the diner and smiled when he saw two highway patrolmen pull into the parking lot. He quickly put his gun in the small of his back.

Shoota saw the policemen as well and told Sharp Shoota to watch himself. Sharp Shoota slid back inside of the car he was driving and moved it into a parking space as the police officers walked inside of the restaurant. Shoota entered the restaurant behind them and went straight to the booth where Lynette was sitting with tears streaming down her face. Prophet stood by the door and watched with a smile on his face. He knew he had just dodged a major bullet, and he sighed, silently relieved.

"What the fuck is this, Lynette? What are you doing here with that Snoover? Please tell me you ain't doing me dirty like that. I can take it if you fucked another nigga, but not the enemy, cuz. Don't do that shit to me, baby."

Her answer to his questions was to drop her head in shame. At that exact moment, she realized she didn't give a damn about Prophet. She loved Big Shoota. Seeing the hurt on his face broke her heart. Prophet was a thrill, a thrill that has cost her the true love of her life. "I can never explain this to you, Shoota. All I can say is I love you and only you. I hope you can believe that."

He sighed with relief and reached his hand out to her. She grabbed his hand and let him pull her to her feet and led her out of the diner. As they walked past Prophet, he smiled and said, "I guess that's that, huh, Lynette?"

Shoota told Lynette to go get in his car and turned and faced Prophet and said, "Cuz, you thought the beef was serious before. You done made this more personal than you can ever believe. I'm going to kill every one of your punk-ass homeboys; then I'm going to kill your bitch ass—real slow—that's my word, loc."

"Not if I get you and your punk-ass homies first, cuz. Fuck sissies!"

Shoota laughed, not wasting anymore of his words. He was about that action, not bumping his gums. He walked away from Prophet, got into his car, and left the Waffle House followed by his li'l homeboy Sharp Shoota.

When they made it back to his house, Shoota told Sharp Shoota to mount the homeboys up and go get every Hoover they can. The war was on another level now. "Cuz, I want to hear about bodies tonight. More Snoovers will be dropped more than ever this night. Ya hear me?"

"I got you, cuz. Let me get a couple of those SARs and watch my work."

Shoota went into the back room of his house and grabbed three SARs and gave them to his namesake and said, "Stay safe and kill them niggas, cuz."

"On Rollin' Sixties, I'm not taking it in tonight until I've got as many as I can, cuz!" Sharp Shoota said as he left the house.

After Sharp Shoota was gone, Shoota went into the bedroom and grabbed a small straw and stuck it in each nostril, inhaling a large amount of cocaine. He sighed and sat down at the end of the bed while he waited for Lynette to come out of the shower. When she came into the bedroom she sat next to him and said, "How will you ever be able to forgive me, Shoota?"

He shrugged and said, "I don't know. This shit hurts. You cheated on me with a Snoover. What the fuck was you thinking? I could have taken this shit if it was any other nigga. Fuck, I'd rather you fuck a slob nigga before fucking one of those bitch-ass Snoover niggas. Damn, Lynette you got me really fucked up right now."

"I know, babe, I'm—"

Shoota didn't really let her finish her sentence. He slapped her so hard she saw stars as she fell to the floor right in front of his feet. He didn't even realize what he was doing as he started kicking her in her face and body. She screamed and tried to get to her feet, only to be knocked back to the floor by a powerful blow to her head. Shoota lost total control with the help of the cocaine flowing through his bloodstream. He socked her, kicked her, slapped her, and punched her all over her body. When he finally calmed down about ten minutes later, she was lying on the floor unconscious, bloody, and barely alive. He looked at her with a wide-eyed dazed look on his face. He didn't feel a bit of remorse for what he had just done. He just felt contempt for the woman he loved more than anything in this world.

He shook his head to try to clear his thoughts, but all that did was make him angrier. He stood and went to the dresser where his pistol was. In a dreamlike state, he grabbed the gun and racked a live round in the chamber. He stood over Lynette and said, "I'd rather bury you than have you after you've lain down with a Snoover. This isn't out of hate, Lynette, it's out of love." He then pulled the trigger twice and blew two large holes inside of her chest. The first shot killed her, and the second shot gave him some relief from the pain he was feeling. Then he went back and snorted some more cocaine and sat at the end of the bed and stared at the woman he just murdered. His woman.

Damn.

Shot woke up to something smelling really good. He was famished and felt as if he could eat more than he usually did. He walked into the kitchen to see his woman standing in front of the stove frying some bacon. He stared at Daun who was wearing a pair of boy shorts and a bra. *That's a whole lot of woman right there,* he thought as he watched her. Feeling his presence, she turned and smiled at him. "Good afternoon, Daddy. I know you're hungry because I'm starved. You worked me over something good."

"*I* worked *you* over? No way! *You* did all the work, love," he said as he stepped to her and gave her a hug and a kiss. "You know what we did, right?"

Smiling, she said, "Mm-hmm. We most likely made a baby as deep as you were inside of me. I swear I felt your nut hitting my stomach."

"How do you feel about that?"

She paused to take the bacon out of the skillet and said, "If I'm pregnant, then it's time for me to be a mom and slow it all the way down. I've always sworn that when I had a child I would leave the wicked way of life alone."

That made him smile. "You are a special woman, Daun, I love you."

"Mmmm, but are you *in love* with me, Daddy?"

He pulled her to him and gave her a deep kiss and said, "Yes. I am *in love* with you, Daun. You've become my universe. The stars and the moon all revolve around you as far as I'm concerned. I don't ever want to lose you."

"As long as you can remain real and romantic as you are right now, Daddy, losing me is something you never have to worry about. You're all the man I want and need. I will do my very best to keep you right. I will honor and respect you always. I will never lie to you, and I will do whatever it takes to keep you happy with me. I mean that from the bottom of my heart."

"I believe you. Now there is one thing I need you to do for me so I will know for certain that I am the one and only love of your life."

She stared at him with a serious and determined look on her face when she asked, "What is it, Daddy? There isn't anything in this world I wouldn't do for you."

He smiled and said, "Hurry up and finish cooking that there food. I'm starving. Feed Daddy and Daddy will know without a doubt that you're loving me with all of your heart, love."

She smiled and said, "And he has jokes too! Wow. I am extremely lucky. Your breakfast is coming right up, sir," she said and went back to cooking his food.

By the time Cotton woke up, he had over twenty-five missed calls on his phone. He climbed out of bed and went into the other room so he wouldn't disturb Janeen. He saw the missed calls and picked the ones that would bring in the most money and called them back first. By the time he made it to Sharp Shoota, he had arranged to meet ten people for at least ten kilos of cocaine. *Today has the makings of a really good day,* he thought as he called Sharp Shoota to see what he wanted. Boy, was he shocked when he heard what the Crip had to say.

"What's up, Cotton, cuz? Man, you might want to stay off the East Side because niggas been dropping all afternoon. The city is so damn hot any nigga looking like a street nigga getting scooped."

"What the fuck is going on?"

"Some Snoover niggas got dropped in Creston Hills. About four more got dropped in the parking lot of the flea market. And from what I've been told, when some of the fools who got hit up went to Baptist, some more got dropped at the Emergency Room. So if you have any business with them niggas, I think you need to change your plans."

"So you're basically telling me that your people have been putting in some monster work, huh?"

There was a silence on the other end, and that was answer enough for Cotton.

"Who got hit?"

"Big Homie, Henn, and some names from Snoover from what I've been told. Right now, I'm out of the way getting some rest. Just wanted you to know the BI."

"All right, Sharp Shoota, you stay safe, man."

"No doubt, loc. Just another day in a real Crip's life. Holla at ya," Sharp Shoota said as he hung up the phone. He sat down and stared at Big Shoota who was still tripping the fuck out with what he had done to Lynette. Sharp Shoota shook his head and said, "Shake that shit off, cuz. You did what you did, and it's a done deal. We got rid of the body, so that's just another body added to the body count for the Rollin' Sixty Crip gang! No one crosses us, cuz."

Shoota stared at his mans and nodded. Then, in a hoarse whisper, he said, "Cuz, we've only just begun to kill."

Chapter Sixteen

With the city being so hot, Shot decided not to let Cotton make any moves without him, so while they were out and about taking care of business, Janeen and Daun were together having some much-needed one-on-one time. After spending the day shopping from mall to mall, they ended up going back to their beautician and got their hair done. After that, they went back to Daun's house to relax and wait for the men to return so they could see what they would do for the evening.

"Damn, sister, ain't that fucked up that happened to Lynette? I mean, they found her body on the South Side battered and shot twice in the chest. Who would do some cold shit like that to her? Whoever did that shit is in a world of trouble when Shoota find out who they are, I know that much. That man is probably losing his damn mind right about now."

Shrugging her shoulders, Daun's response shocked her sister. "I don't know, sister. I don't see how anyone would have the courage to do some shit like that to Lynette. You just gave the prime reason for that . . . No fool out here is foolish enough to get at Shoota's woman like that. Not even Prophet, and he was obviously fucking her."

"So, are you trying to tell me what I *think* you're trying to tell me?"

She nodded and said, "Yep. I think Shoota did that shit to her. Somehow, he must have found out what she had going on with Prophet, and he lost it and took her out."

"Come on, that sounds like some stuff out of a Lifetime movie, sister."

"No, this is some real-life shit, and it happens all the time. When a man is in love and finds out he's been betrayed like that, there's no telling what he's capable of doing. Especially a cold-ass killer like Shoota. I don't know if I'm right, but my gut tells me he did that shit to her." Daun grabbed her purse and said, "I'm about to test my theory here and see what I can find out." She pulled her phone out of her purse and dialed a number she swore she thought she would never dial again as long as she lived. When the other line was answered, she didn't waste time with any greeting. "Tell me, Prophet, how do you feel about what happened to Lynette, you fucking prick?"

Prophet started laughing and said, "Well, well, looks like my Daun has finally came to her senses. You done shook that joke nigga you been with and ready to come to your real daddy?"

"Is *that* what you think this call is for, you sick fuck? That's sad. You just can't accept that I've found a real man. A man that isn't afraid to take it to your ass. A man that treats me right in every way. A man that has more dick than you could ever dream of having. You are a sore loser for real, you jerk. But like I said, how do you feel about what happened to Lynette because of the dirty mack game you two were playing?"

"First off, that's her and her man's business. I told her to leave that nigga and come be with me, but she made the wrong choice. She wanted to stay with that nigga. Now look what happened to her ass. If she would have stayed with me, all would have been right. She would have been safe with me, and we would have been good."

"Safe with you? Are you fucking *kidding* me, you sadistic bastard? You most likely would have killed her sooner or later with all the sick shit you're into."

"She would have never been treated like how that punk-ass nigga Shoota did her. That was some fucked-up shit. Talking about not being able to take a L. That just shows how weak that pussy nigga is, cuz. See, if I was as weak as he was, I might have came after you and fucked you off the same way that bitch-ass nigga did Lynette."

Laughing, Daun said, "If you even *think* about trying to get at me, your world will come to an end so fucking fast. It's truly a pleasure to have a man who won't hesitate to look at your bitch ass. So, please know that I am kinda hoping you will try to get at me or Shot, because you already know you're a rat and a coward. Bye, Prophet!" Daun hung up the phone laughing.

With a frown on her face, Janeen said, "Do you *really* think that was wise, sister? I mean, come on, wasn't no need for that kiddie shit. You piss that nigga off and make him try to get at you, then more shit will get started. Not cool there."

"Maybe not, but fuck him. I'm with Shot, and I'm happy. I'm safe, and I know without a doubt Shot won't let nothing happen to me. Like I said, fuck Prophet. The real reason why I called that fool was to see if my gut was right, and just like I figured, I was 100 percent correct. Shoota did that shit to Lynette. That coldhearted bastard found out about Lynette fucking Prophet and murdered that girl."

"Prophet told you that?"

"Pretty much." She then gave a replay of the conversation from Prophet's side of things and blew her sister's mind.

"That is some real sad shit. I hope that coward dies a million deaths for what he has done to Lynette."

"Odds are he will get the Karma he deserves because I got a feeling all his beef with them Hoovers and the Sixties stems from Shoota knowing Lynette was fucking

Prophet. That crazy-ass man done went and put the green light on the Hoovers, and they been winning for real."

"I know, those Hoovers been dropping like flies. I saw on the news where Big Homie and Henn from Hover got it, as well as C-Dub. I thought the Hoovers were about that, but looks like they've tucked their tails and running scared."

Shaking her head, Daun said, "No way. If I know Prophet like I think I do, that crazy fool is planning an attack right now to get back at the Sixties. Shoota knows it too, so this summer is only going to get hotter, because there's going to be plenty more bodies from this war, trust that."

"Maybe we should shake the city for a minute and get out of Dodge."

"Why? This is not our problem. I will tell you this, though, if Shot decides it's too hot and heads back to California, I'm not letting him leave this state without me right with him."

"You love him that much, sister?"

Nodding her head, she said, "I love him more than I have ever loved a man in my life."

The seriousness in her sister's tone told Janeen that Daun was really in love, and she was happy for her. "Damn, I wish I dug Cotton like you dig Shot. Don't get me wrong, Cotton is cool, the sex is way out freaky and good, but that's all it is for me, sister. I don't even have the urge to tell him I love his ass when he's serving me that big chocolate dick. And you know if a bitch is coming and won't say that shit, then it's not heart love; it's only love of the dick."

"You are too silly. It is what it is, though."

"So, if you leave with Shot, what will happen to little ole me?"

"Little ole you better start loving Cotton, then, whether it's his heart or dick. 'Cause if my Daddy says he's out, I'm out. Period."

By the time Shot and Cotton made it back to their place, both were tired from driving around the city all day making moves. They had to be extra cautious, so that meant more driving than usual. Staying away from the hot spots in the city was difficult because the main people they dealt with were on the NE Side of town, and right now, the NE Side was the hottest. The Hoovers were basically hiding, and that meant, for the time being, things would slow down on the streets. But once nighttime hit, Shot figured the Hoovers would come out to play and get back at the Sixties for all of their homeboys who had been shot up and murdered thus far.

"I'm telling you, champ, this may be too much trouble to continue trying to get money out here. It may be time to call this city a wrap and go regroup and prepare up another state."

"The money is good, but the law is turned all the way up, boss man, so I'm definitely feeling you. Where would the next state be?"

Shot shrugged and said, "I'll have to get at my peoples and see. You know how it is . . . We may just have to fall back and kick it some until things can be put in order."

"I've made some nice changes out here, so the kitty is getting fat. I don't have a problem heading back to ATL or Miami for a few months."

With a grin Shot told him, "Yes, I bet you don't. What, you're going to get back out there and become King Trick again?"

"Not tricking when you got it, boss man."

"Whatever. What about Janeen? You going to take her with you?"

"No way! Like Sharp Shoota said that time, that's taking your sand to the beach. Trust me, boss man, there's plenty of sand in South Beach, baby!"

"Whatever."

"What about you? When you head back West, you're going to take Daun?"

Shot thought about that question for a moment, and then said, "Yes, if she wants to join me, she's more than welcome."

"You know you fall in love too damn easy. When we first hooked up, you was on some player shit for real. Then you met Nola, and it was a wrap for that shit. Things go south with your ex-piece-of-game and now you fall right back in love with Daun. Granted, Daun is a bad one, but you don't need to fall in love just because she's fine and pretty as fuck, boss man. You don't even know her for real, and you talking about taking her West. That's nuts."

"It may be nuts, but I've learned to always trust my instincts, champ. I never second-guess my moves on the streets, nor my heart. So you can chill out with the lecture on me and my get down and go put that paper up. I need you to go on and scoop the Sin Sisters up and bring them back here. By the time you get back, I'll be finished handling things with my people in the West. The business needs to be discussed about whether I should slam this town and bounce."

"I feel you. So what are we going to get into tonight?"

"I don't know, but whatever it is, it's going to be way out of the way because there is no way we're going to do any clubs or that Lil Boosie concert. I have a funny feeling this will be the night the Hoovers flex their muscles and try to get some revenge."

"Maybe. They will either get they man or they ass locked up because the law gon' be all over the East Side tonight."

"Oh well . . ."

"All right, let me handle this shit. Give the ladies a holla and let them know I'm on my way," Cotton said as he carried a small duffel bag filled with money they made throughout the day.

When Cotton left, Shot pulled out his phone and called JT in Los Angeles and gave him a detailed report on the state of the streets in Oklahoma City. When he finished, JT asked him a question that he felt the answer would determine whether he would bring the Oklahoma City part of Operation Cleanup to a close.

"Do you feel the violence will ease up soon, son?"

"No. They are going to go at it for a minute. A lot of blood has been shed, but it's only been one-sided. It's about to flip and become even bloodier."

"Do you feel with the moves you've made it will impact the streets of Oklahoma City for better once we have the sweep team come clean up?"

"Definitely. The Hoovers will take a major hit, and so will the Sixties."

"What about the Bloods and the other sets out there? Do we have enough is what I'm asking, son? Trust me, I don't want to pull the plug on this mission too quickly. When you leave there, I want those streets to be calm somewhat. I want them to feel the loss of the power that they've held on to for far too long."

"We've touched a lot of people, and I know for a fact that if we remove Shoota and Prophet from the streets, along with their main men, then, yes, the streets will feel it tremendously. As for the Bloods and the other sets out here, we've touched them all up pretty good. We've done some good out here, JT."

"Can there be more, though? Can we at least make it until the end of the summer?"

Shot thought about that question for a minute, and then said, "I don't see why not. But what concerns me most is the violence. By not moving and taking these jokers down, we're taking a serious risk of more murders happening out here. So far, there's been no innocents hurt by this war with the Crips and Bloods. But how long do you think that will last? Are you willing to take that risk of blood being spilled by innocent people, JT?"

"We're in this to do some good, and there is no way I want anyone hurt, but you know the mission, and you know that we're cleared to do what we have to in order to bring as many criminals out there down. So I can't let the thoughts of innocents into my mind. It's about to be July. Let's ride it to Labor Day, and then we pull out."

"Understood."

"What about the females with the credit scam? What have they been up to?"

Shot stared at the phone and remained silent for a moment, and then sighed.

JT recognized that sigh and muttered, "Shit, son, not again."

"I don't know what it is, champ, but it seems like I keep falling in love, and it's driving me crazy."

"Love? Are you fucking kidding me? What the hell are you doing falling in love? I thought you loved Nola?"

"I thought I did too, champ, I thought I did too. Let me go. I have work to do."

"Yeah, get to work!" JT hung up the phone and shook his head wondering if it was time to pull the plug on the entire operation. For the first time since he'd met Shot, he was doubting his abilities. He thought about that for a few minutes, then smiled. "No way. Shot is the best man for Operation Cleanup. If he keeps falling in love, then that may be a good thing. Keep up the good work, son," JT said aloud as he turned his laptop on and sent a detailed e-mail report to the director of the FBI to update him about the progress being made out in Oklahoma City.

Chapter Seventeen

Word on the street was that Lynette had been messing around with Prophet from Hoover, and that was the reason Shoota killed her. But no one had proof of that, so for now, that's all it was, a rumor. Only Sharp Shoota knew the real as far as the Sixties were concerned. Bridget, Lynette's sister, didn't think that Shoota killed her sister because that would be cold. The fact that Bridget and Lynette were extremely close also made her confident in believing that Shoota didn't have anything to do with it. If Lynette was creeping around with Prophet, she would have told Bridget, that was something she was positive of. That's another reason why she ignored the rumors about her sister and Prophet. But there was a nagging feeling in the back of her mind, and she wondered if Shoota could do something like that to the woman he loved. The only reason her family hadn't gone after him was because of her, and she prayed she was right with her feelings and that he didn't have anything to do with killing her sister and keeping her family at bay. If she found out that Shoota *did* kill Lynette or had anything to do with it, she would kill him herself. These were her thoughts as she began to get dressed to go put her sister to rest.

It was the morning of Lynette's funeral, and she was on Big Shoota's mind big time. Actually, his mind was all over the place. Ever since he murdered her, he'd been a nervous wreck. Not only was he scared out of his mind of the police having him as the prime suspect for the murder, it was also the combination of Lynette's family swearing if they found out he killed her there would be hell to pay. His nerves were totally shot. He was snorting more and more cocaine since the murder was committed, and the more he snorted, the more paranoid he became. Killing people was nothing new to him, but Lynette was his woman, his world. Murdering her did something to him that he was unable to comprehend. For the first time, his crazy life, his conscience, was getting the best of him. He was hurting from his actions, and those feelings were completely foreign to him.

He sat at the dining-room table and snorted some more cocaine and sighed. He felt he needed to be extra high in order to deal with Lynette's funeral. He didn't want to go, but knew he had to attend the service or he would look guilty to those who felt he did kill Lynette. He knew that all eyes would be on him because the rumors had been swirling around the city ever since Lynette's body had been found on the South Side. Even though he made it obvious to all of his people that he was on the warpath and blamed the Hoovers for killing Lynette, it didn't change what everyone was thinking. He had to get his act on at a Denzel-type level in order to make it through this service and convince everyone that there was no way he could kill the woman he loved the most in the entire world. *Fuck,* he thought as he shook his head, and then snorted some more cocaine. *It's about to be one hell of a fucking morning,* he thought as he sat back in his seat and started crying. "Damn, Lynette, why you had to fuck with that bitch-ass nigga Prophet? Fuck!" he screamed.

***

"Are you sure attending that funeral is the right thing to do, boss man? I mean, that's really none of our business," Cotton said as he grabbed his black sports coat and slipped it on.

"It's a sign of respect for Big Shoota. We've done some good business with him, and I feel it's appropriate that we show our respect."

"I feel all that, but, damn, my man, you know they been at war with the Hoovers like crazy, and this would be the perfect opportunity for them nuccas to come and get at the Sixties while they're grieving their man's loss."

"True. But I don't think Prophet would be foolish enough to order a move like that. The heat from that would bring that fool down so fast he would never be able to bounce back. Even Detective Bishop wouldn't be able to save him."

"If you say so, but we still need to be strapped and prepared for any surprises."

"Since when did you ever see me *not* prepared for any surprise, Cotton? You know better," Shot said as he grabbed two 9 mm SIG Sauers and put them in the small of his back. "Come on, we're picking up Daun and Janeen. We're all riding together."

"That's another thing I'm really not feeling. Why we taking them with us?"

"They knew Lynette, and they want to pay their respects, so why not take them with us? Plus, I'm still not all the way right with Daun being too far away from me with that joker Prophet lurking. I have a funny feeling sooner or later he will make a play at her, and when he does, he will be dealt with."

"Damn, Nola *has* been replaced for real, huh?"

Shot stared at his man for a moment, then said, "Who?"

***

"You do know it's now been over four months since we saw that bitch-ass nigga Bubba, right? I told you we should have went after his bitch ass. We ate a lot of money from that chump, and just as soon as I can, I'm getting his bitch ass," Janeen said as she slipped on a modest but expensive black dress. After slipping on some black Jimmy Choo pumps, she continued on with her rant. "He got to die, sister, I mean that shit."

"You right. I tried to give that bitch a pass, but he played us. We let this ride, then we lose clout, and our names get weakened. I'm going to tell Shot that he can go on and go back home 'cause we need to make some moves, and I don't need him babysitting me anymore. Then we'll go on the hunt and find that pussy-ass Bubba."

"Humph . . . And you think your man is just going to accept that and do as you ask him to?"

"Yep. He respects my business, and if I tell him I need to handle some things without him, he'll understand. I'm telling you, sister, that man is so fucking perfect that it scares me sometimes. How can a man be that damn good to me?"

"Because you deserve a good man, that's why. That, and the fact that he's a boss nigga for real. He gets his bands at a high level, and he conducts himself in a respectful manner at all times. You're winning with that nigga, I will give you that."

"Damn, I can't remember the last time I was with someone that you gave such high approval to."

"You can't remember it because that shit never happened before!" They both started laughing as they finished getting dressed.

Lynette's funeral was packed not only with her friends and family members, but with almost every Rollin' Sixty

Crip in Oklahoma City. It was standing room only when Shot, Daun, Cotton, and Janeen made it inside of the church. Shot let his eyes roam all over the church, and he could tell that every last Crip inside of the church had weapons on their person. "Prophet would be a fool to try something here today; he'd get slaughtered," Shot said to himself as he listened to the preacher give Lynette's eulogy.

When it was time for the final viewing of Lynette's body, Shot couldn't believe his eyes when he saw Prophet enter the church and walk down the aisle with his head up, showing absolutely no fear at all. He went straight to Lynette's father and whispered something in his ear, and then shook hands with the grieving parent. He then said something to Lynette's mother and sister. He then turned and went and stood in front of the casket and stared down at Lynette's body. Shot instinctively reached for his weapon because he knew something was about to go down as he watched each Rollin' Sixty Crip inside of the church look as if they were about to run up on Prophet and murder him right there in front of everyone inside of the church. He was shocked to say the least when he saw Shoota stand and wave his hands to all of his homeboys, signaling for them to stand now. He then stared at Prophet and gave him a nod. Prophet returned the nod, then turned and left the church.

"What the fuck was that, Daddy?" Daun whispered.

"Your guess is just as good as mine, love. Come on, let's pay our respects and get out of here." They then went and viewed the body and shook hands with some of the family members. Shot stepped to Shoota, and they shook hands.

"Thanks for coming, cuz. I appreciate that gesture," Shoota said somberly.

Shot stared at him briefly and said, "I know this is a hard time for you, my man, and I want you to know my prayers are strong for you and your girl's family."

Shoota nodded and sniffed loudly. Shot could only wonder whether his sniffs were from his crying or the cocaine he had obviously been snorting. He could tell by his eyes that Shoota was definitely faded. "If you have some time, get at me later, loc. I need to chop it up with you on some serious shit."

Shaking his head, Shot said, "Not today, my man. Shop's closed. Plus, you're in no shape to conduct anything. Go on and grieve properly, my mans, and holla at me tomorrow."

Shoota nodded, and they shook hands again. He watched as Shot turned and grabbed Daun's hand and left the church, followed closely by Cotton and Janeen. Sharp Shoota whispered in Shoota's ear and asked, "Why the fuck didn't you let the homies slay that punk-ass nigga Prophet, cuz? There was no way he should have been able to leave this fucking church alive. It's not like we don't have a few crash dummies we could've had get at that nigga, loc."

Shaking his head, he said in a low tone to his little homeboy, "I've caused enough pain to Lynette's fam, cuz. I couldn't cause them any more. Don't worry about that nigga, loc. Before the week ends, he'll be a dead man. He thinks he's safe, but I got a line on where the bitch been hiding at. Tonight, it goes down."

Sharp Shoota gave a nod and said, "That's right, loc. Come on, cuz, it's time to say good-bye to your girl." They both stood and stepped in front of the coffin and stared at the body of Lynette.

Shoota knew that every pair of eyes inside the church was on him at that moment, so he took a deep breath as the tears slowly slid down his face. He bent forward and gave Lynette's cold cheek a kiss and whispered, "I'm so sorry, baby. I'm so sorry. I know I'm going to burn in hell for what I did to you. I'm so sorry." He then turned and walked back to his seat as the family stood and began to have their final viewing of their loved one. When Lynette's mother started screaming, his heart felt as if it was about to stop. He actually couldn't breathe. After a few seconds, he caught a breath and sighed, then stood and marched out of the church with tears streaming down his face and shame in his heart.

Once they were inside of Shot's car and on their way to have some lunch, each person became caught up in their own thoughts. Daun and Janeen were both thinking about how they were going to get at Bubba and punish him for beating them out of their money. Cotton was thinking about the dark-skinned cutie Shirin who had been blowing him up the last few days. He was digging Janeen, but after losing the love of his life, love just wasn't in the cards for him any longer. Janeen was cool, but he wanted a variety, and he felt he'd given her way more time than he ever thought possible. He wondered how in the hell he was going to be able to shake her with boss man all caught up with her sister. Shot's mind was on Shoota. He couldn't believe what he was thinking, but he saw it in Shoota's eyes. *Guilt. He killed that girl. That is one cold-blooded man. It's going to be a pleasure when he, along with the rest of the scumbags out here dealing drugs and death to our people, are locked up in a federal prison for the rest of their lives,* he thought to himself as he drove toward Kevin Durant's restaurant.

Daun sighed and said, "After we finish eating, Daddy, me and Janeen need to go handle some serious business. I'll give you a call in a day or two when everything is everything, okay?"

"A couple of days? Are you going out of town, love?"

Not wanting to lie to him because she knew there was no lying in him, she told the truth. "No, we're going to look for some people who need to be handled for their disrespect. Please don't ask me any more, Daddy. I need to handle my business."

He remained silent as he pulled into the parking lot of the restaurant. After he parked and killed the ignition, he said, "Do what you need to do, love."

"Are you upset with me, Daddy?"

He shrugged and said, "Would it matter? Would it change anything, love?"

Her silence was his answer. He got out of the car and led the way inside of the restaurant. They had the tensest lunch together that they had since becoming a couple. Cotton tried to lighten the mood, but Shot's mind was all over the place. Should he stop her? Letting her go do whatever it was she was going to do could compromise his position. He pretty much figured it out, they were going to go hunt down that guy Bubba that beat them out their money. What if she got caught? Or what if she was hurt? He couldn't let her do this. He had to find a way to stop her and her sister from doing something that could get them in trouble. He set his fork down and stared at Daun for a minute and was about to speak, but she cut him off by shaking her head no.

"I will never interfere with your business, Daddy; please, please don't interfere with mine. Please."

Shot stared at her with a frown on his face. He then gave a nod of his head and started back eating his food. So be it.

Chapter Eighteen

"I can't believe we've been all around this fucking city and can't find that bitch-ass nigga Bubba," Janeen fumed as she pulled into the driveway of her home. Once they were inside, she continued on with her rant. "I'm telling you, sister, even if I got to sit down the street from his motherfucking mama's house all day and night, that's what I'm gonna do. That bitch got to pay for crossing me. I mean that shit."

Daun sat down on the sofa and stared at her cell phone. She couldn't believe that Shot hadn't called her or texted her once they split up earlier. She could tell he wasn't mad at her, but he was definitely disappointed, and that hurt her more than him being upset with her decision to go hunt down Bubba. The more she thought about things, the more she felt like fuck Bubba. Hot Shot meant more to her than some damn money or what people thought of the Sin Sisters' rep. She was about to shake town soon anyway. She looked at her sister pacing back and forth in her living room and shook her head. "Will you sit your ass down, girl? You wearing a hole in your rug ain't gon' help us find that bitch. I'm telling you, though, if we don't find him tonight, I'm leaving it alone. He'll slip up eventually. I ain't got time to be looking for him every fucking day, I know that much."

"Damn, that Shot has to have some supergood dick because I never thought you would fall weak and let a nigga get away with doing us. Where has my sister disappeared to?" Janeen said sarcastically as she went into the kitchen and returned with two Coronas in her hand. She gave one to Daun and said, "But you know, you're right. If we don't find that fuck tonight we can fall back, because sooner or later, he *will* slip up. That clown don't have the mind-set to go somewhere else and start his life over. He's city-born and -raised, and he don't know nothing about the life to move and fuck this city. So he'll pop up, and sure as shit, I'm doing that bitch."

Daun was pleased to hear her sister agree with her, so she chose to ignore the comment she made about Shot. She sipped her beer, and then sent him a text message. After a few minutes when he didn't text her back, she frowned, then shrugged and set the phone next to her and said, "So, where are we going to look for that ho-ass Bubba next?"

Janeen smiled and said, "Let's hit some strip clubs. You know that tricky creep used to hang at the booty houses from time to time. Maybe he'll be stupid enough to be out tonight."

"That's a good idea, sister." Daun stood and finished off her beer and said, "Let me pee, and we can get out there. It ain't like there's that many booty clubs out here. We can get on this shit now and hopefully get that bitch or be back home in a few hours."

"Back home in bed, my ass. You sweating your man. I saw your ass texting his ass and from your demeanor, it looks as if old Shot is salty at ya ass and not hitting you back."

"Mind your business and get your ass ready to go when I come outta the damn bathroom."

Laughing, Janeen said, "Yes, ma'am!"

Daun stopped in the doorway that led to the bathroom, turned, and gave her sister the finger.

Still laughing, Janeen said, "Love you too, boo!"

***

Shot was lying down staring at his phone and the back-to-back texts he received from Daun. He wanted to text her back, but he had to let her know that he wasn't feeling what she was doing. He knew it was her business, and he had no right to be tripping on what she had to do, but at the same time, he was doing what was best for her. If she continued on living the way she was living, she'd either get hurt or put in jail, and that was something he didn't think he could stomach. *Love is painful, for real,* he thought as he set the phone down and tried to get some rest. As soon as he closed his eyes, his phone rang again. He started to let it ring and go to voice mail, figuring it was Daun, but something told him to answer. When he heard how nervous Cotton sounded, he was glad he did answer.

"Boss man, I got me a tail. I think someone's trying to get at me."

"Are you sure?"

"Hell, yea, I'm sure. I hooked up with Blood fool Jerry, and after I left him on the North Side, this black Altima got on my bumper about two car lengths back. I've bent several corners, and they're still on me."

Ever since Cotton had been followed and held captive by some Bloods in Dallas, he made sure he took his time to watch his back so that it could never happen to him, ever again. The mere thought of that day made his heart hurt because that was the day his girlfriend, Moesha, was raped, which led to her committing suicide right in front of him.

"All right, where are you now?"

"I decided to stay on the highway. That way, they can't make a move on me."

"Good. Where?"

"I just switched the 40 East headed toward Midwest City."

"This is what I want you to do. Get off the freeway and jump right back on and head back west on the 40 toward downtown. I'm on my way, and I'll call you, and we'll see who this is and that their intentions are."

"Make it fast, I'm running low on gas."

"Don't worry, I'm walking out the door right now," Shot said as he grabbed his guns and was inside of his Audi within two minutes.

Ten minutes later, Shot called Cotton and asked him where he was. He knew his little helper was scared and there was no way he would let something happen to him—no way. "They're not even trying to hide the fact that they're on me now, boss man. They're right on my fucking bumper."

"Put your gun on your lap and don't let them get on the side of you. I'm connecting to the 40 West now. Keep heading that way toward Yukon. I should be with you before you hit the El Reno."

"I got you. How you gon' play this?"

"When you get to the El Reno Exit, get off and pull into the gas station right off the highway. I'll be there no less than two or three minutes after you, and then we'll see what they talking about. Cock a live round in your weapon, Cotton."

"I did that shit when I realized I had a tail, boss man. Hurry your ass up!"

Shot hung up the phone and made sure both of his weapons were locked, cocked, and ready. As he pressed his foot down harder on the accelerator, he flashed back to his time in the war zones of Iraq. When it's time for action, all extraneous thoughts vanished. Focus—don't think—react—and trust his training. That's what JT had taught him, and he tuned those skills in Iraq to become one of the best special ops operatives in the marines. Fight. Fight until you breathe no more, he said to himself as he passed the Yukon Exit speeding toward the El Reno Exit.

When he pulled into the gas station right off the high-way, he saw that Cotton had pulled in front of the gas station instead of pulling up to one of the gas pumps. *Good thinking,* he thought as he pulled right next to him and got out of his car with both of his guns out as he stood behind Cotton's car and tapped on the trunk, telling him to get out of the car. Three men dressed in all-black got out of the Altima that was pulled in the gas station at one of the pumps. "Bad decision, dummies," Shot said to himself as he stepped toward them with Cotton right next to him, with his gun in his hand held down by his side.

Once they were a few feet from the men who had tailed Cotton, Shot said, "Is there a problem? What's up with you guys following my mans here?" None of the men said a word. Instead, they reached for their guns.

Stupid move. Extremely dumb. Shot was much faster than any of the men because he already had his guns in his hands, something they obviously didn't pay attention to. Shot let off three rounds that hit one of the men in the chest and made the other two run and duck for cover behind their car. Cotton started shooting his gun at the parked car, and Shot had to stop him before he ran out of bullets. "Don't waste your ammo, Cotton. Make each shot count," Shot said as he let off three more shots that hit the rear tires of the Altima. He then pulled Cotton back toward their vehicles, hoping that the men would be stupid enough to think that they were retreating in fear.

And that's exactly what they thought was happening.

When they saw Cotton and Shot backpedaling toward their cars, they stood from behind the Altima and started charging at them. Cotton didn't give a damn about what Shot said as he unloaded his gun and hit one of the charging men in the face. Shot smiled but kept his focus on the remaining charging man. He aimed carefully, even though the man was firing his weapon at them, and dropped him with two precise shots to both of his legs. Once the man was down and Shot saw that he had dropped his gun, he rushed to him and knelt down next to him and asked the man who was bleeding profusely, "Why are you getting at us like this? Who are you?"

"Fuck you, nigga! You're a fucking dead man, bitch. You fucking killed my homies. You dead, nigga. You fucking dead!"

Shot sighed loudly and said, "I don't have any problems with you, but you brought this on yourselves. If you want to live, tell me who sent you after my mans."

"Fuck you, loc. You and that black-ass nigga gon' die!"

"*We* gon' die? You bitch-ass country nucca, you gon' die first!" Cotton screamed as he stepped over the man and aimed his gun at his head. Before Shot could stop him, Cotton used the last bullet he had in his gun and shot the man in his forehead. "Now, who dead, you bitch? Punk-ass fools think they can get at me like this. Fuck him!"

Shot was shocked, but the shock quickly wore off when he realized what had just happened. He grabbed the dead man's arms and raised up his sweatshirt and checked him for tattoos. He gave a nod of his head when he saw the 107st HCG tattoo on his left forearm. Hoovers. He stood and pulled Cotton toward his car and put him inside and gave him strict instructions.

"Gimme your weapon and head on home. Do the speed limit, Cotton; take your time and drive like everything's fine. I'll meet you there. Do you understand me?"

"Yeah, I got you, boss man. I fucked up, I know, man, but all I was thinking about was that bitch Foe-Way and how they did Moesha. I-I fucked up, huh?"

Shaking his head no, knowing the trauma he was going through was extremely hard for his mans, Shot said, "No, you did what I was going to do anyway. It was us or them, Cotton. Us or them. Now, do what I said, and if you get pulled over, make sure you don't run. Let the law do what they do; you'll be good, trust me. I should be at the house no more than five minutes after you; now go!"

Cotton nodded and started his car and eased out of the gas station and got back on the highway headed back to their place. Shot got into his car and sped out of the gas station as well. But instead of heading back east the way he came, he got on the 40 West and drove in the opposite direction from Cotton. He pulled out his cell and called JT in California and let him know what had just taken place. He let him know Prophet had sent some Hoover Crips to get at Cotton, and they had to lay them down. He gave JT the exact location where the shooting had taken place and told him that this was an ugly situation.

"No shit, son. But don't worry, your main man has everything under control. You just make sure you make it back to your safety zone. We don't need you arrested."

"My thoughts exactly. Give me a holla when you've worked your magic, JT."

"Will do."

Shot got off the next exit, then got back onto the highway headed back east toward Oklahoma City. He was calm because he knew that JT would take care of everything. He was more concerned with Cotton and this messed-up situation with Prophet. The Crip had just done the one thing that Shot never accepted. He tried to take his life. For that, the gloves were now off. Prophet wanted to play the gangster game he was playing with someone who killed before in the name of the U.S. Marines. A man who killed for this country. A man who killed in order to keep breathing. Now, he was going to kill a man who tried to take his life. Survival of the fittest, and he was positive that *he* was the fittest for the drama that was about to come Prophet's way.

"You're a dead Crip, Prophet. That's a promise," Shot said aloud as he grabbed his phone and called Daun to make sure she was okay. When she answered, he told her that he needed her and her sister to meet him at Cotton's place as soon as possible.

"I can't do that right now, Daddy. I'm about to take care of some serious business," Daun said as she sat down next to Janeen inside of her car, staring at Bubba's bright green 1972 convertible Cutlass parked in the parking lot of Zoomer's strip club in Del City.

Shot grit his teeth when he spoke. "Listen to me, love, and listen to me good. Prophet just tried to take me and Cotton out. I need for you to abort whatever it is you and your sister is doing and get to my spot now! Don't test me here, Daun. Do what I tell you! Please!"

Ever since she met Shot, she loved how cool and calm his demeanor was, and to hear that calm demeanor vanish made her snap to attention. "Okay, Daddy, we'll be there." She hung up the phone and told her sister what Shot said.

"Fuck! Let's just bum-rush the club and snatch that bitch outta there before we bounce, sister. We got his ass! It took us three damn hours to find the right strip club. I ain't trying to let this bitch get away."

Shaking her head, Daun said, "No. Shot wants us at his spot as soon as possible, sister. Let's get it. Now that we know this bitch ain't shook the city, we know where to find his ass. We'll take care of his ass before the week ends. Right now, we got to check and make sure that Shot and Cotton are good."

Janeen let out a loud sigh, shook her head, then started her car and eased out of her parking spot. "You lucky as fuck I love fucking that black-ass nigga Cotton."

Daun didn't hear her sister speak. She was too busy worrying and hoping that Shot wasn't hurt. She feared that something had happened to him, and those fears gripped her heart like a cold piece of steel had pierced it. *I'm on my way, Daddy, just like you told me to. Please be all right when we get there. Please,* she prayed silently.

Chapter Nineteen

By the time Shot arrived home, Cotton was in the shower trying his best to get his mind to accept that tonight was the night he killed a man for the very first time. As he scrubbed his body, he prayed that it would be the only time in his life that he had to take a human life. While Cotton was taking his shower, Shot used that time to think and process the situation a little more calmly. He knew that it was time to turn up, and that meant it was time to display a part of him that he had hoped to keep away from Oklahoma City. But once his life has been threatened, he only knew one way to respond. Violently. He sighed as he went into his room and pulled a large duffel bag from under his bed and took out several different handguns. He had everything from 9-mm Berettas to .40-caliber Glocks. He checked and rechecked every pistol; he wanted to make sure everything was in proper working order. When he finished, he went into the living room just as Daun and Janeen arrived. He opened the door for them and told Janeen that Cotton was in the shower and maybe she should go check on him. He then gave her a quick version of what happened. Janeen gave a nod of her head in understanding and went silently into the bedroom to undress so she could join Cotton in the shower. Daun stared at Shot for a moment, and then sighed. "Are you okay, Daddy?"

"No. That man sent someone to hurt Cotton. His message is quite clear. He's going to come after me next.

But before I let that happen, I'm going to take it to him and put an end to this for good."

"Then what?"

"Then it's time to get out of Oklahoma City and move forward."

"Am I welcomed to join you?"

He stared at her, and with a smirk on his face, he said, "That depends, love."

"On what?"

"On whether your business is more important than how I feel about you and your well-being."

"Don't. Don't say that, Daddy. You know it's not even like that. Bubba beat me and my sister for a lot of money, and you already know that, that is bad business and cannot be overlooked."

He was silent, then said, "Were you able to handle your business?"

"Almost, but I was ordered to leave before we could handle things."

He grinned at her and said, "Thank you for following orders. Now, listen to me, and listen good. I know you have to do what you have to do, but you need to be careful out there. That fool Prophet is going to try to move against you as well. He's at the point where he has to save face, and with all of the drama that's going on, it's only added more pressure to the situation. This beef between the Hoovers and the Sixties has everyone on the streets looking at Hoovers as if they've shown weakness. That's not good. Prophet sending those men at Cotton tells me it's about to get real heated in this city."

"What we have to do won't take long at all. We'll snatch Bubba's bitch ass and be done with it. No problems."

He shook his head and said, "Nothing always goes as planned, love, so you need to make sure that all of your 'i's are dotted and your 't's crossed."

"I understand. I'm sure glad I have a man to keep me in check when I need checking."

"Mmmm, I wonder if you can ever truly be checked. You are a handful, love."

She smiled and said, "Since you feel I'm a handful, why don't you take me in that there bedroom and fill your hands," she said in a seductive tone that made Shot feel some twitching in his loins. He stood and grabbed her hand and led her into the bedroom so he could fill *both* of his hands with the thick and sexy Daun.

The Valero gas station right off Interstate 40 in El Reno was packed with police. Yellow crime scene tape was spread around the gas station to make sure no one entered into the crime scene. Three dead men were lying at different spots in the gas station, and this was major news for a small city like El Reno. El Reno PD wasn't used to dealing with three homicides at one time, and they were moving and acting like it. The captain of the El Reno Police Department arrived on the scene and made sure that everything was being handled properly. He ordered his officers to make sure they went and secured the gas station clerk so he could be interviewed. He had been told that there weren't any other witnesses and that seemed to frustrate him mightily.

"Well, shit, Billy Joe, how the hell are we going to find out who did this shit?" He snapped his fingers and pointed toward the gas station's video cameras and said, "Please tell me someone has already been inside and secured the videotape from those damn cameras."

Officer Billy Joe Hopkins smiled at his superior officer and said, "Yes, sir, that was one of the first things we did when we made it to the scene."

"Good job, damn good job. I cannot wait to see who the hell did something as crazy as this."

Billy Joe heard more sirens wailing and turned to see two black Chevy Tahoe SUVs pull into the gas station. Once the SUVs came to a screeching halt a few feet from where Billy Joe and the captain were standing, four FBI agents jumped out of the lead SUV and approached the police officers.

After flashing their credentials to the police officers, the man who seemed to be in charge spoke to them in an arrogant and authoritative manner. "My name is SAC Nickolas Paulson, and I've been ordered here to take over this investigation. We have solid leads that this was a crime committed that is currently under investigation by our office." He then gave the captain two pieces of paper that were signed by the U.S. assistant attorney granting them full control over the crime scene. This infuriated the captain, but after reading the papers, he knew he had no win in the matter, so he gave the papers back and called in his men.

"It's all yours," the captain said sarcastically as he turned toward Billy Joe and said, "Make sure you give the special agent in charge here the videotape that you secured, Billy Joe. Then meet me back at the station house." The captain then went to his squad car mumbling how he couldn't stand the FBI.

After the captain and the other El Reno police officers left the crime scene, the FBI agents inside of the other vehicle assisted the coroner as they did their jobs quickly and efficiently. It took them under two hours to get everything bagged and tagged, the bullet casings along with everything else they felt needed to be recorded. Once the three dead men were loaded inside of the coroner's wagon, SAC Paulson pulled out his phone and made a call to his superior. "Everything is in order here. The bodies are now on their way to the morgue in Oklahoma City."

"Were there many witnesses?"

"No, sir. Only the gas station clerk."

"News people?"

"Negative, sir."

"Good. I was hoping we could get there before they made it way out there. Good job, Agent Paulson. Is there anything else?"

"Yes sir, there's the video surveillance tapes."

"Please tell me we're in possession of them."

"Yes, sir, we are."

"Good. Bring them in and make sure you put them in my hands just as soon as you make it back to headquarters."

"Yes, sir. We're leaving here momentarily."

"Good. See you when you get here," the head FBI agent said and hung up the phone. He then picked the phone right back up and made a call to Los Angeles, California. When the other line answered, the FBI agent said, "Everything has been taken care of, JT. The bodies are being delivered to the morgue as we speak. The witness gave a statement, and it's all recorded, along with all the other evidence left on the scene. We also have in possession the gas station's surveillance tapes. Your man is safe."

JT nodded into the receiver and said, "Thanks, Jim. Appreciate your speed on this matter."

"No need to thank me. When I get a call from the big boss, I don't ask questions, you know that. Not trying to piss the director off."

JT laughed and said, "Yeah, I know. I would have called in this favor on my own, but I knew you would give me a lot of questions, and there wasn't any time for that. Sorry."

"No problems; you just keep your word and make sure my office gets some of the glory when you've finished doing whatever the hell it is you're doing on my turf."

JT laughed and said, "Will do, Jim. Take care."

"You too."

After JT ended the call, he called Shot and let him know everything had been taken care of. "You do know that we're going to have some explaining to do. The director wants a conference call at 10:00 a.m. sharp in the morning, so I advise you to make sure you call me on time."

"Come on, JT, you know I am not with all that stuff. Why don't you give it to him how I gave it to you and let him know everything is good. It couldn't be avoided. They made their move on Cotton, and we did what we had to do."

"I understand that, but the director wants to speak with you, and there is no way I'm telling him you don't want to have that talk. So make sure you call me at 9:55 a.m. exactly."

"I thought you said ten?"

"I want you to call me five minutes before so we'll be right on time."

"Yeah, right."

"You do know that I know where your mind-set is right now, son. An attempt has been made on your life, and if I know you like I know I do, you've already pulled out all your weapons and made sure that they're ready to rock and roll. I want you to kill those thoughts, son, and stay focused on the mission."

Shot's silence on the other end of the line pissed JT off because he knew Shot wasn't trying to hear what he was saying.

"Dammit, son, do you hear me?"

"I heard you, JT. But you know as well as I do that I cannot, and I will not, let this go. They got at me, now I have to return the heat so they will know that Hot Shot doesn't play any of that. Let me do this my way, JT. You know how it goes down, and in order for everything to remain as we've worked it, this *has* to go down."

JT understood what Shot was telling him. They worked extremely hard to get Shot's cover cemented in the streets. If he didn't give some form of retaliation, he would look weak, and looking weak in the streets—no matter what state you were in—was *not* something a man wanted attached to his name.

"Okay, do what you have to do, but if you can, no more bodies, son. I don't think the director's heart would be able to take me calling him again in the evening asking him for permission to get your tail out of another jam like this. He likes you. He respects your work, but you can only get away with so much. Do you hear me?"

"Yes. Talk to you at 10:00 a.m. your time."

"No. I said 9:55 a.m. *exactly*, Hot Shot."

"Yes, you did," Shot said as he ended the call and went back into the bedroom where Daun was resting peacefully after their sexing. He smiled at her and said, "You ready for some more, baby? I don't think I got my hands full enough during that thirty-five-minute romp with your fine self."

Daun smiled and moved the covers off of her body and opened her legs wide and said, "Well, come on in and get a mouthful of this good pussy, Daddy."

Shot did just that.

Chapter Twenty

Shot woke up the next morning and did his morning workout, then went for a run around his neighborhood, trying to make sure that what he was about to do was the right thing to do. He didn't want to mess up the good work he was doing with Operation Cleanup and running and thinking usually helped him think things through more clearly. His life had been threatened, and that was something he didn't take too lightly. Prophet and every Hoover would feel his wrath before he let them even *think* about getting at him or Cotton again. The beef they had with the Rollin' Sixties was nothing compared to what he was about to bring to them.

By the time he made it back home, he was still in the same mind state . . . The Hoovers needed to get it, and he was going to give it to them. Period. By the time he finished showering, Daun, Cotton, and Janeen were sitting in the dining room eating breakfast. He stepped to the kitchen and grabbed a bottle of orange juice and poured him a glassful. Then he joined the others in the dining room with a smile on his face.

"Good morning, all. So what's on the agenda for today?"

"Shit, boss man, I was about to ask you the same thing. I mean, after what happened last night, I just knew you were going to be mad as hell and ready to tear shit up," said Cotton.

"Yes, things have gotten a tad bit out of hand and need to be addressed properly. You do know me well, my friend. But you should also know that I refuse to move on emotions. When I move, everything has to be calculated to a tee. I will not let this interfere with the business. But best believe, Prophet and his associates, homies, or whatever, will be dealt with accordingly." He checked his watch and saw that it was ten minutes to twelve, so that meant it was ten minutes to ten on the West Coast. *Time to call JT,* he thought.

"I won't waste my breath trying to tell you to let that shit slide, Daddy, but you do know how those Hoovers don't play fair," said Daun with worry in her tone.

Shot stared at the woman he cared for deeply and said, "Neither do I, love, neither do I. Now, I need to make a call to the West and get at my people. Excuse me for a little bit," he said as he went into the bedroom and called JT precisely at 11:55 a.m., 9:55 a.m., West Coast time.

JT smiled when he answered the phone and said, "I love it when you follow orders, son. Hold on while I get the director on a secure line." Two minutes later, JT came back on the line and said, "Special Agent Gaines, the director is on the line."

"Good morning, sir," said SAC Jason Gaines, aka Hot Shot.

"Talk to me, Agent Gaines. Talk to me and help me understand what has taken place out there. Help me understand why I had to make some serious calls to clean up three deaths. Talk to me and help me decide whether I should pull you from Oklahoma City and put an end to the good work we've started with this operation," the director said in a stern tone.

Never a man to mince his words, Shot got straight to the point and told the director everything that had taken place. When he finished, he waited for the order to be pulled from Oklahoma and was pleased to hear that he wasn't.

"I understand what you've said, and I agree, that particular situation was handled in self-defense. These things will happen from time to time. This is something I am aware of. In order to fight these types of criminals, you have to be given enough leeway to operate. Your first priority is to remain alive, so I cannot fault you for doing what you did. I'm sure that if it could have been avoided, you would have avoided killing those men. So with that said, I am going to keep you active. But you have to refrain from taking lives, if you can. I would never ask you not to protect yourself. At the same time, you know I report everything that is reported to me directly to the president. Telling him that you had to kill three men is something I'm sure he will be highly agitated by. Given the circumstances, I'm positive he will look at things objectively, like I have. Your handler SAC Tackett has informed me that things have progressed nicely and that this part of Operation Cleanup will be brought to a close by the end of the summer."

"Yes, sir, things are going well. Right now, I have enough to bring down a nice size of Oklahoma City's most unsavory criminals in the gang life, as well as the drug trade."

"That's some good news for the president. You do know that he picks the states that you are going to."

"No, sir, I didn't know that," Shot said as he thought, *How in the heck would I know that?*

"Well, he does. He has expressed to me that your next operation will be back on your home turf. California. The Sureños Mexicans and the Mexican Mafia are getting outrageous, and it's time we introduced them to Hot Shot."

"They're hard to infiltrate, sir. They only deal with their own."

"True. But I have all the confidence in the world in your skills. They may deal with their own, but when it comes to weapons and being able to maintain their strength, I'm positive that you will find a way inside and help bring them down at least a little bit."

"Yes, sir."

"Good. So finish up out there and try to refrain from killing anyone else."

Hot Shot didn't respond, so JT said, "Did you hear the director's last *order,* son?" JT put emphasis on the word "order" because he pretty much knew for certain that Shot was planning some form of retaliation for those Crips attempting to kill him. He knew him all too well. Shot sighed and said, "I heard him. I will do whatever it takes to make sure this mission is complete, sir. I will be as aggressive as I have to be. I will get the job done, and I won't let you down, sir."

"Good. Very good. Okay, gentlemen, I'm off to the White House to give my report to the president. Have a good day," the director said and ended the call.

JT laughed after the director was off the line and said, "Boy, you are something else."

"What are you talking about, JT?"

"You got around answering that question. That way, you can honestly say you didn't lie to me or the director. But you know I know better."

"Again, what are you talking about?"

"The director told you to refrain from killing anyone else."

"Yes, and?"

"And, your answer was, 'I will do whatever it takes to make sure this mission is complete, sir. I will be as aggressive as I have to be. I will get the job done, and I won't let you down, sir.'"

"I know what I told him, JT. Your point is?"

"My fucking point, son, is you didn't give the director the answer he wanted to that direct order! Stop playing! You know damn well that you're already planning to make a strong move on those assholes who tried to shoot you and Cotton. I know you don't lie, but that evasive shit you pulled with the director ain't flying with me, son. So I'm going to say this and leave it alone. You move on from them. I don't even want to hear anything about it. You won't have any assistance from me. It will be strictly off the books, so if you need cameras pulled from gas stations or police officers pulled off your ass, it ain't happening!" JT hung up the phone and sat back in his seat with a smile on his face. He shook his head and laughed. "I can see that bastard smiling right now."

The phone rang, and JT answered it quickly when he saw that it was the director of the FBI calling him. When he answered, the director said, "Do you know that I'm aware my order wasn't answered properly?"

"Yes, sir, I do. I just read Agent Gaines the riot act for that a moment ago."

"For the record, right?"

"Yes, sir, for the record."

"Off the record?"

"Off the record, I think those Crips in Oklahoma City are in a world of trouble."

The director laughed loudly and said, "Those were my exact same thoughts. Go, Hot Shot, go!" Both men laughed together because they knew that Hot Shot had just had the leash removed from his neck.

Back in Oklahoma City, Shot hung up the phone and was smiling just like JT thought he would be. It was time to tear this city up a little bit, he said to himself as he stood and returned to the dining room where everyone was still eating. When Cotton saw the smile on Shot's face, he knew it was on.

"You got the green light?"

"Yes."

"Oh shit," said Daun.

"I hope you slay all them bitches," said Janeen.

Shot shook his head and said, "That's not my intention. You take the head and the body will fall. Whoever gets in my line of fire will get it, though. Now tell me where the Hoovers' main locals are and where I'll be able to find Prophet and his strongest men."

Daun and Janeen told him how the Hoovers floated all over the city from the Northeast Side to the North and Northwest Sides of the city. Creston Hills has a strong part of the Hoovers, and they were known to be the deepest there. And odds were high that they would be where Prophet would be holed up as he made his plans to get at the Sixties and Hot Shot.

"Well, it looks like tonight, Creston Hills is where I will begin my blitz."

"You need my help, Daddy?"

"No. This is something I have to take care of alone," Shot said as he stared directly at Cotton. "That means you too. I don't want you in the way when I move, because you'll do more harm than good to me. I need you for other things, understand?"

"You know I know how you rock it, boss man. I ain't tripping," said Cotton.

"Good. Now I need you to go to Radio Shack and get us a couple of police scanners along with the manual on the areas. Also, snatch a couple of long-range walkie-talkies. You're going to be my ears when I move."

"Gotcha."

"Well, since you guys will be playing Mission Impossible with the Hoovers tonight, I guess we can go and get on our business, sister," said Janeen.

Daun stared at Shot and hesitantly replied, "Yeah, I guess you're right."

"I'm not going to interfere with you and your sister's business, love. Please be careful. I don't need to add more men on my list to hurt."

She smiled at her man and said, "Okay, Daddy."

"All right, then, since it's still early, why don't you come take me around the city and show me these Hoover locals so I can get the lay of the land."

"I'll go with Cotton to do his shopping. Shit, getting them scanners and walkie-talkies sound like some shit that we need to do together, sister. I like your get down, Shot. You don't be bullshitting when it's time to put it down, I see," said Janeen as she got out of her seat.

"No, Janeen, I don't," Shot said in a deadly tone. It was about to get even hotter in the streets of Oklahoma City.

Here comes Hot Shot, Hoovers!

Chapter Twenty-one

Prophet grew up in the neighborhood of Creston Hills, a small middle-class neighborhood of hardworking Oklahomans. He knew his neighborhood like the back of his hand. So when the heat got too hot in the city, whether from the police, Bloods, or the Sixties, he always made it a point to return to his turf to take refuge. Hiding wasn't his forte, but right now, he knew that he had to be able to remain safe while deciding what moves to make strategically. He knew that by his homeboys missing Cotton that Shot would be looking for him as well. He smiled because he wanted to make sure that he handled Shot personally. The word on the streets was that Prophet was running scared from the Sixties because of the blatant disrespect he showed by attending Lynette's funeral. That couldn't be further from the truth. He was making sure every move he made was aggressive and on point. At that very moment, seven Hoover Crips were on their way to serve some severe warfare to the Sixties of the Northwest Side of town. On the Far North Side of town, he was also sending a message to the Bloods by sending ten more Hoovers to let them feel his wrath. No one fucked with Prophet and the Hoover Crips without him getting back at them tenfold.

While he sat back at his cousin's house on Mira Mar Street right off of the corner of NE Twenty-third Street, he was waiting for his homies to get back at him and confirm that the work had been put in on the Bloods as well as the Sixties. Little did he know as he sat back and waited for a report on the damage his homeboys caused his foes, *he* was being stalked.

Hot Shot was cruising around the Creston Hills neighborhood in a stolen black Dodge Dart. The compact car didn't have much get-up-and-go, but it would serve its purpose. Hot Shot was a drive-by gang member. When it was time for him to do what had to be done, he preferred to do everything up close and personal. His training in special ops as well as hand-to-hand combat gave him the edge over these street peasants, who knew absolutely nothing about war, *real* war, where men, women, and children died for their country. Every time Shot murdered when he was overseas, it was in the name of his country. A country he loved and respected and would gladly give his life for. Those thoughts gave him a peaceful feeling and helped him decide that tonight he wouldn't be taking lives in the name of his country. Tonight was about revenge, plain and simple. He knew right then that he couldn't do that. He wasn't a cold-blooded killer. He was a trained FBI agent with a mission to complete. Going after the Hoovers and killing them would make him feel great, but long term, it would bother his conscience.

He shook his head as he drove past a group of Hoovers standing in a driveway of a small house. He passed them and turned the corner and parked his vehicle. He checked his weapons to make sure that they were locked, cocked, and loaded. He wasn't going to murder anyone tonight, but he was going to cause the Hoover Crips a whole lot of pain. The only Hoover that had to die was Prophet. He was a ruthless coward that had to go. If he did, by some chance, avoid Shot's gun, then he would rot in a federal penitentiary, that was for certain, Shot thought as he climbed out of his car dressed in all-black army fatigues.

The streets in Creston Hills were dark because there were very few streetlights in the neighborhood. Something that served to the Hoovers' advantage when it came to their enemies and the police, as well. Tonight, this would serve as a detriment to them instead of a positive.

Hot Shot easily blended into the night with his dark clothing. He was standing across the street from where several Hoover Crips were drinking and smoking what smelled like PCP to him. He shook his head in disgust as he watched the false bravado they were trying to portray. After ten minutes of watching the Hoovers, Shot decided it was time to start delivering his message.

He noticed that each of the Crips was armed with what looked like small handguns, either 9 mm or .380-caliber guns. They didn't stand a chance when it came to the firepower he had with him . . . two seventeen-shot 9 mm and two MP-5 fully automatic submachine guns. Each weapon equipped with silencers and flash suppressors. He took a deep breath to calm his heart rate, and then calmly walked in the middle of the street and began to unleash a volley of death aimed at the gang members. He was dropping them with well-placed shots from the MP-5. Without a word being spoken, he continued to shoot with deadly precision. The only thing was, he wasn't aiming to kill, only to injure. Shoulder shots, leg shots, arm shots, and a few shots to some hips, knees, and shins to make sure no one would be able to run or give chase when it was time for him to make his departure from this side of Creston Hills. Their screams made him smile.

"Aww, cuz! I'm hit!" screamed one Hoover.

"What the fuck is going on, loc? Who the fuck is shooting at us, cuz?" another Crip yelled.

Once Shot was positive that he had the situation well under control, he stepped toward some of the fallen

Hoovers and said, "Make sure you tell Prophet that when he comes after a man that he doesn't miss. The only reason you're not dead tonight is because I've chosen not to take your worthless lives."

"Man, who the fuck are you? We don't got no problem with you, cuz," whined one Crip who was bleeding profusely from three gunshot wounds in his thigh and right arm.

"I'm a Hoover killer. Tell Prophet, Shot is going to retire him, so get ready to meet his Maker." Shot turned and eased back into darkness and disappeared just as easily as he came. Once he was back inside his car, he drove around the corner and saw three men with orange and blue Denver Broncos jerseys on. Orange and blue were the colors of the Hoover Crips. He stopped the car and rolled down the window.

"Say, do you guys know where I can find Prophet?"

One of the Crips pulled out what looked like a .45-caliber automatic and said, "Cuz, you must be outta your damn mind if you think you can roll through the turf asking about the big homie. Who the fuck you think you is, loc?"

The Crip didn't realize that Shot's 9 mm was aimed directly at him as he slowly approached his vehicle. Shot smiled as he squeezed the trigger and gave the Crip a three-round burst from his weapon, hitting the surprised Crip in the groin, his right hand, and his left shoulder, dropping him to the ground in tremendous agony. The other two Crips saw their homeboy fall and were confused because they hadn't heard a shot and their minds couldn't register what was happening. By the time they realized that their homie was shot, it was too late. They too were on the ground in pain from shots from Hot Shot's gun. Shot got out of the car and stepped to the Crips and stood over them. "Tell Prophet that Shot came through. I'm going to keep coming until I find him. Now, you can save yourself and your homeboys a lot of pain if you tell me where I can find your big homie."

"I-I don't know, cuz. He's somewhere in the hood, though, that's all I know, cuz. Please don't kill me. I don't want to die, cuz," the Crip pleaded.

"Not tonight, buddy. You're not going to die tonight. But it's best to stay out of the way and heal up because I'm coming back every single night until I get Prophet. Make sure you get word to him. He messed up trying to get at me." With that said, Shot calmly got back inside of the car and proceeded to comb the Creston Hills neighborhood. Every Hoover Crip he came across, he hit them up with a few shells to their body, never once taking a life, only wounding them. He felt good with the decision he made, and his anger slowly subsided as he continued his hunt for Prophet.

Prophet received several calls on his cell informing him that a bunch of his homeboys had been shot up in the neighborhood. He couldn't believe that shit because he hadn't heard anything. No gunshots, nothing at all. He thought someone was trying to fuck with him, so he called his mans Squirt and told him to come and get him from his cousin's home so they could roll through the turf and see what the fuck was going on.

"Cuz, I think you need to stay your ass put. I just got a call from SliccLoc, and he told me he was at the hospital with two hits to his legs and that some nigga named Shot was rolling through the hood strapped with some heavy shit blasting every homie he sees, cuz. And the nigga shit is silent."

"Silent? What the fuck you mean by that shit, loc?"

"I mean that nigga got some fully auto shit with silencers, cuz. Everybody he hit up he gave the same message."

"What?"

"To tell you that you fucked up by getting at him, and he would be through every day until he gets you. He's only hurting the homies, but he says he's going to kill you."

"Fuck," Prophet whispered as he tried to digest the information he had just been given. He now heard ambulance sirens all around the neighborhood and knew that Squirt was telling the truth. Fuck! "All right now, cuz, I need you to slide through and get me the fuck out of the hood. We're going to go out to the south and kick shit at my bitch Shanna's pad. Then we're going to find a way to find this nigga and get his fucking ass."

"Cuz, you must didn't hear me. The nigga is rolling through the set putting it down on some serious war shit. It's best you lie low there until the morning; then we'll get you up outta there."

"I don't like being stuck in here, cuz. I feel like I'm a sitting duck or some shit."

"The nigga don't know where you're at, loc. You good for now. And for real, the hood is crawling with the Ones right now, so odds are, he's out of the way now. So sit your ass tight and I'll hit you up when I know more," Squirt said as he ended the call.

The thought of police combing the neighborhood gave him some solace, but at the same time, he thought about how the money he was supposed to be making in the hood would come to a screeching halt with damn near all of the young homies shot the fuck up. "Yeah, this nigga Shot gots to go. He fucking up my money and my peoples," Prophet said to himself as he grabbed his phone again and called Detective Bishop. When Bishop answered the phone, Prophet wasted no time and got right to the point. "Man, Bishop, you need to get at them feds or some-fucking-body and get that nigga Shot. He's fucking riding around my hood shooting all of my fucking homeboys!"

"So that's Shot doing that shit to your guys? What you do to piss that guy off, Prophet?"

"Fuck that goofy shit, Bishop. You need to do your fucking job and get that fool before he kills all my people!"

Laughing, Bishop said, "So you want me to do my job, huh? You mean to tell me that the super OG, extra hard Prophet from 107 Hoover Crip is scared of this guy? Come on, say it ain't so, Prophet."

"Fuck you, Bishop. You know what it is, cuz. I don't fear shit, but this bitch-ass nigga on some creep shit. He ain't been getting at us on no face-to-face shit. If it was like that, we'd get right at it and see who's who with this shit, dead ass! You need to get at that fool, though. Come on, Bishop," Prophet said, not caring one bit how he was sounding.

"First off, what do you expect for me to do? Call the FBI and tell them that I got word from one of my informants that their man they were watching is driving around his neighborhood shooting up all of his boys? They would laugh at my ass before hanging up in my face. You don't have any proof that it's this guy Shot who's doing this shit to your ass. It may be the 456 Pirus getting back at your ass for shooting at them earlier tonight."

"What?"

"You heard me. We picked up two of your homeboys fleeing the North Highlands after doing a drive-by on Eighty-third."

"Fuck!"

"Oh, it gets better, Prophet. Or it could be some of the Sixties because we got word that some of your homeboys tried to get at them on the Northwest Side, and Loco C and Gangsta C ended up getting hit up by some of Big Shoota's homies. Dead on the corner of Thirty-ninth and May. Looks like you and your homeboys are having one extremely fucked-up night," Bishop said and laughed.

All Prophet could say was "Fuck."

***

Shot knew it was time for him to make his way back to the house and call it a night. He eased out of the back end of Creston Hills and made a right turn on Tenth Street and made his way out to Midwest City. He then hit the highway and headed west on Interstate 40 and drove through downtown looking at the lights of this newly redone highway and smiled. He picked up the walkie-talkie and told Cotton that he was on his way back home.

Laughing, Cotton said, "Damn, boss man, you did that shit. From what I've been hearing over the scanner, there has been over thirty-five people shot in the Creston Hills neighborhood. No fatalities, though. What, you on some hurting shit tonight? I thought you were going to hunt them down and kill all the sons of bitches."

"No. Death is only for Prophet. The rest just gets a whole lot of pain." Switching subjects, Shot asked, "Have you heard from them Sin Sisters?"

"Nope. I guess they're out there doing some hunting of their own, boss man."

"Yes, I guess you're right. I'll see you in a few," Shot said and ended the call thinking about Daun and praying that she and her sister were okay.

Damn.

Chapter Twenty-two

"Okay, we've been in this parking lot for over two hours, sister, and it looks like that bitch Bubba's going to stay in that damn club until it closes. I still say we should just roll in there and sit right next to his ass and let him know what it is," said Daun, highly agitated.

Shaking her head, Janeen said, "No way, sister. That bitch would scream for security; then we lose the advantage. We need to be patient here. If he doesn't bounce up outta there within the next hour, then we make the call to Peaches and see if she can make it happen for us."

"I'm not really feeling adding Peaches in this mix. Then you know what *that* means."

"I was thinking the same thing. That's why I'm trying to be patient here and not put her in the business."

"Ugh! This shit is driving me nuts. Sitting here listening to this damn scanner talk about those fucking shootings around the city has my nerves fried here."

"I know Shot told you not to call him, but if it will give you some peace of mind, you need to go on and at least send him a text to make sure he's straight."

"No. I'll wait for his call. I trust him and know he's all right. I feel it. But I'm still worried."

Before Janeen could say something, Daun received a call from Shot, and she smiled as she answered the phone.

"Hey, love, you okay out there?" Shot asked in his normal, ultracool and calm tone. The way he sounded, no one would ever have thought he'd just shot off thirty Crips.

"I'm fine now that you've called me, Daddy. Where are you?"

"About five minutes from the house. What about you? When will you come to me?"

She smiled into the receiver, and Janeen rolled her eyes at her sister. "Right now, we're playing the waiting game. But we should be through here soon."

"You just make sure that you be safe and get at me soon as you're headed in. If you need me for anything I'm a phone call away. Okay?"

"Okay, Daddy. We got this, though."

"Call me if it looks remotely like you are having any difficulties."

"I will."

"I love you, Daun."

"I love you too, Daddy," she said and ended the call.

"Okay, now that the lovey-dovey shit is done and your boo is obviously good, can we focus on the business at hand?"

Daun smiled at her sister and said, "Yep, we sure can, 'cause look, there goes Bubba's punk ass coming out of the club right now."

Janeen turned and smiled when she saw Bubba walking toward his old-school Chevy with a slight stagger in his walk. "The dumb fuck is faded too. Look how he's walking. Let's get his ass." Janeen grabbed her SIG 9 mm, and Daun cocked a live round inside her .40-caliber Glock and didn't say a word as she opened her door getting ready to attack Bubba. Janeen got out of the car and quickly approached Bubba who was parked two cars away from where they were parked. Bubba was so drunk that he didn't realize the sisters were on him until it was too late. Janeen slapped him on the side of his head so hard that he fell to his knees. "Bitch-ass nigga, you thought you could get away from us? Now you about to die," Janeen said in a deadly tone.

Holding the side of his head trying to slow the heavy blood flow coming from his wound, Bubba cried, "Come on, Janeen. I'm working this shit. I should have all your ends in a week or so. No need for this shit. You do me then we all lose. You kill me won't get your money."

"It's not about the money no more, bitch; it's about principles. You don't take shit from the Sin Sisters and live to talk about that shit," Daun said as she pulled him to his feet while Janeen held her gun to the side of his head. "Now walk, bitch. You try anything, you getting two to the dome."

The sisters led Bubba to Janeen's car and put him in the backseat with Daun sitting next to him with her gun poking him in his side. Janeen got into the driver's seat and eased out of the strip club's parking lot without anyone seeing them.

"Damn, cuz, them bitches tried to get at us for real," said Sharp Shoota. "Tried that shit and got they ass served. That nigga Bozo did that shit, and that was some straight gangsta shit. Niggas can't get a 6-O and think that they gon' get away with that shit."

"You fucking right, loc. What's even crazier is my cousin who stays in the Highlands hit me and told me the Hoovers tried to get at some Piru niggas over there and got faded too. So they taking Ls all over the place," said Big Shoota.

"That's dead ass, cuz, 'cause from what I've heard from the homies is somebody has been blasting them Snoovers all night in Creston Hills."

Laughing, Big Shoota said, "Them hoes having a bad night for real, loc. But it ain't over. We got to be the ones who lay that bitch-ass nigga Prophet. He was bold enough to come to Lynette's funeral only because he knew we wouldn't get stupid. That was the last slap in the face, though. Before it's all said and done, I have to have his head, and that's on Rollin' Sixty Crip."

"Cuz, that nigga on some hide-and-seek shit. We gon' have to be patient and wait for him to pop up in order to do him."

Shaking his head, Shoota said, "Nah, cuz, when you on the hunt, you got to be able to have the proper plugs to get your prey in these cold Oklahoma City streets, ya hear me? And ya big homie has those plugs. That nigga has been bouncing from one spot to the next in Creston Hills. You know that's his backyard, so that's where he feels safest. But what he doesn't know is that I know he's moving. I was going to get at his ass tonight, but when you hit me and told me all about the busting over there, I had to fall back. He's not hanging out. He's staying tucked, but that shit is too close for comfort. He's getting ready to move, and when he does, I will be notified. When I get that call, we move and take his ass out."

"Who the fuck you got on your line serving you that type of info, loc?"

Big Shoota smiled and said, "That nigga ain't the only nigga who fucks with bitches from the other side. That nigga Squirt's bitch from Hoover has been eating the dick up for the last year or so. She's been riding around with Squirt all night, and she has kept me in the loop with Prophet. Squirt told him to stay down until shit cools off because it's way too hot over there, and it's not safe for him to move. He'll most likely rest there tonight, and then try to bounce in the morning. If I get the call that he's still there in a few hours, we're going to take it to his ass before the sun rises."

Sharp Shoota smiled at his big homie and said, "I like, cuz, I like that shit!"

"Yeah, me too," Big Shoota said as he dipped his head and snorted two long lines of cocaine and sighed.

Janeen and Daun had Bubba tied to a chair inside of the small house located in Arcadia. This was one of their rent houses out in the country that they kept especially for these types of situations. Though they never had to use this place, they always knew that one day they would. That's why they chose to never rent out the small two-bedroom home. Bubba was in tears as he watched as the Sin Sisters were preparing to murder him and dispose of his body. His heart was beating so hard that he prayed he would have a heart attack to save him from the punishment he was about to receive from the two. God, he wished he would have gone with his first mind and not let his girlfriend Melinda talk him into beating Daun and Janeen out of their money. Now that bitch was going to enjoy all his ends, and he was as good as dead. Fuck! He had to find a way out of this shit, and he knew the only chance he had was to give the Sin Sisters the money. Fuck Melinda! He wanted to live.

"Come on, Daun, I got your money! Don't do this to me, please! I'm begging you, I got every penny of it. I was trying to flip it so I could come up so when I gave y'all yours, I would be good. I swear to God if you take me to my girl's pad in Edmond, I will give you every penny of what I owe y'all!"

Hearing that he had their money made Janeen and Daun pause. If they could get their money, there wouldn't be any need to kill this clown. Though they weren't afraid to kill if they had to, the sisters had nothing against moving without taking Bubba's worthless life.

"Bubba, if you are trying to play us and try some stupid shit, then instead of blowing your brains out with one to the head and tying these forty-pound dumbbells around your ankles and throwing your ass in Arcadia Lake, we'll ravage your body in ways you've never dreamed of—*then* kill your ass slowly. I've recently finished a book by Eric Jerome Dickey called *A Wanted Woman,* and the shit the lead character did to the men who crossed her out has put some real vicious shit in my head. So make sure you are telling us the truth here," Janeen said seriously.

"Talk, bitch, and speak the gospel or get ready to take one to the dome," said Daun.

"Like I said, all of your money is at my girl's house in Edmond. All you got to do is take me there, and I'll give you the money, and I swear I ain't trying to cross you. It will all go straight up, I promise to God."

Daun and her sister exchanged looks and a few seconds later, they nodded. "All right, Bubba, we're going to make this long-ass drive back to the city. When we get to your bitch's pad, we're walking your ass in and get the money. Any bullshit and you *both* will get it. Do you hear me?" asked Janeen as she began untying him.

"I swear there will be no more bullshit, Janeen. All I want to do is live."

"We'll see," she said as she stood him up from the chair and marched him outside back to her car. Once he was in the backseat with Daun right back by his side with her gun poked hard in his side, they left Arcadia and headed toward Edmond, Oklahoma.

Twenty-five minutes later, they pulled into the driveway of a modest-sized home in the city of Edmond. They got out of the car and let Bubba lead the way toward the front door. He pulled out his keys and unlocked the door and led the way inside of the house. Once they were in the living room, he pointed toward the bedroom and put his index finger to his lips, signaling for them to be quiet as they went inside of the bedroom where Melinda was sleeping soundly. When he cut the light on, Melinda opened her eyes and was shocked to see the Sin Sisters standing at the foot of her bed with a gun aimed directly at her. "What the fuck is going on? Get the fuck outta my house!"

"Bitch, if you don't shut the fuck up, you're about to get a bullet to those fake-ass titties you paid for," Daun said staring at Melinda, daring her to say another word.

"Be cool, babe, this shit is a wrap. I'm giving them they money. They was gon' kill my ass," Bubba said as he walked toward the closet with Janeen right on his side—just in case he tried to pull any sneaky shit. Bubba knelt and pulled out four Nike shoe boxes and set them outside of the closet. He opened the contents and showed everything to Janeen. Each shoe box was filled with stacks of hundred-dollar bills wrapped in bundles of $5,000. "There it is, all of y'all's money, the entire $500,000. Now, keep your word, Janeen, and let me make it, please."

With disgust in her voice, Melinda said, "You weak, bitch-ass nigga. Something told me to take that money and move it to my mother's house. A grown-ass man scared of some females? You straight bitch, Bubba!"

"Bitch, shut the fuck up! It's *my* life that was on the line, *not* yours. I ain't trying to die behind this shit."

"Okay, you two lovebirds can discuss this shit after we've left. Shut the fuck up! Bubba, go to the bed and sit next to your bitch," said Daun as she watched as he did what she instructed. Janeen scooped two of the four shoe boxes and gave them to Daun. She then turned and grabbed the other two while Daun kept her gun aimed on the couple. They then backed out of the bedroom and walked out of the house, both relieved that they didn't have to kill Bubba and had their money. Tonight turned out better than either of them thought it would.

Just as Daun opened the passenger's side of the car, Melinda and Bubba came storming out of their home with guns in their hands. Janeen was first to react because she was facing the couple. She screamed for Daun to look out and started firing her gun just as Bubba started shooting. Melinda aimed her gun at Janeen and started shooting at her at the same time as she was shooting at Bubba. Daun took two shots to her stomach, but was able to get off two shots from her gun, hitting Melinda in her neck and face, killing her instantly. Janeen's three shots hit her mark in Bubba's chest. She watched as he fell to the ground, just as one of Melinda's shots hit her in her chest. Melinda fell to the ground right next to Bubba's dead body and died right next to her man.

Janeen staggered around the car to her sister and tried to help her get up, but she was too weak and fell right next to her, gasping for breath with blood pouring from her chest wound. When she saw all of the blood on her sister's shirt, she screamed, "Nooooooo!" That was the last word Daun would ever hear as she closed her eyes for good. Janeen cradled her sister in her arms and rocked her back and forth until she too closed her eyes and died.

The Sin Sisters were no more. They were dead with $500,000 sitting inside of the car. Money and death—a deadly combination.

Chapter Twenty-three

For the last eight days, Shot had been in a state of shock. He could not believe that Daun was dead. His mind was in denial, but the reality hit him hard when he viewed her body at Temple and Sons Mortuary. Daun looked so peaceful, almost as if she were asleep. Shot stood in front of her casket and let the tears slide down his face. He loved that woman and was going to do whatever he had to do to protect her. He knew it wasn't his fault she was dead, but he still blamed himself. He should have put his foot down and not let her go hunting for that Bubba character. It gave him solace to know that Daun and Janeen at least killed the man and woman who murdered them. Eye for an eye. He felt empty now, though. The pain tearing through his heart took him back to when he had to bury his mother, father, and baby brother. Why was he losing his loved ones? Everyone he seemed to love he lost. Why? Why was this happening to him when all he was trying to do was some good?

Cotton came into the room with him and stood next to him and remained quiet. After a few more minutes, Shot turned, and they left the room and went into the next room and viewed Janeen's body. Janeen looked at peace as well, but to Shot, it seemed as if her last facial expression was one of pure agony, and that further broke his heart.

The two men went outside of the mortuary to see Detective Bishop standing in front of Shot's Audi.

"Wrong time for this, man," Shot said to himself as he prepared to aggressively deal with this police officer.

"Can I help you?" Shot said as he pulled out his key fob and hit his alarm to open the doors.

"We need to talk, Hot Shot. I'm Detective Bishop of the Oklahoma Police Department. Your name is ringing some serious bells around the city, and I want you to know that we don't take too lightly to you California boys coming out here raising hell on our streets."

"I don't know anything about raising hell out here. I'm a man who handles my business in a peaceful manner," Shot said as he turned toward Cotton and said, "Get in the car, Cotton." Once Cotton was inside of the car with the door closed, he turned and faced the detective. "Whoever told you anything about me lied to you. I don't have any issues with you or anyone out here. I lost my girl to some senseless violence. There's no one to retaliate on about this since the couple who murdered my girl and her sister are also dead. So I don't have a clue about what you're saying."

"Hoovers. Prophet. Creston Hills. Ring any bells?"

"No."

Shaking his head in disgust, Detective Bishop said, "All right, you can play that game, boy; just know that your days are numbered. You think you can come out here and deal that death and hurt people whenever you fucking like, but you are a damn ignorant nigger, and you're going to die on the streets—either that or get life. Hopefully, we'll be able to get your black ass the needle."

"You're a man of the law, yet you stand there and disrespect me as a man, a black man. Let me tell you something. You can't touch me, and I know you know that. You keep on, and I promise I will make sure you regret disrespecting me. If you ever, and I mean *ever,* call me that N-word again, I'm going to do more than make you regret that."

"Are you standing there threatening the law, *boy?*"

Shot smiled. "Boy? I'm a grown man, Detective. A grown man that can hurt you in more ways than you can ever think of. I don't do threats, Officer. I give my word, and I stand on it. Respect me and stay out of my way."

"I don't respect criminals. I lock they ass up. You're not worthy of any damn respect, you piece of shit. You're dirt. A scumbag nigger that has a jail cell waiting on your ass. I'm going to make sure I do everything in my power to make sure I get you in that cell, nigger!"

Hot Shot shook his head sadly and said, "I really hate that you keep on disrespecting me." Cotton rolled his window down and heard the exchange between Shot and the police officer. When he heard the detective keep on calling Shot a nigger, he prayed that Shot wouldn't do what he thought he would do.

His prayers weren't answered.

Shot hit the detective in the stomach with a powerful right, followed with an overhand left that knocked the detective out cold. Then Shot stood over the unconscious detective and said, "I told you to stop calling me that N-word. Jerk." He then turned and got inside of his car and left the parking lot of the mortuary, knowing that he had just made a horrible mistake. JT and the director were going to have a fit about this one, he thought as he turned onto Kelly Avenue and headed toward Twenty-third Street.

Two days after Daun and Janeen's double funeral, a funeral that neither Shot nor Cotton attended because Shot knew there was a warrant out for his arrest for assault on a police officer, they were sitting at their house having a drink in memory of the Sin Sisters. He had refused to let Cotton go to the funeral because he

didn't want to have to deal with him getting arrested for
his own foolish mistake. They were two women that they
cared for. Though Shot's feelings were stronger for Daun
than Cotton's were for Janeen, both men were mourning.
Getting drunk seemed like a fitting tribute to those
beautiful women.

Shot knew he should have informed JT of what happened with him and the detective, but right now, he
just didn't give a damn. He figured that what he had
done would only add to the rep for his cover and further
solidify his cover on the streets. Yes, that sounded real
good to him. Maybe he would be able to use that in his
defense when the director went nuts on him for what he
did. He sighed and downed another glass of his peach
Cîroc. *Love is so damn painful,* he thought to himself as
he poured another drink.

"You know we can't be sitting up in here getting bent all
day when there's money to be made out there, boss man,"
Cotton said as he sipped his drink.

"I know, but we need to lie low for a minute until we
can have this situation taken care of."

"How you gon' do that shit? You knocked a fucking
police officer out, boss man! You tripped all the way out!
We got too much heat on our asses now to make any
more bread. I say we get the fuck on and slam this shit
down."

"No. We're good. All I have to do is make a call to the
West, and this shit will be handled."

"I know your peoples out West are strong, but I don't
see you getting out of this shit without going to jail."

"That may be true, but I'll post bond and all will be
good."

"So, you're ready to go to jail?"

"That's what happens when something like this happens. I'll post and get an attorney; then my people will
take care of the rest."

"If that's the case, then, why haven't you handled this shit already? I mean, we're missing bread at an alarming rate here, boss man."

"I haven't made the call yet because I've been dealing with the loss of a woman I loved. I'll handle it, Cotton."

"I know you will, boss man. Damn, this city is wilder than I thought it was, for real. What about that Prophet situation?"

"What about it?"

"How are you going to proceed with that? The heat is wicked. If you try to move on the Hoovers again, you're going to get knocked. You might as well let that one lay."

"No. Prophet will feel my wrath. No man gets at me without feeling the pain. I may have to be a tad more patient, but he has to die."

"Damn, boss man, I've never seen you this hell-bent on getting at a nucca. I know you're get down is real wicked when angered, but you letting this become personal. Personal interferes with the business, and that's one thing you have instilled in me. Never let personal interfere with the business. Think about that one, huh?"

Hot Shot let those words sink in as he sipped some more of his vodka. He trained his mans Cotton well. It was time to handle things the right way. He still wanted to teach Prophet that he was not to be messed with, though. No one, *no one* has ever tried to get at him or his mans. Prophet would feel his wrath one way or another. For the time being, he had to deal with the predicament he caused. He sighed and said, "All right, Cotton. Give me a few minutes to make a call and get this situation dealt with." He stood and went into the bedroom and called JT. As soon as JT answered the phone, he started yelling.

"I cannot fucking believe your ass! You actually knocked out a fucking police officer, Shot! A fucking detective, at that! Don't you fucking know that the entire OKCPD is looking for your ass? How fucking dumb can you be, son?"

"I screwed up, JT. The combination of Daun's murder and the disrespect he was spitting at me made me lose it. I warned him repeatedly to stop disrespecting me, but he kept on, and before I knew what happened, he was lying on his back out cold."

"Fucking inexcusable! The director has already been informed by the U.S. assistant attorney because she's been notified by the captain and the chief of police there in OKC. We had to give them your real name so you have an active warrant for your arrest. I've already gotten in contact with an attorney for you. You need to call him ASAP so you two can arrange for you to turn yourself in. You can post bond, and we'll deal with things on this mess later. Once you get out, you get on the business so we can close this one down because you're on some superthin ice. The only reason why the director isn't pulling you is because he feels this little hiccup can only add to your power."

Shot smiled into the receiver of his phone but remained silent.

"Take that fucking smile off your face, son. This is serious. You cannot be out there hitting on police officers. The bad guys, yes, do what needs to be done, but in no way is your aggression to be aimed at fellow lawmen. Am I fucking understood?"

"Yes, JT. I screwed up. I apologize."

"What did he say to tick you off anyway?"

"He called me 'boy' several times with the 'N-word.'"

"Jesus H. Christ. You got to learn to let that N-word stuff go sometimes, son."

Shaking his head as if JT could see him, Shot said, "No way."

"I know. I remember when you beat the crap outta that kid from Kentucky calling you that. It took all the influence I had to keep you from the stockade. Where did you get this sensitivity for that word?"

"My father. He told me that as a black man, we need to respect ourselves. That would be the only way others will respect us as black men. That lesson stuck because I watched my father knock out a friend of his who refused to stop using the N-word around him. If that mild-mannered man could knock out his friend for that disrespect, then I knew it was something that had to be important to my father. No man will ever get away with calling me that. *Ever.*"

"I understand. Now, do what I said and get at that attorney," JT said as he gave Shot the number of the Oklahoma City attorney that would handle this assault-on-a-police-officer charge Shot had. "Handle this and get back to work. You're really turning into a damn headache, you know that, Shot?"

Shot smiled into the receiver and said, "I love you too, champ."

"If you love me, then help my ulcers here and do some good, son."

"Affirmative," Shot said and ended the call. He stood and went back into the living room where Cotton was sitting still sipping on his vodka. After he was seated, he told Cotton that he had to get with his attorney and turn himself in.

"You do know they may try to beat your ass when you get inside there, right?"

"I sure hope they don't go that route, or it *will* get ugly."

"Damn, boss man, you can't be in there fucking up the law. You'll never get outta that fucking place."

"No man will ever hurt me without me hurting them, Cotton. That's just how I get down."

"You're really trying to make this shit worse out here, boss man."

"It can't get any worse, Cotton. I've lost the woman I wanted to build a life with, and now I got to go to jail and deal with this craziness. I honestly don't think it can get worse, for real." Before Cotton could respond, Shot's cell phone rang. He checked the number and saw that it was a local number that he didn't know. After he answered the phone, he wanted to tell Cotton that he was wrong about saying that it couldn't get any worse. When he heard Nola's voice, he realized that, yes, things *could* get worse indeed.

"Hello, Nola."

"What the fuck has gotten into your ass, Hot Shot? Do you know you not only have every Hoover Crip in OKC wanting your ass dead, but you also got the fucking police looking for you for assault on a police officer and they want to question you for over thirty fucking shootings? Have you lost your damn mind?"

He smiled and said, "I've missed you too, Nola."

Chapter Twenty-four

The next morning, Shot went and met with his attorney, Devin Smith, at his downtown office. Nola accompanied him to his attorney because she wanted to be with him through his ordeal. That sign of loyalty gave him mixed emotions because he felt he was not being loyal to Daun's memory by having Nola with him. At the same time, he felt good to see her come stand by him. His feelings for her seemed to have resurfaced a tad too easily, and that made him even more confused. His woman had barely been buried, and here he was thinking about his ex.

Confusing.

After the attorney explained the procedure to them and what the process would be to get him bonded out, Shot was ready to go deal with whatever the police had to throw at him. He knew they were going to try to get him to talk or make a mistake and say something incriminating, and that wasn't going to happen. He had the FBI behind him, so he knew that all he had to do was refuse to say anything. His attorney assured him that he would be right by his side through the entire interview. Once that was concluded, they would be separated while he was arrested and processed into the system. By the time they would have him booked in, the process to bail him out would be set in motion. Cotton had already gone and acquired the bail bondsman, and they were now awaiting the call from Shot's attorney.

As they left the office to head to the police station, Shot drove and followed his attorney toward the city jail. Nola sighed and said, "I feel somewhat responsible for all of this happening to you, honey. I should have never left your side. I hope you'll be able to forgive me. There was too much going on inside of my head, and I didn't know how to deal with everything. It was as if I was overwhelmed; my head was spinning with worry for my family. On top of that, the loss of our baby did something to me that I can't even put into words."

"I understand that, babe, but you blocked me out. No matter how hard I tried to talk to you, you pushed me out of the way and that made me feel as if I was being punished for loving you. That was unfair and very hurtful, Nola."

"I know there's nothing I can say to help ease the pain I caused, honey. All I am hoping and praying for is that you give me another chance. I love you, Hot Shot. You have to know that."

"At one time I thought I knew that for certain. You know I don't do lies, babe, but I honestly don't know how to respond to that. I don't know. I feel strongly for you, but what happened to Daun is still so fresh to me. I feel like it would be disrespectful to her memory to just up and try to pick up where we left off."

She nodded and said, "I understand. Let's deal with this; then we can proceed one day at a time. Time heals all wounds, honey."

"True. But right now, with everything else going on, I don't know how much time I'm going to have left."

"Don't say that, Shot. Don't. This is nothing. You'll be out of here in a few hours; then it's back to business. I'm staying out here with you, and I will help you any way I can. You know my family out here is in them streets, so getting the money ain't an issue."

Shaking his head, he said, "It's not about the money. It's about the beef. Those Hoovers are trying to get me, and I will not let them try again. I have to make my move."

She stared at him and smiled. "Whatever move you have to make, I'm with you, Shot. I'm with you all the way, honey. I'm never leaving your side again."

Her words made him smile, and he felt good. Only time would tell how this was going to work out. For now, though, he had to mentally prepare for what he was about to deal with.

He pulled into the parking lot of the city jail and gave his keys to Nola. "All right, you go on and get with Cotton at the bail bondsman. I'll see you in a little bit."

"Okay, honey," Nola said as she got out of the car and walked around to the driver's side. She grabbed his hand and smiled. "Give me a kiss, Hot Shot, with your fine ass."

He smiled and gave her a peck on her cheek. She frowned, and he laughed. "You don't think I'm going to make it that easy for you, do you?"

With a pout on her face, she said, "Hopefully, you'll feel different after a few hours in there."

He turned and looked up at the city jail building and said, "You may be right about that." He waved and followed his attorney inside of the city jail.

As soon as they entered the building, Shot saw Detective Bishop standing with several other police officers. Bishop was sporting a pretty nice-size lump on the right side of his cheek. Shot grinned as they went past him to check in with the police officer standing behind the glass partition. A few minutes later, a police officer came and escorted the attorney and Shot inside of the station. The officer left Shot and his attorney inside of a small interview room. Three minutes later, a detective came into the room accompanied by Detective Bishop. The lead detective introduced himself as Detective Branch.

"You are facing some pretty serious charges, Mr. Gaines. So before we proceed, I have to read you your Miranda Rights." The detective then read Shot his rights. Once he was finished, he said, "You are being charged with an assault on a police officer. Do you have anything to say about that charge?"

Shot gave his attorney a glance. Mr. Smith gave him a nod, giving him permission to answer that question. They already agreed that since Shot wasn't going to deny what he did, he would answer all questions pertaining to the assault on Detective Bishop. Any other questions the attorney would answer.

"I'm guilty as charged, sir. Your detective disrespected me as a man several times until I couldn't stand it any longer, and I hit him twice. Once in the stomach and once to his face, leaving him unconscious in the parking lot of Temple & Sons Mortuary."

"I appreciate your honesty, Mr. Gaines. Can you be a tad bit more specific about the 'disrespect' that was shown to you by Detective Bishop?"

Shot shrugged and stared directly at Detective Bishop. Though Hot Shot felt he was a slimeball, he was a fellow lawman. Shot didn't want to taint his career, so he said, "I'd rather leave it at that. He said what he said, and I did what I did."

"Are you certain this is the way you would like to handle this? If Detective Bishop did something to provoke you, he can be brought up on charges as well. This is your right."

"I understand. I'm good. All I want to do is get this process started, so I can get out of here as fast as possible."

"Understood. Now there's more here than just the assault charge. We have some information that links your name to several shootings that happened last week in the Creston Hills neighborhood. Can you tell me about the beef you have with the Hoover Crips?"

Shot sat back in his seat and let his attorney take over from there.

"My client has absolutely nothing to say to anything pertaining to any other crimes except for what he has already admitted to."

"So he's refusing to answer any more questions?"

"That is correct. If you have anything else you want to charge him with, then we are prepared to deal with that as well."

"We're hoping that maybe he could help us out here with this, Mr. Smith. There has been way too much violence on the Northeast Side and the Northwest Side of town, and we felt Mr. Gaines here can shed some light on some of it."

"Again, my client will not answer any questions that are not directly involved with what he has already admitted to doing."

Detective Branch sighed and stood from the small table. "Well, I guess that concludes this interview. I'll have another officer come get Mr. Gaines and begin the process of booking him."

"Thank you, Detective," said the attorney as he leaned and whispered something into Shot's ear.

Shot listened to his attorney but never took his eyes off of Detective Bishop who was still standing in the doorway after Detective Branch left the interview room. "You got something to say to me, Bishop? Go on and say it," Shot said and continued to stare at the detective.

"You should have told the man everything I said to you. It may help you out later on with this."

"I'm good. I don't get down like that. Like I said, you said what you said, and I did what I did. It is what it is."

"I meant everything I told you the other day. I'm going to try my best to get you off the streets of Oklahoma City."

"That's your job. My job is to make sure that doesn't happen."

"Asshole," Detective Bishop said, but he wore a smile on his face as he turned and left the interview room.

Thirty minutes later, Shot had been photographed and fingerprinted. As he was wiping off the ink from his fingers, Detective Bishop appeared and had a few words with the jailer who was processing Shot into the jail. The jailer smiled and gave him a nod. *Here we go with the foolishness,* Shot thought. The jailer then grabbed Shot by his arm and led him inside of the jail where the cells were located. As soon as Shot was put inside of a cell with four men who looked to be gang members, he knew what Bishop had told the jailer. He saw the orange and blue gang attire the four men were wearing and knew that they belonged to the Hoover Crips. He went and put his back against the far wall of the cell and waited for the fun to begin. Detective Bishop appeared outside of the cell a few minutes after the jailer departed and smiled at Shot.

"You got a pretty mean fight game, Shot. I wonder how good that fight game is when dealing with more than one man."

Shot returned the smile and said, "Trust me, it's great. I'm sure you set this thing up, so why not sit and watch my work?"

Shot's arrogance irritated the shit out of the detective, so he said, "Say, there, Loco D, you know that fool that they say shot up all your homeboys last week is standing right there. What you and your homeboys gon' do about that?"

"You need to gon' with that bullshit, Bishop. We ain't trying to catch no case fucking with this nigga. Save that weak shit, cuz."

Bishop raised his right hand and said, "I swear to God, that's Shot right there. The one that knocked out Big Herc. The one that has the beef with the Hoovers and

Prophet. Do what you feel you got to do, and you will have no charges whatsoever brought against you." With that said, Bishop started laughing and left the cell block area.

When the men inside of the cell hear the door close behind Bishop, they each stared hard at Shot. "They call you Shot, cuz?" asked Loco D.

"Yes."

"You the one that got at the homies in Creston Hills, loc?" asked one of the other Hoovers.

Shot knew that the cell may have some recording devices so he stared at the young man but didn't answer his question.

"You heard a Hoover Crip ask you a question, cuz. You need to answer my homeboy," said Loco D.

"I've never been one to admit to do anything wrong. That's not my way. But if you want to know whether I have beef with your set, then the answer is yes. If this will help speed up what's about to go down, then whatever you think I done to your homeboys, then do what you want to do. As a matter of fact, I don't like Hoovers. Does that help some?"

"Cuz, let's smash this bitch-ass nigga. On Hoover, cuz, you ain't leaving this cell conscious!" Loco D said as he rushed Shot. Shot braced himself and exhaled as he waited for Loco D to get in range. Two strong blows to the face and stomach and Loco D was out of the fight. The three other men stood and tried to circle Shot. Shot let them so it would be easier for him to disperse them. The larger man of the three rushed Shot and paid for that move with a kick to the nuts and a powerful upper cut that raised him off of his feet. Before his body hit the ground, Shot was on the attack. He rushed both men into a corner and began raining blows to both of them simultaneously. Kicks, knees, and fists flying as fast as an action hero in an action movie. The fight with the four Crips was over in less than three minutes. Each man lay on the floor of the cell unconscious as Shot went and stood in front of the cell waiting for his bail to be posted.

Bishop came into the cell about twenty minutes later and stared with a shocked expression when he saw Loco D and his three homeboys on the floor knocked out. He laughed and said, "Well, I'll be damn. You do have a mean fight game, boy."

Shot frowned and said, "There you go with that 'boy' stuff again. You don't get it, do you? You need to respect a man, Detective."

"I don't respect any criminals, and that's all you are to me, *boy*. A low-life nigger criminal."

"I tried to do right by you, Detective; now, you have become an enemy of mine. It's going to be my pleasure to have your career ruined."

"You can't touch me, you piece of shit. You just remember what I said. *I'm* going to be the man to have your ass get the needle."

Shot nodded and said, "Remember what I told you. I don't do threats. I promise you that after I leave this city, you will no longer have a position with the OKCPD. You don't know who you're dealing with, but you *will* find out the *hard* way. Now, will you please get someone in here to give these young men some medical attention? Because if they wake up trying to act tough again, I will be forced to give them some more of what they deserve."

"You cocky bastard."

Shot laughed and said, "I've been called far worse by far better people, you prick."

Chapter Twenty-five

"You lie!" screamed Cotton as he sat in the backseat of Shot's Audi as Nola drove them back to their home once Shot was released from jail on a $500,000 bond. "They put you in a cell with four Hoovers? And you beat *every one* of those nuccas' ass? Come on, boss man, for real?"

"Since when have you ever known me to lie about anything, Cotton? Look at my hands," Shot said as he raised his hands up and showed Cotton the bruises and swelling on his fists. "They didn't start hurting me until after they moved me to another cell by myself. The adrenaline had worn off by then, and the pain set in. I asked the jailer for some aspirin for the pain, but they just laughed at me." He shook his head. "It's crazy how they treat men inside of that place."

"If you think that's something, the county jail is even worse," Nola said. "I've heard stories from my family members who've been on lock, and 'scary' isn't a strong enough word, for real, of what they told me about that place."

"All men, even men convicted of crimes, should still be treated with some form of respect."

"Not on this planet, boss man. Anyway, so now that you got a court date, are we going to fall back some or what?"

"No, we're going to turn up. Get this money and do what we're here to do. Make the calls to your people who wanted them bars and let them know I'll have a fresh pack within three days. Make all the orders for the weed, cocaine, and anything else. It's time to get this bread. The lawyer said he will be able to put this case off as long as my money can stand it. That's funny because that means I won't be seeing jail any time soon."

"Your money is *that* long, honey?" asked Nola.

Shot smiled at her but didn't answer. He told Cotton, "There's still work to be put in. Holla at Sharp Shoota and see what the Sixties are up to. See if they're back in money-getting mode or banging mode still."

"You're not going to fall back on that Prophet issue, huh?"

"He has to die, Cotton. If not, then one of us will get it. I don't know about you, my man, but I enjoy breathing."

"Me too!" Cotton laughed nervously as he pulled out his phone and started making calls, seeing if any of his people needed anything from him. It was time to turn up like his boss man said.

"Damn, cuz, you heard that it was that nigga Shot who put all that work in on the Snoover niggas in Creston Hills?" asked Sharp Shoota.

"Yea, loc, I knew I liked that fool Shot. But he didn't get that nigga Prophet, and that means that move is up to us," said Big Shoota.

"What is that Snoover nigga bitch talking about, cuz?"

"She hit me with a text and told me that when they went to go scoop that nigga Prophet, he had already shook the spot. He must have a fucking spidey sense because he didn't even call his mans and let him know where he was bouncing to. That's cool, though; he'll get at that nigga Squirt sooner or later, and when he does, that big-mouth-pussy-whipped sucka will tell his bitch, and she'll get at me. Until then, it's time to focus on the ends. Niggas need to eat out there on them streets. The homies have been hitting me up from the country, and they need us to get them some work. So round up your clique, cuz, and get them ready to move by tomorrow. Then get at Cotton and see if we can get ten bricks, about thirty pounds of that Az, X, and some Oxy. Time to get back focused on the money. Getting at them Snoovers has been costly."

"I got you," Sharp Shoota said as he pulled out his phone and started making calls to do what his big homie told him to. While he was on the phone with one of his other homeboys, he received a call from Cotton. "Damn, cuz, you must have read my mind. I was about to get at you to let you know we need to hook up."

"Okay, that's the business. When can we hook up so we can handle that list you need to give me?"

"Whenever you ready, loc."

"All right, give me about an hour and I'll hit you and we can meet at that Jimmy Eggs over on Britton."

"That's what's up, cuz. And tell your mans Shot we heard about that business with them Snoovers."

"Will do," Cotton said as he ended the call. He turned and faced Shot who was sitting at the dining-room table with both of his hands stuck inside of two big salad bowls filled with ice. "That was Sharp Shoota, and he wants to place an order. He told me to tell you he heard about the work that was put in on the Hoovers."

"Looks like the streets are definitely talking."

"That could be a double-edged sword, honey. If the streets are bumping their gums, that means so are the rats. You got to be careful out there, Shot," said Nola.

"I know, and I will."

"One thing for certain, you won't be putting anything down for at least a day or so with those big swollen mitts you packing right there," said Cotton as he stood and went to the kitchen and grabbed a bottled water. "So get ya rest up, boss man. I got this."

"You listen to me and you listen good. Don't be on no wild man stuff out there. Make the moves and make them cautiously. If you even *think* something is grimy or about to get wicked, you follow protocol and get right at me. Swollen hands or not, I'm your muscle when you need me, and I'll make sure I do what needs to be done to keep your ass safe. Don't get tough guy on me. Call me if you need me, Cotton. I mean that."

The sincerity in Shot's voice touched Cotton so deep that for one of the few times in his life, he was speechless. He had grown to not only look up to Shot, but respect him and love him like an older brother. And though they never spoke about it, he knew that Shot felt the same way about him, and that made him feel good. Being raised an only child, he always wanted a sibling, whether older or younger. Now he had a big bro, and that made him feel real good.

"I got you, Shot. I got the double strap thang going on. But you Batman, and I'm Robin, and I have no problem hitting the Bat signal if needed," Cotton said and grinned.

Shot shook his head and laughed. "Okay, Robin, be safe."

After Cotton left the house, Shot pulled his hands from the bowls of ice and stood and went into the bedroom followed closely by Nola. "What are you about to do, honey? Do you need me to help you with anything?"

He turned and faced her and said, "I'm about to take a long, hot shower to wash all that jail stink off of my body. Then I need to take a nap."

With a smirk on her face, Nola walked past him and went inside of the bathroom and started drawing him a hot bath. When he entered the bathroom, he said, "I said a hot shower, Nola."

"I heard what you said, honey. You don't need a shower; you need a hot bath so you can soak and let me wash you and take care of you." She then stood and faced him with a look of hunger in her eyes. She began to take off his clothes, one piece at a time. When she had him naked she stared at his girth and moaned while licking her lips. "Damn, I miss that big-ass dick."

"Nola," Shot warned weakly. He knew he wanted her, but he was still battling himself with this. Daun was no longer alive, but she was still a deep part of his heart. Though this was the God honest truth, he stood completely still as Nola dropped to her knees in front of him and put his dick inside of her mouth. She began giving him some head that felt so good that all he could do was stand there and enjoy the supreme sensations she was causing him. She worked him with her mouth so expertly that he came within two minutes, and she swallowed every drop of his semen. She then stood and let the sundress she was wearing fall off her shoulders and peeled out of her thong. She turned and bent over the side of the table and slapped her ass, signaling for him to enter her from behind. "I don't have a condom, babe."

"So what? I'm on the pill now, nigga, so come give me that damn dick! It's been too damn long."

Shot paused with her usage of the N-word, but he was so turned on, he didn't have time to speak about it. He eased behind her and slid easily inside of her sex, and it felt as good as if he had returned home after an extended vacation. The way Nola was throwing her ass back at him had him feeling as if he was the one being fucked instead of the other way around. Her aggressiveness shocked him, but pleased him as well. He blamed it on the length of time they spent apart from each other. She was hungry for him, and that turned him on greatly. When she started to come, she screamed extra loud.

"Give me that dick, Shot! Give me that good dick, nigga! Yes! Fuck this pussy to death! Fuck it! Fuck it! Yes!"

Shot pounded her harder and harder until he felt his nut rising and he said, "Tell me this is mine, babe; tell me it's all mine. Tell me how I like for you to tell me."

"It's yours, Shot. It's all yours, honey. Fuck this pussy like you own it 'cause you do! It's all yours, Shot!"

"Say my name, baby. Tell me you belong to Hot Shot. Say it how you know I like it."

"Oh shit! I'm coming again, Hot Shot! I'm coming again, Hot Shot! Ohhhhh, it feels so good, honey!" she screamed as she began an intense orgasm which, in turn, caused him to erupt inside of her and make his legs feel as if they wanted to buckle. When he finished and was able to regain his bearings, he stepped back and stared at Nola as she slid over the side of the tub and into the warm water. She turned on the nozzle and added some more hot water to the tub and finger waved for him to come and join her inside of the Jacuzzi tub. Once he was in the tub with her, she lay her head on his shoulder and said, "Damn, I miss that. I miss you so damn much, Hot Shot."

He closed his eyes and let his head rest on the rim of the tub as he relaxed in the hot water. Something was off, but he couldn't put his finger on it. He had a nagging feeling that he was missing something important, and he didn't like how that was feeling at all. He closed his eyes and rested while trying to figure out what was slipping past him.

Prophet did, in fact, have somewhat of a spidey sense because he never second-guessed his first mind. The more Squirt told him to stay put at his cousin's house, the more he realized he needed to get as far away from Creston Hills as possible. He knew that his homie would never cross him, but at this stage of the game, he trusted his gut more than anyone else. That's why he chose to take his cousin's Ford Focus and slip out of the neighborhood out to Midwest City to where he had a friend who would love to have him for company for a few days.

When Debbie opened the door she welcomed him into her home, as well as to her body. He fucked her silly for the first couple of hours, and then passed out and slept peacefully. He enjoyed sexing her, but he hated how she wasn't with the pain he wanted to inflict on her. She wasn't having that shit, so it was strictly some vanilla sex. Her pussy was so good, he wasn't that disappointed. Plus, she was giving him some much-needed cover, so he was good.

The next morning when Deb got up to go to work, she asked him if he would be there when she got off, and he told her yes. She smiled and went to work one happy woman. She wanted Prophet, and if she played her hand right, maybe, just maybe, she would have him, she hoped as she hopped into her Ford Explorer and went to work.

Once Deb was gone, Prophet grabbed his phone and began making calls to his people. He had to get a line on Cotton and that nigga Shot. He had to have that nigga before he would be able to move around again. That nigga showed that he is not to be taken lightly, so it was time to get just as aggressive. When Detective Bishop answered the phone, Prophet said, "Look, Bishop, I heard that nigga Shot faded four of my homies in the city jail yesterday."

"That's right; beat the crap outta they ass and knocked each one of those wannabe tough guys' ass," laughed Bishop.

"I also heard he knocked your ass out in the parking lot of Temple & Sons. So save the slick shit, will ya?"

Not finding Prophet's statement funny, Bishop said, "What the fuck you want, Prophet?"

"What the fuck you think I want? I want that bitch nigga Shot's head! You fools had his ass on lock and let him walk. What the fuck is that? You know he's the one who got at all of my fucking homies in Creston Hills."

"We couldn't hold him. No witnesses. He moved too damn good 'cause no one could say it was him positively. If they did see him, no one was talking. You know they were keeping it real Hoover tight and gangsta."

"Fuck you and your fucking sarcastic shit, Bishop. I need to get a line on that nigga so I can end this shit."

"What are you asking me, Prophet?"

"I need to know who posted him bond."

"Why?"

"You don't need to know why, Bishop. You cannot know. Just give me the name of the bondsman he used, and I'll take care of the rest."

Bishop thought about what Prophet was saying and smiled into the receiver. "Hold on for a sec." Bishop made a call downstairs to the jailer and asked what bondsman bailed out Jason Gaines. Once he was given the name of the bondsman, he clicked back to Prophet and said, "Jimmy McWright's bondsman got him."

"Those white boys out on the South Side?"

"Yep."

"All right, then, thanks, Bishop."

"Whatever. You just make sure you don't get your ass killed. That Shot ain't to be taken lightly. He's much tougher than I thought he was," said Bishop reluctantly.

"He's been lucky so far, but that nigga's luck is about to change," Prophet said as he lay back and thought about his next move. He smiled as he dialed 411 and got the number to Jimmy McWright's bail bondsman office.

Chapter Twenty-six

The next few weeks everything seemed to fall back in order as far as the money was concerned. Cotton was running all around town doing what he did best, and Shot was making sure they had all of the product they needed to keep everything running smoothly. JT was ecstatic that things were back running smoothly and was on schedule to bring down a large number of Oklahoma City's gangsters and drug dealers. He was proud that Shot seemed to have put the revenge plot against Prophet on the back burner. Even though he was not disillusioned one bit, he knew that before everything was said and done, Shot would make his move against the man who threatened his life. He sighed as he thought about that and figured they'd cross that path when they came to it. Until then, he could bask in the glory of the good that was being done. The director would be pleased with his reports, and that's all that mattered to him.

Shot had to admit that Cotton's aggression toward getting the money out in the streets of Oklahoma City was of a high order. He was very impressed with how Cotton handled his business. He's developed a no-nonsense attitude, and it paid its dividends. The money he was making was getting larger and larger by the day. They could barely keep the product on hand. That was definitely a good thing. Cotton smiled as he finished counting the last of the money he'd made for the day.

"All right, boss man, you need to make that call to the West 'cause I got people on hold until Saturday, and they will be driving me nuts if I miss or have to put them on hold."

Shot set the money inside of a large duffel bag and said, "No need to worry. Everything should be here by then. I'll go have this money sent so by the time we're done with the next package, we'll be stocked back up."

"That's the business."

"I'm meeting with Nola and taking her out to lunch, then maybe to the lake and kick it and chill. What's on your agenda for the rest of the day since we're out of work?"

Cotton shrugged and said, "Spending a little time with Shirin. She's finally forgiven me for shaking her for Janeen. She wants to go see that new movie *Think Like a Man Too*. So we might do that and maybe get something to eat afterward."

"That's cool."

"I see you've let Nola back in fairly easily. Thought you would at least make her tough it out some. Guess that soft spot you got for her broke you down, huh?"

"I don't know. I won't front and say I didn't miss her or that my feelings for her never left. But something about the way she gets down puzzles me."

"What you mean?"

"I can't put it into words. It's like she's not the same to me."

"Trust, when a woman loses a child like that, it does something to their psyche, you know, some mental shit or real. That, combined with her family getting knocked, threw her off some. The more you two kick it, the more comfortable she will be, and things will slowly get back to normal for you two."

"Since when did you become Dr. Phil?"

"I'm a man who knows women, and trust me, I'm learning more and more each day. Never underestimate them and never try to figure them out, for real. That's the most important lesson to remember, boss man."

"I guess you're right. I'm still feeling guilty about getting back with her so quickly, though. I mean, it wasn't even forty-eight hours after Daun was buried, and there I was making love to Nola. That still doesn't sit right with me, and I don't think it ever will."

"Life goes on. It sounds kinda cold, I know, but Daun did her thing the way she chose to, and it came back and bit her in the ass. You can't punish yourself for the decisions she made. You can't stop living your life because she's no longer here. You loved her, and that love will never fade. She will forever have your heart in that special way. Look at it like I do when it comes to Moesha. She's gone. I can't change that fact. I know she loved me and wanted me to be happy. If moving on with my life makes me happy, then I'm sure that beautiful woman is smiling down from heaven at me wishing me well. I have an angel above watching over me. That thought keeps me focused on the now. I'm alive. I'm free, and I'm enjoying my life. My money is right and getting better every single day. Life is good, and it's too short not to keep it moving."

Laughing, Shot said, "All right, Dr. Phil, you've proved your point. I'm still going out to Trice Hill Cemetery and put some flowers on Daun and Janeen's grave. I need to give a proper good-bye to her. After that, I'll get the ends off to the West and go scoop Nola."

"That's a bet. Do me a fave, though, and scoop a dozen roses for Janeen for me. I'm not one to be going to talk to the dead. That shit is depressing."

"Whatever, jerk. Be safe and hit me up later to let me know everything is everything and that Shirin isn't holding you hostage."

"Trust, that fine chocolate mami can hold me hostage just as long as she wants to!"

"Whatever," Shot said, and they both laughed.

It had taken over two weeks for Prophet to finally find a way to get the address to where Shot stayed. He tried everything from trying to bribe the secretary who worked at McWright's bail bondsman, to threatening her. When that didn't work, he thought about trying to break into their South Side office, but the bail bondsman was a 24-hour business, and they always seemed to have someone in the office. Finally, he decided to go down to the bail bondsman's office and get at the owner and see if the direct approach would work. He brought $10,000 along with him because he was determined to get what he wanted, and that was the address to where that bitch Shot was resting his head at. Before he made his move against Shoota and the Sixties, Shot and his mans Cotton had to die.

When Prophet left the bail bondman's office, he wore a satisfied smile on his face. That was the best $10,000 he'd ever spent. He now had the location to Shot's home out Far North. He knew the area well because he used to have an apartment out that way. So, he hopped right onto the highway and drove by the address he received from the owner of the bail bondsman. As he drove past Shot's home, he smiled when he saw Cotton's Ford Raptor parked in the driveway with Shot's Audi parked right next to it. "Yeah, cuz, you two niggas are as good as got," Prophet said aloud as he kept driving down the street. He didn't want to expose himself so he left the neighborhood and headed back to Midwest City. He was now in a supergood mood. He would wait for Deb to return from getting her hair done, and then take her back to her house and fuck her real good. Afterward, he would strap up and get Squirt and few other of his most trusted homeboys and make their move north to Shot's home.

Yeah, that's the plan. Shot dies tonight, he said to himself as he turned onto the highway, headed back to Debbie's home.

Shot was standing over the final resting place of Daun, his lost love, and let tears slowly fall from his eyes. He missed her. He missed her smile, her laugh, and the way she would look at him every time she called him Daddy. He was saddened by the fact that he would never have the opportunity to hold her in his arms again. He was hurting now because he still felt as if he'd failed her. He would never stop kicking himself in the ass for not demanding that she didn't make that move with her sister to go after Bubba. "I failed you, love. I let your free-spirited will deter me from doing what I knew I should have done. You're gone because I didn't put my foot down and follow my first mind. I know you would never blame me, but I blame myself. Now you're gone, and I'm here demeaning your memory by getting right back with Nola. Am I not a prick or what? Jeez, love, what do I do here? I mean, I'm truly confused. For the first time in my life, I don't know how to move with this. A part of me wants Nola so bad that it hurts. To have her again gave me such a great feeling. But afterward, I felt confused. Was it because I felt bad for being with her so soon after you died? Or is there something else with this? I don't know. What I do know is you're a strong part of my life, and I'll never forget you or the time we spent with each other. I love you now just as much as I loved you when you were alive. Please know that."

He shrugged his shoulders and thought about what Cotton told him. "Life goes on, love. I got to keep living. I guess now that you're in heaven and can see everything, you know that I'm an FBI agent. That was a secret that I would never have been able to reveal to you. Sorry. One thing for certain, though, I wasn't letting you or your sister get into any trouble. I was taking you West with me and make a good, honest woman out of you." He smiled at those words and said, "Well, I was going to try. Please don't think I was ever against you, love, because I wasn't. I have a job, and I'm determined to do it to the very best of my ability. I'm a good guy. You know I like how you used to tease me when we watched *Scandal*. I'm wearing the white hat you love. I am making progress slowly, but I am doing some good for our people, the honest black people who deserve to be able to walk down the streets in their neighborhoods without fear of being gunned down by rival gangs beefing with one another. Or their children getting strung out on all types of drugs. I'm trying to rid the streets across the United States of as many bad guys as I can. Operation Cleanup was designed to do some good, and that's what I'm doing, love. Watch over me, along with my parents and my baby brother. I pray for your souls every single night. I know God has you in His loving hands, and that gives me peace.

"When you see me make aggressive moves that may seem overly aggressive, try to understand that I'm doing that in the name of doing some good. I have to fight these evil, mean men with the same form of aggression. They don't play fair, and neither will I. It's all in the name of the good, Daun. The name of good. Good-bye, love. I love you," Shot said as he stood and stared at the dozen roses he left on her grave. He turned and stared at Janeen's grave and smiled sadly as he set the dozen roses Cotton had him buy for her. "Cotton misses you, Janeen. He's experienced this type of love loss before. I think he's trying to keep you blocked from his mind because his heart can't take this type of pain. He sends his love. I'm sure you know that. You keep a close eye on your sister for me. No more Sin Sisters now; you're God's Angels. Watch over us down here."

Shot wiped his eyes, then went to his car feeling somewhat better, but still in a state of confusion. He grabbed his phone, left the cemetery, and called Nola. He told her that he was on his way to pick her up, then take care of some business. Then they would be able to chill out and spend the rest of the day together and do whatever she wanted to do.

She smiled into the receiver and said, "You already know what I want to do, honey. I want to make up for lost time. Come to my suite at the Skirvin and fuck me silly all day long, and I'll be great! You know what I'm saying? I mean Tony the Tiger *Grrrrrreat!*"

"You got jokes. I thought we'd go get a bite to eat somewhere, then go out to the lake and chill out and talk. I miss how we used to sit back and talk and plan. Remember how you used to like for me to take you out to the beach and we'd walk barefoot in the sand and talk about our future?"

Nola was silent for a moment; then she said, "Yeah, I remember. If you want to do the lake thing, I don't have a problem with that, honey . . . as long as you know I need that there dick up in me real deep before the day is over, ya hear me?"

"Yes, I hear you. You sound as crazy as Cotton now."

"What? You don't like me being straightforward with telling you what I want?"

"It's not that, it's just—don't worry about it, babe. It's all good. You know I got you with whatever you want and however you want it."

"Promise?"

"Promise."

"Good. What business do you need to take care of after you come and pick me up?"

"I need to go send some money to JT. It won't take me long, just a stop by the post office real quick."

"You and that damn post office. What do you got going on there? An inside plug or something?"

"You forgot how I blast the ends to the West? As many times as you have gone with me, I would think you would remember the get down."

"Shit, honey, so much has gone on since the last time we were together, and my mind ain't on shit like that. Okay, do this. Go do whatever it is you got to do at the post office, then come and get me from my suite. I have to make a run to Del City and see my cousin about something. I'll be back before you get here."

"Okay."

"Then we'll do lunch and the lake thing. If I'm lucky I might be able to give you some good head at the lake. Would you like for me to do that, honey?"

Laughing, Shot said, "Now you already know the answer to that question, babe." His phone started ringing, and when he saw JT's face on the caller ID, he said, "Okay, babe, let me go. This is JT calling me on the other line. I'll give you a call when I'm leaving the post office to make sure you're back from your cousin's."

"That's fine, honey. Tell black-ass JT I said what up! See ya in a little bit," Nola said and hung up the phone.

Shot hit the ignore button on his phone sending JT's call to voice mail and sat back in his seat. He was replaying the conversation he just had with Nola. After a few minutes of sitting there, he started his car and headed back toward the city. Suddenly, everything was crystal clear to him.

Damn.

Chapter Twenty-seven

After Shot sent the money to JT, he left the post office and went and picked up Nola. He took her over to Kevin Durant's restaurant where they enjoyed a nice meal with very little conversation. Shot's mind was all over the place because there were way too many questions swirling around inside his head. When they were leaving the restaurant, he made his mind up on the course of action he was going to take to answer the many questions he had for Nola. They arrived at the lake and found a nice spot and sat down on the grass and relaxed.

"You remember that time we went to the beach and you told me that you could live in LA forever, babe?"

"Mm-hmm. I love that the water is so different from the lakes I grew up going to," Nola said as she scooted a little closer to him.

"Tell me then, why was it so easy for you to leave me and go back to Texas?"

"Don't do this, Shot. Let's leave that alone and enjoy this peaceful afternoon, honey. We're headed in the right direction now. Let's not back slide, okay?"

"Okay. Tell me, have you heard anything about Simon and how he was murdered?"

"The word on the streets is that his body was found at one of Juan G's trap houses in Oak Cliff. Some even said it was you who did that to Simon. But I knew better than believing that shit. That's not your style at all."

"Mmm. So, how are things going with your brother and sister? I know it must be extremely hard for them right now. Is Weeta Wee and Keeta Wee with Tiny Troy?"

"Yes. They're at Beaumont Medium. Troy calls me every other day telling me how messed up it is up there. They're all on the same unit so they are doing okay 'cause they have one another's back."

"What about Lola? How is she doing?"

"She's having it pretty rough from what she's told me. It's hard for her because of her attitude. She's had several fights. They recently moved her from Bryan, Texas, way out to Waseca, Minnesota. As soon as she arrived out there, she had a fight a few months later with her celly. She's in the hole now waiting to see what they are going to do to her. She beat the crap outta some girl who has life and got all up in her face in the middle of the night. She's trying to stay out of trouble, but it's like the females in there keep wanting to try her. I really hate this happened to her. This is extremely hard for my family right now, honey."

"I can only imagine. You having to hold everything down for them is a tremendous amount of pressure on you. That explains a lot to me, though."

"What do you mean? Explains what?"

"Your memory loss."

"What memory loss? What are you talking about, honey?"

Shot stared at her for a full minute before speaking. He eased her off of his arm and said, "Stop with the games, Lola. Stop insulting my intelligence. Did you *really* think you could fool me? I mean, your sister and I were closer than you could ever imagine. Yes, you look exactly like her, but your mannerisms are totally different. You may have been able to keep me lost if you wouldn't have had sex with me. That was the first sign that something was wrong. But you still had me fooled until you kept saying certain things to me that I knew you knew."

"You are really tripping right now, honey. *I'm* Nola."

"So you're going to keep with this farce, huh? Okay, Nola, since you want to play this game to the end, I'm going to ask you some questions that I know for a fact only you know. You answer them, then I will admit to be tripping."

"Whatever. I can't believe you brought me out here to be on some stupid shit."

"Will you answer my questions?"

She stared at him for a moment, and then sighed. "Yeah, I'll answer whatever you ask just to prove your ass wrong."

"Thank you. Who killed Simon?"

"I told you they say you did, but I really don't know."

"Wrong answer, Lola. *You* killed him. Or should I say your sister *Nola* did. She shot him when he came to my place trying to kill me."

The shocked expression on Lola's face told Shot exactly what he already knew. "You need to quit this game you playing, Shot."

"Next question. How come you didn't know how I sent the money to JT?"

Realizing that Shot was on to her, Lola sighed and didn't answer his question.

"Not wanting to answer me now, huh? I figured as much. Well, let me tell you how you screwed all of this up. First off, Nola went with me several times to go send money to JT, so she knew how I moved at the post office. Furthermore, Nola knows JT and has spent time with him on several different occasions."

"So what does that prove?"

"She knows that JT is a white man, not a black-ass man like you have referred to him as."

"Shit."

"Exactly. Now you need to explain to me what the hell is going on here. Why are you here and Nola's in jail serving time for the crimes *you* committed with your brother and cousins?"

"I can't answer that, Shot. You just need to leave this alone."

"Leave this alone? Are you out of your fucking mind? My woman is in jail doing time for her twin sister, and you think you can tell me to leave it alone? Lola, if you don't tell me what's going on, I'm going to be forced to do something I really don't want to do to you."

She frowned at him and said, "You aren't the type to put your hands on a woman, Shot, so save that weak-ass threat. Just take me back to my room. You know enough now, so leave it alone."

"I don't know anything other than the fact that Nola is in the feds and you're here. I need to know why! I need to know what happened to my child! I need to know why you two did this craziness! Talk to me, Lola! I swear you better tell me what's going on!"

"I can't! I can't tell you shit, and no matter what you say, I will *not* tell you shit! I fucked this up by wanting to see what was so fucking special about you. I should have never fucked with you. I should have stayed away like Nola told me to. I will tell you one thing, and this is the honest-to-God truth."

"I don't think you're capable of telling the truth, so leave God's name out your filthy mouth."

"Whatever. Nola loves you more than anything in this world. But she would never not be there for the family. She will do whatever it takes for family. She's proved that by her actions. I wish I had the heart my sister has. Now, will you take me back to my room so I can get my shit and get my ass back to Dallas?"

Before he could answer her question, his cell phone started ringing. He checked the caller ID and saw that it was Cotton. "What up, champ?"

"Where you at, boss man? We need to talk, and I mean like right now!"

"I'm out at Lake Hefner with Lo—Nola."

"I need you to meet me on the Northwest Side. I'm at one of Big Shoota's spots, and I think you need to hear what he has to say to you."

"I'm in the middle of something. Give me about an hour and I'll get back with you, Cotton."

"No! You need to get here like right *now,* boss man! This is some serious shit! You have constantly told me about bumping my gums on the phone so don't make me go against that with this shit. Get here. We're on Northwest Thirty-ninth. How fast can you get here?"

"Less than fifteen minutes."

"Get here then!" Cotton yelled and ended the call.

Shot stood and grabbed Lola and helped her to her feet. "Look, I got to make a run somewhere, and I need you to roll with me; then I'll take you to your room. But you *are* going to tell me everything, Lola. I mean that."

Shaking her head she said, "No, I'm not. I can't. You can yell and fuss all you want to, Shot, but I ain't telling you shit else."

Once they were inside of the car, Shot chose to be quiet as he sped out of Lake Hefner. Thirteen minutes later, he pulled into the driveway of Big Shoota's trap house. Big Shoota, Sharp Shoota, and Cotton were standing in the driveway next to Cotton's truck. Shot got out of the car and stepped toward the three men. "What's good? What's so important that has Cotton cursing at me like he's lost his mind?"

"Cuz, your mans had to make sure that you understood how serious this situation is," said Big Shoota.

"Okay, I get that. Now tell me what's what."

"Prophet and four other Hoovers know where we stay and most likely are on their way to the house right now to lay and wait and get at us," said Cotton.

"How would they know where we rest our heads?"

"That fool Prophet paid the owner of the bail bondsman who bailed you out of jail for knocking Bishop out to give up your address."

"And how do you know this for sure, Shoota?"

"I got a bitch in the Hoover camp who fucks with that bitch-ass nigga Squirt."

Shot frowned at the usage of the N-word but ignored it. "And?"

"And the snake bitch got at me about thirty minutes ago and told me that Prophet got Squirt and told him to meet him out in Midwest City at one of his bitch's pad. Debbie or Deb, something like that. She told me that Squirt told her that they knew where you and your mans Cotton lived and how Prophet got that info. They went out to Midwest City and waited for two more of Prophet's main dudes. They're going to either bum-rush your tilt when you get there, or wait 'til late night and try to catch you and Cotton slipping and take y'all out."

"It's real, Shot. We've been using this broad to get info on Prophet so we could make our move on him. But when she told the big homie about how they were about to move on you and Cotton, we had to let you know the business, dead ass," said Sharp Shoota.

Shot stood there silent for a moment trying to figure out the best way to play this. After a few minutes he smiled and said, "That's good looking out, Shoota. This is something I could have only dreamed of."

"What do you mean by that crazy shit, boss man? Those fools got the jump on us and gon' try to dead our asses," Cotton said nervously.

Shot shook his head and said, "No, Cotton, *we're* the ones who have the jump on them." He turned and faced Big Shoota and asked, "How many of those SARs do you have left?"

"I got about ten, why?"

"I need to use two of them. If something happens, I'll replace them with something extra for you for giving me this solid."

Shaking his head, Big Shoota said, "Cuz, you don't got to do that shit. It's my pleasure to assist you on this. For real, for real, if you need me to ride with you on this shit, me and the li'l homie here will rock it with you and Cotton."

"No. This is all on me. You, Sharp Shoota, and Cotton would only be in my way. In order for this to pop off the way I want it to, I have to go about this solo."

"Solo?" both the Crips said in unison.

"Yeah, solo. That's how this crazy man gets down," said Cotton.

"I can see this is going to be one long-ass night, boss man. So please put us up on what you got going on in your head."

Shot smiled and said, "I'm going to murder Prophet tonight."

Prophet, Squirt, Mad C., and C-Prince drove past Shot's house and saw that neither Shot's car nor Cotton's truck was parked in their driveway. Since it was still daylight, Prophet decided to go back to Midwest City and wait for the sun to set. Once it was dark, they would return and wait for Shot or Cotton to come home. If Cotton comes first, then the plan would be to hit the house and take him out and wait for Shot to return home, and then do him too. If Shot was the first to arrive, then they would

take him out and deal with Cotton another time because
he wasn't the main focus to Prophet. When they made
it back to Deb's place, they sat down in the living room
and began to talk and go over how they intended on
murdering Shot and Cotton.

"I'm telling you, cuz, we got to be fast with that shit.
Too much noise out that way and it's going to be hell
making it back out this way," said Squirt.

"Yeah, loc, you already know that Far North is nothing
but white folks' lands, and any type of shooting will
attract the law with the quickness," added C-Prince.

"I'm knowing that shit, cuz. That's why I didn't stay out
that way and wait for them to come back home. I made a
call to Sampson from Shotgun and cuz is on his way out
here to bring me some silencers so we can do that shit
real quietlike."

"Silencers? Cuz, that's some movie-type shit! I've never
seen no fucking silencers before," added Mad C.

Laughing, Prophet said, "Well, loc, you're about to see
some in about thirty minutes. We're making a strong
Hoover power move tonight, cuz. Y'all ready?"

"You fucking right, cuz," said Mad C.

"On Hoover fucking Crip, you know I'm ready," said
Squirt.

"As long as I get to pop one in that punk-ass nigga who
shot up the homies you already know I'm with it, loc, ya
hear me?" said C-Prince.

Prophet smiled and sat back in his seat. "Yeah, bitch,
you die tonight," he said to himself, not paying attention
to Squirt's girlfriend texting furiously on her iPhone.

Chapter Twenty-eight

Before Shot left Shoota's trap, he gave Cotton strict instructions to wait for him until he returned from dropping Lola off at her hotel. He then got into his car and told Lola that she needed to tell him everything that she and her sister were up to. She again refused, and it only pissed him off. He didn't have time for games from her, and it was obvious that whatever game Nola and Lola were playing, Lola was going to stand on her end of things. The mere thought of Nola being in jail fighting for her survival made his stomach churn. He felt sick because he knew he was partly responsible for all of what transpired. If something happened to Nola while serving that time for her sister, he would never forgive himself. He sighed and gave up on trying to get Lola to tell him what was going on. Right now, he had to make sure he remained focused on what he had to do. Tonight was all about Prophet. He had chosen to make his move, and this is exactly what Shot hoped for. A perfect case of self-defense. He was confident that he would be able to take care of Prophet and whoever joined the OG in trying to kill him. Yes, tonight would give him the closure he needed. No one tried to take him out and lived to speak on it.

No one.

After dropping off Lola with the promise that he would be coming to Dallas soon to see her, Shot then sped out of the hotel parking lot headed back to Shoota's place. He wished he would have been able to get to his house first so he could get to his weapons. His sniper rifle would definitely come in handy for what he had planned. Since that wasn't an option, he started to plan his assault on the Crips. He would give them the impression that he was slipping and walking right into their hands. Actually, they would be walking right into *his* hands. As he sped back toward the Northwest Side of the city, he debated on whether he should tell JT what was going on. The more he thought about it, the more he felt that he should at least give JT a heads-up. He grabbed his phone and called his handler. "What's up, champ?" Shot said when JT answered the phone.

"Please tell me you're calling me to give me some good news, 'cause I'm not in the mood to hear any bullshit, son."

"Well, the news I have to tell you is good to me. I'm not sure how *you're* going to feel about it, though."

"Talk to me."

Shot gave him the information that he received from Shoota and Sharp Shoota, and then finished with, "Now, if this is how they're going to play, then I'm going to end this tonight. After that, everything will be on schedule to finish up out here."

"You want that guy Prophet, don't you, son?"

"I've only killed when faced with enemies. When my life has been threatened or an attempt has been made on removing me from this world, the only thing on my mind is making sure that that person never has the opportunity to every try me again, JT. So to answer your question, yes, I want to kill that thug piece of dirt. To be totally honest with you, I was going to find a way to do it off the books anyway. This way makes everything nice and clean. They're coming after me, so they will die."

"Thank you for calling me. This remains between us. Do what you have to do to remain breathing, son," JT said and ended the call.

Shot was smiling as he pulled back into Shoota's driveway. He got out of his car and went to Cotton who was
standing in front of his truck talking to Sharp Shoota and
said, "This is how it's going to go down. Sharp Shoota,
I'm going to need you to do me a fave in this."

"No problem, cuz, what up?"

"I want you to roll with Cotton in one of your whips so
you guys can give me a precise location of Prophet and his
homeboys. Once you spot them, give me a call and let me
know where they're set up. The street we stay on is wide,
so they won't be hard to spot. Cotton, you know most of
the cars in the neighborhood, so you should see them
fairly easy."

Big Shoota came outside of the trap house and said,
"I think I can make that easier for you, loc. Let me text
Squirt's bitch and find out what they're driving. She hit me
a li'l bit ago and told me they were sitting out in Midwest
City waiting until it got dark so they could go sit on your
spot and wait for you and Cotton to come home," Shoota
said as he sent a text message to Squirt's girlfriend.

"That's perfect. Cotton, I need your weapon. All I have
on me is mine."

"I thought you wanted to use of the SARs?" asked
Sharp Shoota.

Shaking his head, Shot said, "I'm taking one but only
for an emergency. My H&K 30, along with Cotton's SIG
9 mill, should be enough to get the job done. If things get
sticky for me, then I'll use the SAR."

"Okay, she just hit me back and said they left Midwest
City twenty minutes ago, and they're driving a dark blue
Tahoe."

"Good, that will be easy for you guys to spot. I want you
to roll right by the house and pin-point them for me, then
call me. After that, I want you to head back here with
no hesitation. Do not for any reason come back by the

house. Come here and wait for my call. I'll give you a text to let you know I'm good as soon as I can. I don't want you there when the police arrive. I'll deal with everything with them on my own."

"Cuz, are you sure you want to play this shit like this? From what baby told me, they strapped with some heavy shit. She described them as some big-ass guns," said Big Shoota.

Shot smiled. "That's even better. They're in a position where they feel they're on high ground and have the advantage. But they don't have any advantage, Shoota, I do. Them having big guns also adds to that advantage. They won't be able to move as swiftly as they think they can. I'll drop them before they even have a chance to raise their weapons."

"You talking like you're a commando type, Shot, 'cuz you tripping. I still think you should let us all roll with you, and we fade them Snoovers together."

"No way. That prick is mine, and whoever with him is going to get it too."

"So you're really good enough with a gun to handle four men, loc?" asked Sharp Shoota.

"Yes."

"Cockiness can get you dead, cuz," said Shoota.

"Confidence in one's ability keeps you alive. I'm built for this, trust me." Shot turned to Cotton, who had been unusually quiet, and told him, "Remember how I handled things in your town?"

"Yes, boss man, I remember."

"I got this."

"I know you do."

Shot reached out his right hand and Cotton passed him his SIG 9 mm; then the two men shook hands. "Let's go. Time to make Prophet regret ever coming after us," Shot said as he turned and went inside of his car and waited as Cotton and Sharp Shoota climbed inside of a silver Lexus.

***

Prophet and his three homeboys were parked across the street from Shot's home waiting for him to arrive. The plan Prophet came up with was simple. Once they saw Shot turn into his driveway, they would jump out and run up on him and take him out. Then they would run back to the SUV and speed away. Mission accomplished. Each Crip sat inside of the Tahoe checking their weapons, making sure they were locked and loaded, ready to fire. Prophet wanted to make sure they got the job done right, so he wanted nothing but heavy artillery. C-Prince had an AK-47 with a seventy-five-round banana clip while Mad C. had a fully automatic AR-15 with a thirty-round clip. Squirt had a fully automatic MP-5 submachine gun with a forty-round clip. Prophet had a semi-automatic Uzi with a thirty-round clip. He knew with the firepower they had there was no way Shot would be able to stand a chance against them. If Cotton arrived home first, then they would rush him and take him inside and wait for Shot. If Shot comes first, then Cotton lives another day. Shot was to die without any hesitation; he made that clear to his homeboys as they sat and waited patiently for Shot or Cotton to arrive. They didn't pay any attention to the silver Lexus as it cruised by them at the normal speed limit. Their wait for Shot was about to be over.

"There they go, cuz!" Sharp Shoota said as he drove past Prophet and his homeboys sitting in the blue Tahoe. "Them niggas are right there for real, loc! They about to try and get your mans! Damn, cuz, I sure hope Shot is as good as he claims to be."

"He is. Shot don't play when it comes to this type of shit," Cotton said as he grabbed his phone and called Shot and told him exactly where the blue Tahoe was parked. "They're parked directly across the street from the pad, boss man."

"Blue Tahoe?"

"Yep."

"Good. Head back to Shoota's and I'll give you a call when everything is everything."

"You make damn sure you hurry up too!"

"Aww, you worried about your boss man? I didn't know you cared so strongly about me."

"Whatever. It's my money I care about the most. Something happens to you, I lose a monster connect."

"Kill that. You know you love your dog."

In a serious tone Cotton said, "Yeah, I do. So handle this shit, boss man."

In an equally serious tone, Shot said, "Affirmative." He ended the call and checked both of his pistols, making sure that each gun had a live round in its chamber. Then he inhaled deeply, filling his lungs with oxygen, and then exhaled to calm his nerves and let his heartbeat remain steady. "Time to do this," Shot said to himself as he turned his Audi onto his street.

He saw the Tahoe as he made it to the middle of his street. He turned into his driveway and kept his eyes on the SUV through his rearview mirror. As soon as he came to a stop in the driveway, he saw the doors to the Tahoe open. He wasted no time. He was out of his car in a flash with his guns raised as he stepped calmly toward the rear of the Audi.

The shocked expressions on the Crips' faces as they saw Shot with two guns in his hands aimed at them was priceless to him. He wasted no time as he began firing his weapons. His shots were dead-on. Shot kept his calm as he squeezed shot after shot with deadly precision. C-Prince was the first to die with a well put shot right between his eyes. Next was Squirt who came out of the back of the Tahoe with his gun not even raised yet. He caught two shots. One to his right eye and the second in the heart. Mad C. got hit in the neck, thigh, and nose and was dead before his body hit the ground.

Prophet tried to do a drop and roll and was firing his Uzi at the same time, praying that he was lucky enough to get a hit on the man that was killing his homies as if it was the most natural thing in the world to do at 8:45 in the evening in this middle-class neighborhood on the Far North Side of Oklahoma City. Prophet's spraying tactic gave him some breathing room because it caused Shot to duck for cover behind his car. *Good move, Prophet,* he thought as he waited to see if Prophet was going to press on or retreat. When he saw Prophet stand and start to walk toward him while still firing his weapon, he smiled. *Bad move, Prophet. You should have retreated.* Shot then lay flat on the ground behind his car and aimed at Prophet's legs. He let off two dead-on shots and hit Prophet in each of his shins. Prophet screamed in agony as he fell to the ground. He dropped his gun and was holding onto his shins as Shot stood and ran up on him. Without saying a word, he calmly aimed his gun at Prophet and shot him right between the eyes, then turned and ran back to his car. He grabbed his phone and called 911 and explained to the operator that there had just been an attempt on his life and that he killed four gunmen. He smiled as he listened to the instructions the operator gave him. She informed him that the police were en route and that he was not to leave the location. He assured her he wasn't going anywhere. He hung up, and called Cotton.

"Damn, boss man, is it over that quick? We barely made it back to the highway."

"Yes, it's over. Tell Sharp Shoota to tell Big Shoota he won't ever have to worry about Prophet again."

"Are you all right?"

"Yes. I'll call you after the police do what they have to do."

Shot hung up the phone and called JT and let him know what had taken place.

"The police there yet, son?"

"On their way now."

"Set your weapons down on the ground in plain view so they won't get trigger happen when they roll up and see some bodies laid out like that."

Shot did as he was told, then said, "Done."

"You dirty inside of the house?"

"Nope."

"You do know they're going to take you down to the station to question you, right?"

"Yes."

"You ready for that?"

"Yes."

"This gives you an even more solid case out there in them streets."

"I know."

"You're decompressing right now, aren't you?"

"Yes."

"Taking lives even when defending yourself is never easy, son. I know that was hard for you, but you did that shit in the name of doing some good."

Shaking his head as if JT was right in front of him and could see him, Shot said, "No, I didn't. I killed those scumbags because they were coming to kill me. I killed Prophet because he tried to kill me first. I killed these men because in the streets, no matter whether if it's in Oklahoma, Texas, or anywhere, it's kill or be killed. I will always kill before I am killed, JT. Always. The police are here. I'll give you a call later," Shot said as he raised his hands in the air as six police officers jumped out of three squad cars with their guns aimed at him.

Chapter Twenty-nine

Once the crime scene had been secured by the police, two homicide detectives arrived on the scene and approached one of the officers and were brought up to speed on the situation. Shot has been read his Miranda Rights and was leaning against the trunk of his car waiting to see which way the detectives were going to play this. He realized that bringing the SAR along may have been a big mistake. He would have difficulty explaining why he was driving around with a high-powered assault rifle. *Oh well,* he thought as he watched the detectives approach him. *Here we go,* he said to himself.

"Looks like you've got yourself into a serious situation here, Mr. Gaines. My name is Detective Brown and this is my partner Detective Gonzales. You've been read your Miranda Rights from what we've been told, so you do know that you have the right to remain silent if you choose to do so?"

"Yes, I understand that."

"Do you care to exercise those rights, or will you answer our questions about this incident?"

"I have no problem answering any questions you have, Detective."

Detective Brown nodded and said, "Good, that can go a long way with us bringing this to a conclusion easily."

Hot shrugged and said, "It's an easy situation to conclude. I came home from running some errands, and when I pulled into my driveway, I noticed four men out of my rearview mirror as they jumped out of that blue Chevy Tahoe with guns in their hands. I grabbed my gun, jumped out of my car, and defended myself."

"So you're admitting to shooting and killing those four men?"

"Yes, I am. In self-defense."

"From what we have seen here, those four men were heavily armed with some serious firepower. You mean to tell me that you got the best of them with only *one* weapon, a pistol at that?" asked Detective Gonzalez.

With a grin on his face, Shot answered the detective. "Yes."

"Have you been trained to use weapons? From what I saw, it looks like you're a pretty good shot."

"I'm a great shot. And, yes, I've been trained in every-thing from sniper shooting, pistols, and explosives."

"Army?"

"Marines."

"Okay, give us the entire thing from beginning to end," said Detective Brown. Shot told him everything exactly how he remembered it. How he shot each man, where he shot them, and the order in which it happened. When he finished, Detective Brown asked, "Do you know these men who tried to murder you, Mr. Gaines?"

"I don't know all of them, but I do know the last man I shot. His name is Prophet, and he has been sending word around the city that he was going to murder me."

"So that's why you ride around with your weapon at the ready?" asked Detective Gonzalez.

"Yes. I've also been accused of shooting some of his homeboys up in the Creston Hills neighborhood. That, combined with the threats of revenge, I felt it necessary to make sure I remained armed at all times."

"Would you have a problem with us searching your home?"

"Yes, I would. There is no reason for that whatsoever. There isn't anything in my home that can assist you on this current situation."

The detective gave a nod of his head, then said, "I see you know the law a little bit."

"A little."

"Like I said, a little bit. You see, this is a crime scene, and you are the person who looks to have committed the crime. So, that gives us probable cause to search you, your car, as well as your home."

"If you say so. As long as you have it on record that I objected to the search of my home or vehicle without a search warrant, I don't have a problem with anything you choose to do here, Detective. Like I said, this was done in self-defense. Now, if there's going to be a search of my property and my home, I would like to use my phone and call my attorney."

"That might be a wise idea. Make your call because it looks like we're going to have to take you down to the station for more questioning," said Detective Gonzalez as he stepped away to discuss what they had learned with his partner.

Shot pulled out his cell phone and called JT in Los Angeles and told him everything that happened. He told him that he needed him to call the attorney for him and to have him get to the police station as soon as he could. He then told him about the SAR assault rifle that he had in the front seat of his car.

"Shit. They haven't seen that yet?"

"No. it's covered by my jacket, but if they look closely, they *will* see it."

"Shit."

"You said that already, champ."

"No time for you being a smart-ass here, son. I mean, you *do* need me to get you out of this shit."

"If you say so."

"Shit. Okay, listen, I'll make some calls to get things taken care of if they find the SAR. No biggie there. It's clean, isn't it?"

"That I'm not sure about. I got it from one of the men I've been dealing with. I have no way of knowing if it's been used."

"Shit."

"Would you stop saying that, JT. You're making me nervous," Shot said and smiled.

"Take that damn smile off your face, son. This is serious. What if that damn SAR has a body on it? How in the hell am I going to explain that?" Before Shot could answer, JT continued. "It's one of ours, so we should be good because of the tracking devices we have in them. I should be able to deal with that as well. You just make sure that you don't do or say anything to piss them people off out there. They're going to be all over your ass once you make it to the station."

"This I know."

"So Cotton is nowhere around this?"

"Far, far away. Made sure of that when I came home that I came home alone."

"Those bastards were really trying to take you out. Stupid fucks got what they deserved."

"Yes, they did."

"I'll call the director and let him know what happened and that it was a legit kill. I'm sure he'll call and pass that along to the U.S. assistant attorney. She will then be able to assist. Since you said the house is clean, it won't matter if they get a search warrant, but I'm still worried a little about that damn SAR. That could be a problem, even though it could be explained. Give me a call when you can. I'm calling your attorney now."

"Affirmative," Shot said and ended the call as the two detectives returned standing in front of him with frowns on their faces.

"We've just got word from several of your neighbors that they saw the entire scene here, and what we've been told matches everything that you've told us. So we're not going to call in for a search warrant, but we do want you to come down to the station with us so we can file the proper paperwork and ask a few more questions," said Detective Brown.

"I understand, and I don't have a problem with that. My attorney will meet us downtown at the station."

The detective nodded and turned to walk away. Much to Shot's surprise, Detective Gonzalez stopped, turned, faced Shot, and said, "You can follow us down to the station or ride with us. Your choice."

Shot sighed, relieved that they were not going to search his car and gave him the opportunity to dump the SAR. He said, "I'll follow you guys." He then went and got inside of his car and waited for the detectives to get inside of their car. Once they were on their way, Shot called JT back and told him that he was following the detectives down to the police station and what he intended to do was get rid of the SAR sitting next to him on the front passenger seat.

"Okay, that's a good idea, but it may not be needed. They may be trying to trap you here. I think you should play it cool and go on to the station with them and leave the weapon where it is."

"You may be right. I have nothing to hide. If it comes to any drama, you got my back, so I'm safe."

"Yes, you're safe, asshole. The director sounded like he's getting tired of saving your ass, but after I told him what happened and how you handled yourself, it seemed to ease the tone in his voice. Now that this mess with that prick Prophet is over, it's time to close the show in Oklahoma. Get things in order so we can finish doing some good out there, son."

"Affirmative."

"Remember what I said, don't add any more pressure to this situation once you get down to the police station, son."

"Affirmative."

JT started laughing and said, "You are a handful, son, you *do* know that, right?" Before Shot could answer, JT said, "I'm hanging up now because one more affirmative from you is gonna really piss me off!" Shot was laughing when JT hung up the phone on him.

Shot then called Cotton and told him everything that had taken place and that he was now on his way to the police station for more questioning. "Ask Big Shoota if this SAR I have is hot."

Cotton asked Big Shoota if the assault weapon had been used, and Big Shoota told him that it wasn't. "Nope. Shoota says it's clean."

"Good. One less worry there. All right, I'll give you a call when I leave the police station. Don't know how long it'll be, but it shouldn't be that long. Thanks to our neighbors, everything should go smoothly."

"So they're all dead, boss man?"

"Yes."

"Damn, you a fool with it for real," Cotton said in awe.

"Stay away from the house until you hear from me. Go spend some time with Shirin, understand?"

"I got you, boss man."

"Later," Shot said as he ended the call and pulled into the parking lot of the police station. He got out of the car and was met at the front of the police station by none other than Detective Bishop.

"Looks like you're in fact one lucky man, boy. Killing Prophet and his homeboys may have saved your life. But you better hope your luck holds up because I'm still dead set on getting your ass buried under the jail. I'm praying, actually, that I can get you for those shootings in Creston Hills. I want to be in the room with the other witnesses watching your ass get that lethal injection, you piece of shit."

"I have two promises for you, Detective Bishop. One, you will *never* see me get executed. And two, I'm going to have immense pleasure when I hear about you being removed from your current position. You may not lose your job, but you will *definitely* be demoted. You are a lawman who doesn't respect the badge you've sworn to uphold. I know what you think of me, but you don't know what you're doing or who you're dealing with. I gave you a courtesy because you're an officer of the law. You slapped me in the face for doing so. So it is what it is. And one more thing."

"What's that?"

"You call me 'boy' one more time, here or in there," Shot said as he tilted his head toward the police station, and continued, " and I'm going to catch another assault charge on a police officer because I'm going to hit you *way harder* than the first time. I *promise* you that." Shot stood still and waited for Detective Bishop to try him. He hoped and prayed he didn't, because if he did, JT and the director were going to be pissed off royally because he was ready to hurt Bishop. Bishop thought about how Shot had handled him, as well as those four Crips in that cell, and knew that Shot was not to be tested here. He'd find a way to get him, that was for certain, he said to himself as he turned and led the way inside the police station. Shot smiled as he followed the detective inside. "That was the best decision you've made in a long time, Bishop," Shot said quietly to himself.

Chapter Thirty

It had been a month since the night Shot killed the four Hoover Crips. The Hoovers in the city swore that they would avenge their fallen homeboys, but everyone on the streets knew that they were done. Their muscle was lost when Prophet was buried. The Sixties weren't even getting at the Hoovers any longer. Shoota felt it would be a waste of time and energy. He had his homeboys focused on getting their money right. That was great news for Shot because he continued to supply them, as well as every other serious hustler in the city.

The summer was close to an end, so that meant that his time in Oklahoma City was just about up. He was ready to bring this mission to a close so he could get back to the West Coast and prepare for the next mission of Operation Cleanup. His home turf. The land of the slang and gang bang. The thought of doing some good there made him smile because he was looking forward to being more hands-on with the investigation of the murders of his family. Right now, though, he had to get everything ready for his and Cotton's departure out of Oklahoma City.

Thanks to his attorney, he was able to avoid being arrested for charges of possessing a weapon. Bishop tried his best to get him charged with possession of the gun he used to take out the four Crips because he was on bond for the assault on the detective. But his attorney argued that even though he was on bond, nothing in the law said that he couldn't possess a weapon, especially since his license hadn't been revoked.

With that behind him, he continued to make the moves necessary to bring his mission to a successful end. His reports were filed and he was meeting with U.S. Assistant Attorney Helen Hollier in a few hours to deliver her the damaging evidence that would help her do a major sweep in her district. A feather in her cap that would definitely further her career in a positive fashion. He smiled at that thought because he knew that before he delivered her that great gift, she was going to have to agree to do him a favor in return. Bishop. He was going to make sure that he kept his promise to the detective and get him either fired or demoted for the disrespect he showed him. That and the lack of professionalism he displayed to Shot. No lawman should ever carry himself in that fashion. Shot was going to make sure that Bishop knew that he kept his word. He wanted the man to know that when Shot gave a promise, it was kept.

Shot finished his morning workout, then went and showered. After he was dressed, he went into Cotton's room and was shocked to see Shirin sound asleep, lying on Cotton's chest. He didn't mind Cotton having his friend over because they were about to depart the city, so it was all good. He stepped to the bed and lightly tapped Cotton on his forehead. When he opened his eyes, Shot pointed to the door, motioning for Cotton to follow him. When Cotton came into the living room, Shot told him to have a seat because they needed to have a serious discussion.

"It's time for us to leave this city, Cotton. The money has been good, but it's time to move on."

"Where are we going to next, boss man?"

Shot knew when he told Cotton that they were going to California that he was going to be extremely happy.

"We're going back to Cali, champ. My people want me home to get some things solidified with their operation. Are you cool with making some money on my home turf?"

"I've known a lot of California hustlers getting money in other states, but I've never known of a Texan going to Cali to get money. Are you sure I'll be able to assist you out there without causing any drama, boss man? I mean, it's not like you need me out there to make moves for you on the streets. That's your turf, not mine."

"You don't worry about what you bring to the team. Your position is secure and you will continue to be a very important asset to me and my people. I've let them know that you are irreplaceable. They've accepted that, so it's all good. What I need to know from you is, are you ready to go to the West Coast with me so we can turn up?"

Cotton smiled and said, "Now, you know damn well ya boy is ready to turn up! Shit, the question should be, is the West Coast ready for a true Texas nucca, 'cause you know I ain't playing when it comes to getting that money. And the bitches! Oh my God! I'm going to have a ball in LA. LA is full of big fake booties and silicone titties! I am *definitely* going to get me a few of the baddest becky broads that city has to offer."

Shot shook his head and said, "Crude as ever, aren't you?"

"Call it what you want, boss man, but I call it enjoying this life! When are we outta this place?"

"Two days tops. I have a few loose ends I need to tie up. So while I handle that, you need to start packing things up. There isn't that much we need because we're basically working from a hotel either at the W out there or the Westin. I might snatch us a condo. I haven't made my mind up yet. We'll load up what we need in your truck before we hit the highway."

"Okay, I'm on it."

"No one is to know about our departure, Cotton. You get any calls for any business, you tell them things are on hold for a few days and you'll get with them when you're ready to rock."

"Gotcha."

"Good. So make sure you enjoy your Sooner girl in there because it's time for us to bounce."

"That's going to be bittersweet for real. I'm really digging Shirin, boss man."

"Is that right? Mm, maybe you can send for her once we get things put together if you're feeling her like that. But for now, you aren't telling her anything. When we leave, you can tell her you're heading back to Dallas for a few weeks, understood?"

"No problem."

"Good. All right, I'll see you in a couple of hours. I got some business to take care of. Don't start packing anything until you've taken Shirin home."

"I won't," Cotton said as he stood and stretched before returning back to the bedroom.

Shot left the house in good spirits, but as he drove toward downtown Oklahoma City, his spirits sank some as he thought about the situation with Nola and Lola. "How in the heck am I going to deal with this?" he asked himself as he continued to drive. He pulled out his phone and called Lola in Dallas. When she answered the phone, he ripped right into her. "Look, you need to get at me with the real on this craziness, Lola. I want to know why you aren't in jail and your sister is. This is driving me mad here. Talk to me!"

"The only thing you need to know, Shot, is that Nola loves you more than anything in this world other than family. Her dedication to us is the only thing that would ever make her hurt you. She cried like a baby the last days before she went inside that place. All she wanted was to call you and explain so you could understand the decision she made."

"Explain what? Tell me, Lola! I have the right to know what the hell is going on here!"

"I can't, Shot. I can't, and I won't. Good-bye," Lola said and hung up the phone feeling really bad. Bad because she knew she should have never had sex with Shot. She couldn't help it, though. She was highly turned on by him and was curious to see what he was working with. She knew her sister would kill her if she ever found out and that made her feel shame. Now she hoped and prayed that Shot didn't do anything crazy and put everything they've done at risk. That was a fear that gripped her heart because there was no way she could ever go to jail. She would die in that place. *Please, God, don't let Shot try to contact my sister*, she prayed silently as she went into the bathroom to take a shower and start her day.

Shot hung up the phone with Lola with thoughts of trying to figure out a way he could do exactly what she had asked God to not let him do. He needed to talk to Nola, and he knew in order for that to happen, he would have to ask a gigantic favor of JT, as well as the director of the FBI. Asking wouldn't be the problem, though. Giving the reason why he needed the favor was the major issue. *How can I ask them to get me into a female's federal prison to visit a prisoner without revealing that Nola was Nola and not her sister Lola? Jeez,* he thought as he pulled into the underground parking lot of the federal courthouse.

Ten minutes later, he was sitting across the desk of the U.S. assistant attorney. Helen Hollier was a light-skinned black woman with a short haircut with some snow-white hair. She gave you the grandmotherly feel, and that instantly made Shot feel relaxed in her presence. Her smile was sincere and genuine when she said, "Okay, young man, I will say that you are one hell-raiser. After reading these reports, you are much more than that. You are one hell of an undercover operative. This report, along with the tracking devices in the weapons you sold to the gangbangers here in this city, will be enough for me to bring down not only those you've dealt with on the streets, but many more. Once I sweep up the first wave of these men, the telling will start and I will be able to bring down most of the city's street hustlers. Good job, Agent Gaines. Good job indeed."

"Thank you, ma'am. I cannot take all the credit because if it wasn't for the leeway that my handler and the director have given me, none of this would be possible. So, it's a team effort, not all mine."

"A modest man, a violent man, and an intelligent man who comes across as a sincerely humble man. You are very impressive, Agent Gaines."

"Please, ma'am, you're going to make me blush here." They both laughed. "Before I leave, I need to ask a favor of you, ma'am. A very important favor."

With raised eyebrows, the U.S. assistant attorney sat back in her seat and folded her arms across her chest said, "If there is anything I can do for you, Agent Gaines, I assure you I will. Talk to me."

Shot then went on and explained the conduct of Detective Bishop and how he felt that it was important to the integrity of the OKCPD that he either be removed from the police force or at least demoted from the rank of detective. When he finished, he expected for her to laugh at him and was pleased when she responded in a stern voice.

"To hear this is very disheartening, Agent Gaines, and I can assure you that I will do everything in my power to get that racist pig fired from the force. If I cannot achieve that goal, I am positive that I can make his life a living hell because he will be demoted, for sure. If I have any say-so, he will be doing traffic until he retires or quits. As a proud Oklahoman, I take extreme offense at what you've told me. The work you've done gives you high confidence with me, and I don't doubt your words one bit. But I have to do this by the books. I will alert Internal Affairs of Detective Bishop's conduct and proceed from there. The head of IA owes me a few favors, and it's high time I call him in for one. So rest assured, Detective Bishop won't be calling anyone else that word any time soon."

Shot smiled and stood. He reached his hand across the desk and shook her hand and said, "Thank you, ma'am. I'm just one man, but I was raised to respect our race as well as every man. A man like Bishop doesn't deserve to hold that badge. It's a disservice to your city. Thank you so much for believing me."

"I know an honest man when I see one, Agent Gaines. You definitely fit that mold. Now, you be careful out there with your future missions. I wish you nothing but the best. You will be added to my nightly prayers, young man."

"Thank you, ma'am. All I'm trying to do is some good."

"Well, keep up the great work. The work you've done in Dallas and out here has been extraordinarily impressive. We need more men like you on the good side, Agent Gaines. Be safe and may God keep His hands on you. Now leave me, I have work to do. Many warrants need to be approved because in a few weeks, hell's about to be raised on the streets of Oklahoma City, and I'm serving all the heat that's needed!"

Shot smiled and said, "Yes, ma'am. You go get them."

"That I will, Agent Gaines. That I will."

Chapter Thirty-one

Shot made up his mind when he left the U.S. assistant attorney's office that he had to go see Nola. He needed to know exactly what Nola and Lola were up to. He called JT and explained the situation to him and prayed he wouldn't go nuts.

"Are you telling me that *your* Nola is the one who's incarcerated in Waseca and not her sister, son?"

"That's *exactly* what I'm saying. I need for you to make this happen for me, JT. I have to find out what the heck is going on."

"That's a tall order you're asking me to pull off, son. I don't know how I'll be able to get the director to go for something like this. It's a federal crime that they've committed here."

"I know, JT, but I love her. She's the only one for me, and no matter what happens, I have to protect her. I need you to find a way to make this happen without getting her into more trouble."

Shot's tone touched JT deeply. He knew how Shot suffered when Nola left him. More than that, he knew the pain he went through from the loss of their child. Shot was like a son to him, and when he hurt, so did JT. JT sighed and said, "I'll give you a call back in a few." Then JT hung up the phone and thought about the lies he was about to tell his boss. He sighed and grabbed the phone and called the director. Once the director was on the line, JT told him that there was a situation concerning the

Dallas operation that could possibly affect Shot's cover down the line, and Shot needed to go see Lola Potts in order to make sure things were safe regarding his name.

"What exactly is the issue, JT?" asked the director.

"Right now, just rumors, sir, rumors that may lead people to believe that Shot is working for us. That is a risk that we cannot afford to take. Operation Cleanup is working just as we planned, and we cannot move forward without knowing that Shot's cover remains intact."

"And the only way to ensure this is to set up a visit with this Lola Potts woman?"

"Yes, sir."

"Why do I have a feeling that there's something you're not telling me, JT?"

"Trust me, sir, this is all in the name of keeping Operation Cleanup moving forward."

"You didn't answer my question, JT, and that tells me that it's best that I don't know everything about this. Tell Agent Gaines that he will need to get to Minnesota within the next twenty-four hours. Everything will be arranged for him to have a private meeting with Lola Potts. I'll have it set up as one of my agents are coming to see if we can get her to cooperate with us for an ongoing investigation. You just make sure that after this visit is over, you tell me precisely what's going on. Do you understand me?"

"Yes, sir. Thank you, sir."

"Don't thank me yet. You might not like how I react to the truth once it's told to me," the director said and ended the call.

JT muttered something to himself as he called Shot back and said, "You need to get to Minnesota within the next twenty-four hours. Once you get the answers you need, we're going to have a conference call with the director and give him the truth on what's going on. That was the only way he would work this for you. So it better be worth it, son, because once we tell him the truth, and we *are* going to tell him the truth, the love of your life may be getting some more time in the feds."

"I understand. Thanks, JT. I'm about to book a flight now."

"You're going in as Agent Gaines, so make sure you bring your creds. You're going to have all the time you need because you will be interviewing her trying to see if you can get her to help us with an ongoing operation."

"Got it," Shot said as he hung up the phone feeling relieved, yet worried, all at the same time. He hoped and prayed that he wasn't about to get Nola into even more trouble. He went back to the house and told Cotton that he had to go out of town and would be back in a couple of days so they could head out to the West Coast. "Make sure you get everything ready so when I get back, we can hit the highway."

"Where are you going, boss man?"

"To take care of some business," Shot said and went into his room to pack. After he made his flight reservations for the next morning, he lay down on the bed and closed his eyes thinking about seeing Nola. His heart began to beat faster, and he realized that no matter what he found out, he would never stop loving that woman.

Shot's 7:00 a.m. flight from Oklahoma City's Will Rogers World Airport arrived in Minneapolis, Minnesota's MSP Airport, at 9:15 a.m. The two-hour-and-ten-minute flight to Minnesota gave Shot more time to think about what he was going to say to Nola once she was in front of him. He prided himself for not being a liar, and he was going to stick to that. He was going to tell her the entire truth. The truth. The truth that *he* was the reason why she was incarcerated. Her brother and cousins as well. The truth that *he* was the reason why they lost their unborn child.

He feared he would lose her once she knew that he was an FBI agent tasked with the assignment to bring down as many drug dealers and bad people in Dallas, Texas, as possible. The truth.

Damn.

After getting a rental car, Shot made the seventy-seven-mile trip from MSP Airport to the city of Waseca where FCI Waseca women's federal prison was located. He battled with himself the entire drive there. Once he was inside of the prison's waiting room, he felt sick to his stomach. He couldn't remember the last time he was that nervous.

When the associate warden of the prison came and greeted him, Shot pulled out his credentials and gave them to her and said, "Hello, ma'am. My name is Agent Gaines."

"I received word from the warden that the director of the FBI made this special request. We've already had inmate Potts brought to the interview room in the visiting area. You will have total privacy. Is there anything you'll need from us?"

"No, ma'am. I have everything I need here with me," he said as he patted the notepad he bought from a Walmart when he was in Minnesota, along with a few pens and highlighters.

"Follow me," the associate warden said as she led the way into the prison. Once they were inside of the visiting room, Shot felt dizzy when he saw Nola sitting in there, looking extremely nervous herself. "You can go on from here. If you need anything, just look up toward one of the security cameras and motion that you are ready to leave and someone will come escort you out."

"Thank you, ma'am," Shot said as he took a deep breath and stepped toward Nola. When he was standing in front of her, he said, "Hello, Ms. Potts."

Nola's eyes grew huge when she focused and saw that it was Hot Shot standing before her. It took her a few minutes before she could speak. Finally, she said, "Please don't tell me you're here to tell me something has happened to Nola, Shot."

Her statement made his nerves disappear, and he became angry. He frowned and said, "Stop it." He sat down and pulled out his notepad as if he was about to take notes, giving the security watching them the feeling that he was getting ready to conduct his interview. He sighed and said, "We're about to have a long talk, and we're going to be totally honest with each other. Do you understand me?"

"Wha-what is this all about, Hot Shot? How in the hell did you pull off coming here to see me?"

"All of that will come out in a little while. Right now, I'm going to ask you some questions, and I want the truth. I want you to tell me everything from the beginning to the end. Do. You. Understand. Me. *Nola?*" he asked, putting heavy emphasis on her name.

When she heard him call her by her name, she almost fainted. She put her hand over her mouth and whispered, "Oh my God. How did you find out, Hot Shot?" she asked as her eyes began to water, breaking his heart. He loved her so much that all he wanted to do was give her a tight hug and tell her that everything was going to be okay.

He shook those feelings off and regained his composure. "Lola told me a little, but I figured the rest out on my own. Did you *really* think I could be with Lola and not know she wasn't you?"

Nola wiped her eyes and frowned. "What do you mean 'be with her,' Hot Shot?"

"You know what I mean. She admitted to me that she wanted to be with me so she could see what was so special about me to make sure you love me so much.

She is ashamed and mad at herself for doing that to you. She tried to stick to the script, but she screwed that up in way too many ways." He then went on and explained how he figured out that Lola was not Nola and how she refused to tell him why they did what they did. "Now, you're going to tell me everything right now. Do you understand me, Nola?"

Nola sat there silently for a moment, then finally she gave him a nod and sighed heavily. She felt as if a huge burden was about to be lifted from her shoulders. Even though she was scared she would get into more trouble, she felt comfortable with Shot being here. She loved him more than anything in this world, and she was ready to come clean. She just hoped he wouldn't hate her when she was finished telling him the truth. "It's a long story, so in order for me to give it to you, you're going to have to be patient and not ask me any questions until I've finished."

"Okay. Talk to me, babe."

Hearing that endearment from him made her heart skip a beat. *God, I love this man,* she said to herself. She took a deep breath and began. "When Lola and I were kids, we used to play hide-and-seek around the house and see who could stay hidden the longest, you know, kid stuff. One day we were playing the game, and I knew that Lola liked to hide in a chest that my mother and father kept in the back room. I would always let her think that she won because it was so funny that she would always hide in the same place whenever it was my turn to look for her.

"One day I decided to teach her a lesson so she would learn to find a new hiding spot. So once she went to go hide, I waited for a few minutes, and then started looking for her, even though I knew where she was. I went into the back room and snuck up to the big chest and locked it without her knowing it, then went into my room and started playing with my dolls, thinking I would leave her in there for a little bit to scare her silly. My father came into my room and asked me if I wanted to go with him to the store and he would buy me some candy. I forgot all about Lola and jumped at the opportunity to go with my father.

"By the time we came back from the store, my mother had Lola in her arms rocking her back and forth because she was hysterical from being locked in that chest for over two hours. My mother and father yelled at me for doing that to my sister, and I got the ass whooping of my life, plus punishment for a month. I never forgave myself for doing that to my sister. What made things worse was that Lola could never be in confined places without hyperventilating and almost passing out. She became an intense claustrophobic. She would literally lose her mind if she even *thought* she would be in any closed quarters. Every time she had an episode, it would break my heart because I knew *I* was responsible for my twin sister being this way. My fault."

"Okay, so what does her condition have to do with you being in here now?"

"Think about it. Being in prison you are constantly confined in closed quarters. My sister would never have made it if she would have come in here. I had to make the switch with her and do this time for her. I owed her that much because it's my fault she is claustrophobic."

Shot sat back in his seat and let Nola's words sink in. It made perfect sense. He had to admire Nola's loyalty and dedication to her sister. There was more he needed to know, though, much more. "Okay, now I understand why you turned yourself in as Lola, but what I want to know—no, what I *need* to know—is what happened to our child? Did you really have a miscarriage from the streets caused by your family's situation like you told me?"

The tears seemed to fly out of Nola's eyes when he asked that question, and Shot knew what she was going to tell him. "I'm sorry, Hot Shot. I'm so sorry. I had an abortion. I killed our baby. I had no other choice because I was going to turn myself in for Lola, and there was no way I could do that while being pregnant. At first, I thought about keeping the baby and making these people think I was Lola and pregnant, but that would never have worked because you would have been all over Lola, thinking she was me and I didn't need you in the mix like that. So the only conclusion I could come up with was to abort our child."

She dropped her head in shame and whispered, "I've prayed every single day since it happened, that you would forgive me. I had every intention of telling you the truth once I was out of here. That's why I made Lola promise to me, *swear* to me, that she would stay away from you. Stay clear of you even when you called and tried your best to speak with her. But, damn, that slut had to go on and mess with you. Makes me want to wring her damn neck. The thought of you touching her in that way makes me feel sick, and I swear to God I'm beating her ass just as soon as I get to her. Ugh!" Nola said and wiped her eyes.

"Why didn't you tell me? Why didn't you trust me with this, Nola? *We* could have found a way to make this work together somehow."

Shaking her head, she said, "I couldn't take that chance, Hot Shot. I just couldn't. I told you I love you more than anything in this world, but when it comes to my family I could never not be there for them. I had to do it this way. Please forgive me. Please don't hate me for taking our child from us. Please," she begged.

Shot stared at her for a full minute before speaking. "I could never hate you, Nola Potts. I love you too much for that. I am madly in love with you, babe."

"I love you too, Hot Shot. I'm so in love with you that I hurt every single night in this crazy place with all of these crazy-ass bitches. Thank you, honey, for not hating me."

Shot sighed and said, "Now I have some things to tell you, and I pray you can be as forgiving as I have."

"What? What did you do? God, please don't tell me that Lola is preggo. I would die if that happened."

"No, babe, nothing like that." He took a deep breath, then pulled out his credentials and set his FBI badge on the chair between them and said, "*I'm* the real reason why you and your family were arrested. I'm an FBI agent."

Nola stared at the badge, then looked in his eyes to see if he was playing with her. Then said, "Ain't that a bitch!"

Chapter Thirty-two

"Oh, yes, Mister Hot Shot. Your ass needs to get to telling me these things to make me understand why you fucked off me and my family's lives. I can't believe this shit!"

"First off, you need to calm down and remember that eyes are on us. I'm here in a professional capacity, Nola. Trust me, you don't want to blow this, or you and Lola will be sharing a cell." He took a deep breath and watched as she folded her arms across her chest, clearly pissed off to the highest power. "I'm part of a special operation called Operation Cleanup. It was designed by the director of the FBI, my boss, to take down as many criminals as possible on the streets in urban communities across the U.S. I'm an undercover operative working alone to make deal for guns, as well as drugs, to get in good on the streets so the federal government can get iron-clad convictions and clean up the streets."

"So you're telling me that you're really a fucking fed, Hot Shot?"

"Yes."

"Cotton too?"

"No. Cotton doesn't know what he is doing while helping me in the streets. The only people who know about it are me, the director, JT, and now, you."

"What you're doing is wrong! That's entrapment. You can't set people up like that—it's against the law."

Shaking his head he said, "Not how it's set up. The director is using this as a means to do some good. I'm not making anyone buy drugs or guns from me. I am merely making my services available. Anyone who deals with me goes to jail because I give all the information acquired to my handler, JT, while I'm in the streets. He then gives the information to the federal prosecutor, who does the rest."

"Well, I'll be damn. I fell in love with a fucking federal agent. You're good, *really fucking good*. I would never have thought you were the people. You fooled the fuck out of me. So that means everything you've told me was a damn lie. All of that love stuff was lies."

"No. My feelings for you changed everything. That's why you weren't arrested when your family was picked up. I made sure I kept you out of everything. There was no way I could have you put in jail."

"Humph. So *that's* supposed to make me feel better about this shit? Are you fucking crazy, Hot Shot? You had my family put in jail. This is fucking incredible. You're one cold-ass man. How could you sit there and say that you love me and you did *this* to my family? *You* did this to us. *You're* the reason why our unborn child is not living. Oh my God, I can't believe this shit. I've never been so betrayed like this in my life."

Shot's worst fears were coming true because he saw the hate slowly come into Nola's eyes, and that broke his heart. He knew he had to try his best to convince her that he loved her with all of his heart and hoped that she would be able to forgive him for betraying her. "Listen to me and listen to me good. If I was as cold as you say I am, then you would have been arrested along with your family. Better yet, you would be brought up on more charges, and you and Lola would be in here together, now that I've found out the truth. So *stop* that. Listen to me, babe, and *trust* me."

"Trust you? How can you sit there and ask me that? Everything I thought I had with you was a damn lie. You were only doing your job. You used me to get at my family. You *used* me, Hot Shot. Do you *know* how that makes me feel? You used my body, my heart, my soul. And it cost me and my family our freedom."

"No, you lost your freedom because you felt you had to protect your sister. If there was any other way I could have dealt with this, I would, but by the time everything was set in motion, it was too late. I filed my reports and everything was a done deal. Me falling in love with you wasn't supposed to happen. When it did, I knew there would be a problem. You becoming pregnant killed me because by the time I found that out, it was really too late. There was absolutely nothing I could do but ensure that you weren't arrested, and I did that. Nola, you have to understand that I had a job to do. I am a sworn FBI agent designated to Operation Cleanup to do some good. I couldn't let my feelings interfere with the job I have to do."

"Lies, all lies. I bet you telling me about the murders of your mother, father, and little brother were lies too."

"No. That was the honest truth. Everything I told you about my personal life was the truth. I left out that I was in the marines and served in the Special Forces. I've been in the war in Iraq and many other places. I've been trained in everything from sniper shooting to hand-to-hand combat. I'm a decorated soldier for more medals than I care to have. I was handpicked by JT to do some good, and that's what I do. I'm helping the African Americans who live in the urban communities across America live a little more peacefully by removing drug dealers and gangsters from the streets. I'm not a cold man. I'm an honest black man doing what I feel I was born to do. I love my country, but I love my people more.

I love my people so much that I'm willing to put my life on the line to do some good for them. I'm a black man who cares, Nola. I mean that. I care about my people, and all I want is for a better way for all of us. If that means setting up millions of gangsters and drug dealers, then so be it. If it means killing men in the name of justice, then that's what I'm prepared to do. As a matter of fact, that is what I've done." He then went into detail about the mission he just completed in Oklahoma City.

When he finished, she stared at him and asked, "Did you set up some of my family out there too? Did you set up my family I introduced you to out there, Hot Shot?"

"No."

"Wow, *thanks*," she said sarcastically.

"Don't be this way, Nola. I understand you're upset, and you have every right to be. I can only apologize sincerely for what happened, but I can't change any of that. I love you with all of my heart, babe, I really do."

Her eyes softened at his words, but she was confused. How could she ever trust him again? How could she be with the man that betrayed her this way? "This is way too much for me to handle, Hot Shot. What do you want from me?"

He stared at her and said, "I want your heart. I need your love. I want us to rebuild what we started and be together."

She laughed and said, "Now, how in the hell are we going to be together when I'm in here serving sixty months? What, you gon' ride with me and be my man? You gon' be my man while I do this time and still be out there setting up people doing some good?"

"Yes. My job won't change, and I will continue to do what I feel is right. As for you, I will love you with all of my heart and be right by your side until you come home.

My love for you is genuine, and I will do everything in my power to make sure you know it. I'm going to tell my superiors everything when I leave here and ask them to have you moved to a better facility so we can try to make things right. I'll make sure that I do whatever it takes to show you my heart belongs to you, and only you. I'm going to make sure that Lola remains free so you can finish what you started. I'm going to visit you as much as I can, make sure that your books are straight so you can be as comfortable as possible while you finish up these three years and some change that you have to do. I'm going to love you, Nola, if you let me. I want to spend the rest of my life with you. I want to earn your trust and be with you. I want you to be my bride. I'll marry you in here if you'll let me. I love you that much, Nola Potts."

She stared at him speechless for a few minutes, then simply said, "Damn, honey."

It took all of his restraint not to reach across and hold her hand when he said, "Let me love you, Nola. Let me make some of this craziness right, babe."

"How, Hot Shot? How do I do that, honey?"

"By trusting my heart, the heart that belongs to you."

"So when I come home, then what? We'll be together, and you'll still be doing what you do?"

"Yes. My job is set for the long term. I've just finished in Oklahoma. Now I'm returning to the West to start another mission in California. I'm just trying to do some good, Nola. It's my mission in life, and I can't stop. I *won't* stop."

"Damn, honey," she repeated.

"Tell me you love me."

She stared at him and smiled. "I love you . . . But I hate you too. I hate you for what you've done to my family. But after hearing this, for some stupid-ass reason, I understand. I understand because I know you. I know you're a good man. I know your love for me is real. I feel it. I've felt it every day I've been in this miserable place. Hearing all of this is confusing to me, but one thing is crystal clear to me. You *do* love me. Your actions after the fact have proved that. Especially with knowing what I've done for my sister. I love you so much, Hot Shot."

The way she said his name made him smile. She knew that turned him on like crazy. "Can we make it happen, babe? Can we do this right now? No lies. Everything is on the table now. Can we push forward and find the happiness we both crave for with each other?"

"I want that, I really do. I want you, honey. I want to be with you for the rest of my life. Yes, we can do this. But your ass will have to abide by some serious rules from this point on."

"Anything you say, babe, anything you say."

"I've been down a little over a year, and I already lost fifty-four days for fighting. So that means I still got like two and some change left to do. No fucking. You're on punishment. No sex. Can you go two years and some change without having sex out there, Hot Shot?"

"Yes."

"You fucked my sister. Ugh! How in the hell could you do that? I thought you could tell us apart?"

"I thought I could too, babe. But she is dressing like you and has your mannerisms down to a tee. The only way I figured out she wasn't you was when she said certain things like JT was a black man. Or when she didn't know how I sent the money to JT. Once I figured it out, I knew something was off. After that, I put her in a situation that confirmed my suspicions."

"Like I said, ugh! I cannot wait to get out. I'm beating Lola's ass for doing that shit. I made her swear not to even come close to you. She betrayed me with that, and I should have known her freaky ass would try that shit. Ugh!

"Back to your rules. You are to come see me at least twice a month until I get to the halfway house."

"Done."

"You have to make sure you get your boss to have me moved back to Texas. I need to be close to home. It's too fucking cold out here in Minnesota."

"Done."

"You have to keep your word and never *ever* lie to me ever again. No matter what."

"Done."

She smiled and said, "Once you get me moved to Bryan, Texas, you have to definitely put a ring on it and be my husband."

He smiled at her and said, "My pleasure, babe, my pleasure."

"Damn, Hot Shot. Do you know how fucking horny I am for you right now?"

"Yes, Nola, I do. It's taking all of my control not to grab you and kiss you right here."

She moaned and said, "Damn, honey."

"I love you, Nola Potts."

She smiled at him, and all he saw was the love she had for him in her eyes and said, "I love you too, Hot Shot. Always have and I always will."

Hot Shot felt as if everything in the world was right. He had his woman, the truth was out, and he was ready to proceed with Operation Cleanup. He had only one worry now, and that was convincing the director and JT to make sure the promises he just made to Nola would happen. And that was going to be one tall order.

Damn.

Chapter Thirty-three

During the one hour and fourteen minutes it took for Shot to make it back to Minneapolis, his thoughts were on Nola and how he would be able to make everything right for the two of them. He was willing to do or say whatever it took to get JT and the director to assist him in making sure that Nola was taken care of. He was confident that they would help him because he was going to lay it all on the line and let them know that this is not only what he wanted, but needed in order to continue on with Operation Cleanup. He hoped he wouldn't have to use that threat, but he was prepared to do whatever it took. He went and got a room at a Motel 6 not too far from the airport so he would be able to make his early-morning flight without having to rush. After taking a shower and a brief nap, he got up and called JT.

"So, how did everything go, son? I hope you got what you needed."

"I did," Shot said as he then proceeded to tell JT everything he learned from his visit with Nola.

JT was shocked and speechless as he let Shot's words resonate inside his head. "Damn, you *do* know that they've committed *another* federal crime, son?"

"Yes, I know. I need you to help me here, JT. I gave Nola my word that there wouldn't be any charges brought against her or her sister on this. I need your help in more ways than one because I also gave my word that she would be moved to a facility back in Texas. She needs to be closer to home; she hates the cold out there."

"Well, damn, maybe you should have given her your word that we would get her an early release too. You're asking for things way above my pay grade, son. You know I can't make any of that happen."

"Yes, I know, but the director can."

"True. But what makes you think he would be willing to do it, especially after hearing that they've tricked the BOP and federal government?"

"I love that woman, JT. I'm in love with her, and I asked her to be my wife. I intend on marrying her while she's still inside. I've committed to her fully, and no matter what happens, I will remain by her side. I need this to happen, JT. I need it bad, and I am willing to do whatever it takes, even stepping down from the operation."

"Whoa! I know you're trying to muscle the director, son, but that would be one major fuckup."

"I'm not trying to muscle anyone. I'm merely stating the facts. You want my service on this operation, then you need to keep me happy. The only way I can remain happy is if my fiancée gets what she wants. I'm the reason why she's in that place. I'm the reason why her family is in that place. I'm the reason why my unborn child was aborted. Yes, she made the decisions to do what she did, but her reasons make sense, and I'm the man who put her in that predicament. I'm responsible for this, and I got to make it right."

JT sighed and said, "I'm not going to tell the director this shit, son. This is something he has to hear from your mouth. I'll call you back after I get him on the line. I hope you know what you're doing here, because this could be catastrophic for you."

"I understand that, and I'm willing to do whatever comes with this, JT. I need this, champ."

"Call you back in a few," JT said and hung up the phone. He called the director's direct line and informed him that

Shot was finished with his meeting with Nola Potts and that Shot needed to speak with him to fully brief him on the situation.

"Something is telling me that I'm not going to like what Agent Gaines has to tell me, JT, am I correct here?"

"Yes, sir, you are."

"Care to give me a heads-up on what I'm about to learn?"

"I'd rather you hear what Agent Gaines has to tell you from his mouth, sir."

"That bad, huh?"

"Worse, sir."

The director undid his tie and sat back in his seat behind his desk and sighed. "Okay, make the call and let's get to this."

JT clicked over on his phone and called Shot back, then connected him with the director so they were all on the same line. "Agent Gaines, I have the director on the line."

"Good afternoon, sir."

"Same to you, Agent Gaines. JT has informed me that you have some information for me that I won't take too kindly to. So why don't you get straight to it so we can see how we'll deal with this situation."

"Yes, sir," Shot said as he repeated everything he told JT about the crimes that Nola and her sister did, such as switching identities, and how much he cared for her and asked her to be his bride . . . all the way down to how he felt totally responsible for her actions. When he finished he said, "I'm asking you—no, sir, I'm *begging* you—to grant her request to be transferred back to Texas so she can be closer to her family while she finishes the time she has to do for her sister. I know what I'm asking is illegal, sir. But this is the woman I'm in love with. She means everything to me. No matter what the outcome, I *will* marry her and be by her side throughout this entire situation."

There was silence on the line while the director pro-cessed what he had just been told. JT was sitting at his desk nursing a strong drink of Jack Daniels, praying that the director didn't flip the fuck out on Shot, while Shot sat at the end of his bed in his hotel room praying for some luck as well. After two full minutes the director said, "This is the strangest situation I've ever been a part of. So let me get this straight. You want me to pull some strings to get her transferred back to Texas?"

"Yes, sir."

"That's something that can be done without any prob-lem. But you asking me to overlook the crime that Nola Potts and her sister committed is something totally dif-ferent. That's a serious thing right there, Agent Gaines."

"Yes, I understand that, sir."

"You've let your personal feelings enter this situation, and personal and business is never good."

"I understand that totally, sir. I never in a million years thought something like this would happen. But I can assure you it will never happen again because Nola Potts is about to become Nola Gaines, and no woman will ever be able to get close to my heart while I handle my business for Operation Cleanup. That I can promise you, Director."

"I received a call from the U.S. assistant attorney for Oklahoma City, and she informed me that the warrants are being prepared for over sixty-seven men and women in her district. She also expressed how impressed she was with what you did out there. We're two for two and doing some good, Agent Gaines. That makes me happy, and when I inform the president, I'm positive it will make him extremely happy. Because of that, I have no other choice but to give you this and grant your request. You've pushed me to the limit on this, though. You are doing some good, and that makes us all look great. But you have to tone some of that aggression down. I can't keep backing you when you're out there being overly aggressive."

"With all due respect, sir, I don't understand what you're saying here. I have to be overly aggressive when I'm out there in those streets. It's the field of war out there, sir. I'm fully engaged, and I have to do what's necessary to survive. Not only that, I have to maintain my image at all costs. Granted, things did get a tad bit out of hand in Oklahoma City. I take full responsibility for my actions, sir. But I will not tell you I will tone down my aggression. That would be basically signing my own death warrant. I am out there to do some good, and by doing some good I have to do some wrong. We knew this going in, and things can't be switched up on the fly here because things have gotten a little hectic. I have to have free reign to do what it takes to make my name remain solid in the streets. If you feel that my tactics are too aggressive for your or the president's taste, then I suggest you find someone else to carry on with Operation Cleanup."

There was silence on the line, and JT prayed that Shot hadn't just ruined everything and all of the hard work that they had put in over the last two years. Shot was smiling because he knew he could close his eyes and see the sweat pellets popping up on JT's forehead.

After a moment, the director said, "I respect your candor on this, Agent Gaines. You're right. You're out here putting yourself on the front line, and I don't have the right to tell you what to do for your survival. But I can *ask* you to *try* to avoid certain aggressions."

"I give you my word, sir, I will try to avoid things, if at all possible, but I will *not* run or turn my back on anything if I feel my or my unofficial partner Cotton's life is put in jeopardy."

"Understood."

Shot felt luck was on his side, so he believed now was the time to put in the request to protect Cotton for later on down the line.

"I have one more request, sir, since you're being so generous."

"You are *really* pushing it, Agent Gaines. But since we've gone as far as breaking the law, we might as well get everything out of the way now. What is it?"

"Cotton. My unofficial partner. I don't know how long this will continue to work in our favor, but I want to protect him, sir. He's put his life on the line for me on several occasions. His girlfriend died, and he's done a lot for this operation, all on an unofficial capacity, of course. I want your word that once everything is everything with Operation Cleanup that Cotton will be set free. He's earned his way this far and has been invaluable to me and my moves out there in the streets of Dallas, Texas, and Oklahoma City."

"Now *that* is something I don't have a problem with at all, Agent Gaines. So you don't have to worry about that. But when the time comes, I want you to inform your man of what has taken place and that he is to leave that lifestyle and move on with his life."

"No problem, sir."

"You care about this man?"

"Yes, sir, I do. He's become like a brother to me. We're a team out there, and right now, we're the winning team. He's extremely loyal to me, and I feel he will continue to be an asset to me and Operation Cleanup."

"Okay, then. Is there *anything else* you would like of me? Like maybe giving you permission to have a conjugal visit with your soon-to-be bride? Before you even think about answering that question, please understand that I was joking. You may make her your bride, but you

won't be touching her in that special way husbands and
wives do until she finishes serving the time for her sister.
Understood?"

"Yes, sir. Thank you, sir."

"No need to thank me, Agent Gaines. You're doing
some good, and that means we're doing some good
together. I have to have your back while you're out there.
I have to let you do what needs to be done in order to deal
with those types of men on those cruel streets. I do have
your back, Agent Gaines. You just keep doing some good
and continue to make us all look good."

"Yes, sir."

"Is there anything you'd like to add to this conversation
before I end this conference call, JT?"

"No, sir. I'm just thankful that I still have a job! For a
minute there, I thought this champ was going to have
both of us headed for the unemployment line." The men
laughed. JT told Shot that he was to get to California as
soon as possible. Shot assured him that as soon as he
returned to Oklahoma City, he and Cotton would be on
their way. After that, JT ended the call with Shot and
spoke with the director.

"Do you think we should inform him that the next
mission out here will be with the Mexicans that we've
learned have something to do with the death of his
family?"

"Not right off. We're only speculating right now. Our
sources have been on point, though, so once we have
more concrete evidence, then we'll let him know everything we know. I tried to reel him in some, but that didn't
work."

"I know. That man is a warrior, and he will do whatever
it takes to get the job done and remain breathing. He is
one hell of a soldier, sir."

"True. But he takes things personal, and that's dangerous. When he learns that the Sureños of Southern California had something to do with the death of his family, I'm afraid he's going to go berserk, and we won't be able to control him."

"I share those feelings with you, sir."

"It's your job to make sure that this doesn't happen, JT. Operation Cleanup is something the president is passionate about. He's doing something that no other president has done. He's making a conscious effort to do something for the urban communities. We have to make sure that Agent Gaines doesn't lose it and destroy what we're doing."

"I understand, sir. Maybe we should shy away from this California mission and stay focused on the southern regions for now."

"No. We need to get inside of the Mexican Mafia and the Sureños of Southern California. They're getting too strong, and it's time to address them and knock them down some. If anyone can do that, it's Agent Gaines. It's time for those Mexican gangsters to meet Hot Shot."

"Yes, sir," JT said with a smile on his face.

Chapter Thirty-four

By the time Shot's flight from Minnesota landed, LeBron James announced he was returning to the Cleveland Cavaliers. That was the talk around the world, and Shot had to give the king his props for making such a bold move. Though he was a die-hard Laker and Kobe Bryant fan, he was happy for LeBron. Actually, he was happy—period—at this point. All went well with the director, and he was anxiously awaiting Nola's call so he could tell her the great news. She would be moved back to Texas, and he would make sure that he kept his promises to her. Just as soon as she made it back to Texas, he was going to fly out to see her and start the procedure to make her his wife. Never in his life did he think he would marry, but now, that's all that mattered most to him. He didn't give a damn about her being incarcerated. He could wait and remain true to her for a little over two years. He laughed when he thought about what Cotton would say when he told him that it was Nola who was in jail and not Lola. And he knew he would have all sorts of jokes when he told him he was marrying Nola while she finished doing that time. Love is painful, that is so true, but love felt good when it was right, and loving Nola was something Shot felt was the best and right thing in his life. He was smiling as he left the airport and went to the long-term parking lot to get his car.

When he entered the house, Cotton was lying down on the couch with his phone to his ear laughing. "I'm telling you, crazy lady, there is no way your Thunder will ever win a championship without some help. You ain't working with enough. That was proven this year when the Spurs tapped that ass. Okay, baby, let me get back to you. Shot just came back. I'll holla at you after we've finished chopping it up." He hung up the phone and sat up. "What's good, boss man? Everything good?"

Shot told him that everything was great and proceeded to tell about his visit with Nola. He told him everything except how he was an FBI agent. Keeping that a secret from Cotton pained him now, but he knew Cotton would be better kept in the dark about that. He was safe, and that's all that mattered.

When Shot finished, Cotton laughed and said, "Now, you got to admit that was some gangsta-ass shit they pulled off, boss man. I mean, whoa."

"Yes. That took some balls. I admire her loyalty to her family. I mean, that's like the ultimate sacrifice, for real. To give up your freedom for your sister, and to abort your child in order to do so—man."

"I know that hurt you, boss man, but I can tell by the look on your face that you're good. You really do love that woman, don't ya?"

"I've never loved a woman the way that I love her, champ. We're in it for the long haul. Once she gets back to Texas, I'm flying in and we're going to get married."

"Married? Oh, you sprung for real! You're actually going to marry her while she finishes her stretch?"

Here we go, Shot said to himself. "Yes. I will be 100 percent loyal to my wife."

Cotton started laughing so hard that tears started streaming down his face. "You do know that means no pussy for you! We're going to the West Coast, the land of the most gorgeous women in the world, and your ass will be on some celibate shit. That is fucking hilarious!"

"Whatever. You got everything ready for us to ride? We got a nice drive ahead of us. I figure we can leave early in the a.m. and push it straight to Kingman, Arizona, get a room, then wake up the next morning and push it all the way in."

"I'm with that. Everything is good to go. I'm going to kick it with Shirin for a little bit tonight and console her some more. She's kinda tripping that LeBron left Miami. She's a die-hard Thunder fan but she likes the Heat too. I've been teasing her all morning. What you got up for the day?"

"Rest. I'm about to make me something to eat, take a nice long, hot bath, and then crash so I'll be good for the roll out in the morning. Has anyone been getting at you?"

"You already know. I've given everyone the fifty-two fake-out so it's all good. By the time we get to the West, they'll realize it's a wrap. I'll change my number when we get out there so we can get ready to take out the West. Tell me, though, what's going to be the get down out there? The drugs out that way are supercheap, so how will we be making that bread?"

"You still got a lot of money out there with the drugs, trust me. We're going to do what we mostly do, but the guns will be the bigger business out that way."

"I figured that. Shit, those gangbanging-ass niggas out there love to shoot shit up. It don't matter how much to me, though. As long as I'm with you, I know we're going to eat good."

Shot smiled at his helper and said, "That's the truth, my man, the real all the way. All right, do you. I got to get me something to eat and get fresh. Make sure you don't be out too late. I don't need you lagging on me when we hit that highway."

"You won't have to worry about me. You just make sure you can keep up in that foreign 'cause my truck gon' make it do what it do."

"We aren't racing, and we damn sure don't need to be getting pulled over, so get that out of your mind, champ."

"I got you, boss man. I'm just ready to get to the West so we can get turned up."

"Don't worry about getting a thing, Cotton. We're about to turn all the way up out there. You're going to have a ball and get more money than you ever dreamed of. So get ready. But remember one thing. The Cali way is a different animal than Texas or Oklahoma City. You will have to remain security conscious at all times. No slipping; slippers fall, Cotton."

"I got you, boss man. I'll follow the protocols to a tee. I'm not trying to get laid down out there, and I'm damn sure hoping I won't ever have to lay anyone down. That's not a good feeling at all."

Shot stared at Cotton for a moment and said, "Yes, I know. Everything will be fine. But if it comes to anyone other than us, it is what it is. If it comes to them or us, it has to be them. We're not losing. All we're going to do is win."

"You fucking right!"

Cotton and Shot had been in LA for two months. Shot was having a good time showing Cotton around the city. He smiled at how starstruck Cotton was. They went shopping at the Beverly Center, and when Cotton saw a star, whether it was a rapper, actor, or musician, he made sure he got an autograph or a picture. Shot laughed and called him corny, and that made him think about Nola. She was the same way when he had first brought her to California. So far, everything with them was proceeding as planned. Nola had been transferred to the female federal prison camp, and she was staying out of trouble. They were waiting for the warden to approve their wedding so Shot could fly back and make it official. Nola Potts would become Nola Gaines. The director pulled some strings for Shot so the prison officials would not know that they were getting married and Nola wasn't Lola. Shot was grateful to his superior and made a point to thank him every time they spoke.

While JT had been busy making necessary arrangements for Operation Cleanup Los Angeles, Shot was enjoying the break from the stress. He knew soon that it would be time to get turned up, and he was ready; he was ready to do some more good. That's all he wanted to do, and he was going to make sure that he kept right on doing good for as long as he could.

Look out, LA! Shot's in town, and it's about to get turned all the way up.

THE END

Epilogue

JT and Shot were sitting inside of JT's office when they received a call from the director informing them that Helen Hollier, the U.S. assistant attorney of the Tenth Circuit of Oklahoma, had given him a call and told him that her federal officers just finished serving their warrants for over seventy-five drug and gun traffickers. The news was the biggest bust for the federal government in the state of Oklahoma, and she was extremely proud of the work that Agent Gaines had done. She wanted to thank him again, but the director told her that Agent Gaines was busy preparing for his next assignment and that he would make sure that he gave him her thanks.

"So again, I'd like to commend you on a job well done, Agent Gaines."

"Thank you, sir. I'd like to thank you again for everything you've done for me and my fiancée. I'm in your debt, sir."

"Good. Maybe I can use that debt you feel you owe me to keep you in line some, at least a little bit."

Shot started laughing and said, "I doubt that. But you are my boss."

JT rolled his eyes and said, "Sir, I still go to the gun range twice a month. All you have to do is say the word, and I'll out this joker outta of his misery."

Laughing, the director said, "I'll keep that in mind, JT. Seriously, it's time for you to get things started in Los Angeles. The guns are going to be the main focus. The

Sureños, as well as the Mexican Mafia or La Eme, as they are referred to, are making some serious power moves out there. You being raised in Inglewood really helps things because that's where I want you to start. The Inglewood Trece, aka the I-13s, are the first group we need you to get to do some business with."

"How am I going to just get right in with these Mexicans, sir? I mean, they aren't known to deal with blacks too often."

"This is true. We have flipped a member of the I-13, and he has given us enough information I think that you will be able to use to your advantage. Also, the 18 Street gang has a heavy influence in Inglewood, much to the I-13s' annoyance. That beef will be your way in. I'll let JT fill you in on the rest. You get them to buy as many guns as you can, and we'll come in and rock their little gangster operation."

"Yes, sir."

The director paused and JT knew that meant he had made a decision that he was dreading he would make. "Oh shit, he's about to tell him. Fuck!" JT mumbled.

"Agent Gaines, I'm a man who prefers to keep everything straight up with my agents, especially my agents in the field. I have been going back and forth with this information I've obtained a few weeks ago, mainly because I wasn't sure whether you would be able to handle this and still be able to maintain your professionalism out there in the field. But you're a professional, and I have to keep full confidence in you that you will continue to do some good, no matter how hard the situation may be."

Shot was wondering where the director was going with this, but when he saw the look on JT's face, he knew that it was something JT didn't want him to know. "Sir, are you telling me that this mission I'm about to start has something to do with the deaths of my mother, father, and brother?"

There was silence on the other line for a moment, and then the director sighed and said, "Yes, Agent Gaines, that's *exactly* what I'm saying. We were able to learn from our informant that your little brother Jeremy was involved with drugs and was dealing weight for an I-13 member named Toker. They went to school together, and Toker took your brother under his wing and groomed him to the game by putting him on in a major way. Your little brother was serving some heavy weight around the city. He and Toker got robbed by the 18 Streets for fifty kilos, and Toker didn't have the money to give back to his people. Toker was ordered to kill your brother, but when he refused, the I-13s tried to have him killed but missed. That's when he came to us."

Tears slid down Hot Shot's face when he asked, "The I-13s killed my family?"

"Yes. When they missed Toker they went after Jeremy, and in the process, murdered your mother and father. You have the right to know this, and I want you to know that although I didn't want to tell you this, I had to for various reasons. I want you extra hungry to bring these assholes down. But I want you focused and not bent out of shape with anger while handling this mission. I know you have a built-in rage when you think about the loss of your family. Use that rage to do some good, Agent Gaines. I am no fool either. I know you want revenge, so off the record, I'm telling you that when, and if, you find the men who committed that brutal crime against your family, do what you feel you must do. The reigns are off of you on this one. Do what you want. On the record, I need for you to bring the big men of this operation in. We have some good to do. Sometimes when you do good, you have to do some bad along the way. I'm all right with that. My question to you, Agent Gaines, is, are you mentally prepared to take on this mission?"

Shot wiped his eyes as he stared at JT and the intercom where he was listening to the director speak from and said in a hoarse whisper, "I'm ready, sir. I've never been more ready for anything in my entire life. Thank you for your honesty with this, sir. I will be equally honest with you. I'm going to complete this mission. I'm going to do what it takes to bring all of these assholes in."

JT flinched when he heard Hot Shot curse. He didn't do that, so that meant one thing to JT. Death was coming to a lot of those I-13s.

Damn.

JT's thoughts couldn't have been truer. The only thing on Hot Shot's mind as he left JT's home was revenge. He was about to finally be able to avenge the deaths of his family. It was time to get more turned up than anyone ever imagined. Hot Shot was about to kill—and kill—and kill.

THE END

Author's Note

I must admit that I am really enjoying this series. I relish bringing Hot Shot to life with every new mission. Keeping him in character is fun for me because he's all-around a good guy. Yes, he's flawed, but who isn't? Making sure he doesn't curse or use the N-word gives him something that I feel is missing in our urban genre. I owe that to my mom and her friend who said I use the N-word entirely too much. So, I hope this series puts a smile on their faces.

Trust me, my faithful fans, Hot Shot has just gotten started! I'm taking a break from this series now so I can get some things right in my mind for the deadly mission Hot Shot is about to partake in. It's time for me to give the ladies something. So, be on the lookout for *Stolen Moments* and *Paper Boys*. By the time I finish these next two books, my work will be better and better, and Hot Shot will be ripping up the cities as he attempts to bring positive change in the communities. That is something I've been waiting on for more than fifteen long years. If you've loved my work while I've been incarcerated, then I give you my solemn promise, I'm only going to get better and work even harder now that I am a free man. So, stay tuned because "Spud" is about to get turned up! And, yes, the name of the third installment of the Hot Shot series will be . . . *Turned Up!* May God bless you and yours. Thank you for the love and continued support.

Peace and Love,
"Spud"

7/13/2014